Her love life has gone to the dogs…

Rose Richardson is on the run from her dangerous ex-husband, a crime she didn't commit—and the embarrassment of being an advice columnist with a disastrous personal life. Donning a fake identity, she escapes to a lovely lake house rental in rural Connecticut…only to discover her refuge is already occupied. Leo Drake is devastatingly handsome–and clearly wants to be alone. Rose stands her ground, even while she fears being found out for the fugitive she is. Plus, her sweet dog, Bella, seems to like the brooding widower, so how bad could he be?

A prize winning novelist, Leo lost everything after he lost his wife. But his mysterious housemate just might be the muse he needs to reignite his writing career. Despite his misgivings, Rose has secrets that only draw him closer, firing his imagination, even as his heart struggles with the attraction building between them. Plus, he kind of likes the quirky pooch. And as he tries to untangle his unusual predicament, Bella's antics just might be the key to showing the loner that love is the only inspiration he needs

Books by Sharon Struth

Blue Moon Lake Series
Share the Moon
Twelve Nights
Harvest Moon
Bella Luna

Published by Kensington Publishing Corporation

Bella Luna

A Blue Moon Lake Novel

Sharon Struth

LYRICAL PRESS
Kensington Publishing Corp.
www.kensingtonbooks.com

Lyrical Press books are published by
Kensington Publishing Corp. 119 West 40th Street New York, NY 10018

All Kensington titles, imprints, and distributed lines are available at special quantity discounts for bulk purchases for sales promotion, premiums, fund-raising, and educational or institutional use.

To the extent that the image or images on the cover of this book depict a person or persons, such person or persons are merely models, and are not intended to portray any character or characters featured in the book.

Special book excerpts or customized printings can also be created to fit specific needs. For details, write or phone the office of the Kensington Special Sales Manager:
Kensington Publishing Corp.
119 West 40th Street
New York, NY 10018
Attn. Special Sales Department. Phone: 1-800-221-2647.

First Electronic Edition: December 2016
eISBN-13: 978-1-61650-649-0
eISBN-10: 1-61650-649-0

First Print Edition: December 2016
ISBN-13: 978-1-61650-650-6
ISBN-10: 1-61650-650-4

Printed in the United States of America

This book is dedicated to the dogs I've owned over a lifetime.

For your unconditional love.

For the thousands of times you've made me smile.

Acknowledgements

I'm a lucky person to be surrounded by such great support as I continue my writing journey. I'll start by thanking Dawn Dowdle of the Blue Ridge Literary Agency, my fabulous agent, who works tirelessly for her authors and has given all of us a family-like atmosphere at her agency.

Thank you to Kensington Publishing/Lyrical press for believing in my series, bringing to life the town of Northbridge and all the great fictional folks who live there. A special nod of gratitude to my editor, Paige Christian, whose editing eyes are a saving grace.

To my adorable husband, your love and support are everything.

To my mother, you are the best salesperson an author could ask for.

To my daughters, thank you for listening to me blabber on about my book when I'm stuck on a plot point.

To my miniature schnauzer, Mollie, whose companionship keeps me happy while I write.

To my RWA Chapter—the best group of friends a writer could ask for.

To Terri-lynne Defino, Joanne Stewart, and Rachel Brimble—I'd be lost without your input!

And to my close friends...your constant support for my work is immeasurable. A thousand thanks!

Chapter 1

Rose Richardson stared beyond the car's swishing wiper blades and whispered, "If anybody is up there listening, please send a sign this isn't the biggest mistake of my life."

She held her breath, not sure if the request might mistakenly rouse an onslaught of locusts. Nothing happened.

Through the wet windshield, her gaze drifted to the front of Blue Moon Lake Realty. The rural Connecticut real estate office could've been a home, based on the green awning over a picture window and potted petunias on the stoop. Weatherworn, salmon-colored paint peeled in places and the awning flap had a slight tear. Only a bright neon sign reading Open hinted to the building's business purpose.

A sign. Any sign. Nobody walked out and gave her a thumbs-up, even though lights inside indicated someone was there. She glanced around the near-empty parking lot. A breeze blew a candy bar wrapper from the roadside onto the nearby lawn, not exactly sign-worthy.

Guess she'd have to trust her gut on this decision. How long had it been since she'd put her faith in anybody else, anyway? Ten years? Twenty? More like never.

Rose flipped on the inside light and adjusted the rearview mirror to get another peek at herself. A near stranger stared back. Just as she'd planned.

A shuffling noise made her turn around. Bella stretched lengthwise in the Ford Escort, hogging most of the bench seat.

"What do you think of me as a redhead, Bella?"

The five-year-old basset hound yawned.

Rose could only hope others reacted with the same disinterest. She took a deep breath to calm her nerves and faced back out the front windshield.

Rain danced on the car's roof, a dreary end to her two-day journey. The trip started twenty-four hours ago, when she still had shoulder-length dirty-blond hair, and her integrity. Now everything had changed.

Besides applying a hair rinse that left her with copper-red locks, she'd stopped at a Smartcuts in Virginia for a different style. Newly purchased black-framed fashion glasses fit loosely on the bridge of her nose and slipped for the umpteenth time today. She shoved them back up with her index finger. Okay, so they didn't *really* work for Clark Kent, but desperate times called for desperate measures.

She opened her purse to search for a pack of gum.

Tap, tap, tap.

Rose's heart startled and she jerked her head toward the window.

"Emma? Emma Morris?" A voluptuous woman with an auburn bob cut and wide green eyes stared back. She wore a navy jacket with the real estate office logo on the lapel.

Rose rolled down the window and crossed her fingers that she passed this first critical test using her made-up identity. "Yes, I'm sorry I'm late." Her heartbeat pounded wildly, but she forced a smile. "Are you Meg?"

"I am." Meg held an enormous golf umbrella. "Glad you made it. I've been worried."

"Sorry. Traffic coming out of Boston was bad." Rose swallowed the lie, glad she'd given the car dealer a little extra cash to give her an old Massachusetts plate he happened to have. Money could buy anything.

"Don't worry at all, sweetie. Sit tight. Let me grab the house key so you don't have to come out in this rain." She hurried back inside.

Rose admired the agent's A-line skirt. All Rose's Ann Taylor clothes still hung in her closet back in North Carolina, replaced with items off the clearance rack from the junior's department at the Roanoke, Virginia Target during her drive north. Her new style said "thirty-eight-year-old woman who wishes she was still eighteen," not "senator's wife and nationally known advice columnist."

Meg exited the shabby ranch home and returned to the car, this time on her cell phone. "Just finish your homework. I'll be home soon." She hung up and slipped the phone in her jacket pocket. "Kids. They always call when you're in the middle of something."

Rose nodded, but she didn't understand. Thank God she and John had never had children. With the news that had sent her running from him, her soul felt as uncared for as the house before her. Pain over his actions was a hard stab at her heart, but she lifted her chin in a defiant gesture he'd never see.

Meg handed Rose an envelope. "Everything you need is in here. Two house keys and a signed copy of the lease from Mr. Drake." She placed a hand on Rose's arm. "You're getting a great deal on this place. It's lakefront. The last tenant took off before the lease ended." She dropped her voice and glanced around, even though the area was deserted. "Mr. Drake was furious. He likes having someone in the house, you know? Makes him worry less about the place being empty."

"I don't blame him. Is it far from here?"

"A stone's toss away." Meg grinned.

"Oh, so it's nearby?"

"A few miles. Follow Lake Shore Drive out of town going toward Southbridge. Go past the Litchfield Hills Vineyard. About two miles beyond that, you'll turn. Be careful. Potholes are everywhere. It's been a rough winter, and they still haven't patched the road. I mean, it's May! What are they waiting for?" She shook her head. "Oh, it's rained for the past two days, so hopefully the driveway leading to the estate isn't flooded. There's a town map inside the envelope and a booklet with local services and businesses. Anything goes wrong, you call me right away. One of my cards is in there with my cell number. Mr. Drake is a good landlord and handles problems quickly."

"Thank you, Meg. Hold on." Rose leaned over to the passenger seat and searched her purse for the envelope holding all her cash. Her lifeline. The only way to remain hidden from the lies of her ex-husband. Her hatred for John swelled, but she held it in check and removed enough to cover rent. "Here you go. For the first month."

"I'll print a receipt tomorrow, if it's okay? The computers are shut off."

"Sure."

"Remember, call if you need me."

Rose waited until Meg disappeared inside the office, then tipped her head against the headrest and blew out a relieved sigh.

Maybe she hadn't seen a sign, but she'd gone too far to turn back now.

* * * *

After a quick stop at the local market for a few essentials, Rose navigated the dark lake road. In the distance, twinkling lights from houses scattered along the hills sparkled. The ad for her rental house had said it had water views and solitude.

A perfect place to remain invisible. A perfect place to hide.

There were so many layers to John's dishonesty she didn't know which one had made her run. Five days ago, their divorce had become final. All she had to do, by the terms of their divorce agreement, was live in the same house and stay silent about their split until the elections were over. A nasty trade on her ex-husband's part, but a small price to pay to get what she needed from him. Six months of hell, then she'd be home free.

Or so she'd thought.

An approaching car flicked their high beams and Rose lowered hers. She yawned, tired but anxious to reach the private house rental. The call to her college friend Joanne had been a stab in the dark, but she lived up the eastern seaboard in Connecticut, far away from John's threats and offenses. Joanne had put out her feelers for a rental in a remote area and, within an hour, someone mentioned a quiet house in the northwest corner of the state on a lake. The miracle of social media. Rose would never complain about it being a waste of time again.

The car's headlights brightened a white sign for the vineyard Meg had mentioned. Rose's worries lightened and she forged ahead, eventually making a turn. The narrow road twisted like a curious snake between the trees. Every so often she'd pass a driveway, proving civilization did exist.

At a mailbox with the name Drake in black letters on the side, she slowed. A rusted No Trespassing sign had been nailed to a thick tree trunk. She turned in, thankful to arrive.

Gravel crunched beneath her tires. She inched up the incline of a stone-paved driveway centered between thick trees. The Ford Escort hit each bump as if nothing rested between Rose's rump and the ground. She'd needed to use the bathroom since leaving the real estate office. With each jolt, she paid the price of not stopping sooner.

At a clearing, her headlights illuminated a huge white colonial looming before her, larger than she'd imagined. Pillars marked the sides of a portico entrance and symmetrical darkened windows with black shutters lined the façade. She parked near the walkway, turning off the car and plunging into total darkness.

She turned on the inside light. "We made it, Bella."

Bella stood, flattened her stubby legs in front of her, and arched her behind high in the air. A good yoga stretch. "I know, girl. It's been a long drive."

Rose searched the envelope from Meg and removed a key. She took a deep breath, slipped her purse over her shoulder, and got out. Drizzle misted in the air. Bella hopped out of the back seat and sniffed, her tail high and nose pressed to the ground like a Hoover.

Rose popped the trunk. The light inside glowed, highlighting the darkness of the property. A twig snapped in the nearby woods, making her jump. The tree cluster was thick and ominous, worthy of a Brothers

Grimm fairy tale setting. Beyond the house, a clearing in the backyard showed dotted lights from houses across the way—maybe the other side of the lake.

Grabbing her backpack, she decided to take the rest in tomorrow. All she wanted after such a long drive was to eat and go to sleep.

She opened her Target bags, searching for a nightshirt and toothbrush amongst the new items. While she looked, her purse slipped off her shoulder into the trunk and several things fell out. She ignored them to continue her search. The quiet in the secluded yard got creepier by the second. A little chill spiraled up her spine. Hastening her search, she stuffed her findings into her backpack, and replaced the spilled items from her purse. After a quick neatening of the trunk, she slammed it shut.

"Let's go, Bella." Bella sniffed a nearby patch of tulips and ignored Rose, who snapped on the leash and gave her a tug.

Using the dim beam of a cheap key-ring flashlight, she followed a slate walkway to the door. It took a minute to work the key, but the lock finally clicked and she pushed the door open.

Her eyes adjusted to the pitch-black entrance. Shadows teased her already jumpy nerves as she dropped her belongings on the floor and patted the wall. It took a few seconds to locate the switches, and she flipped them up.

An overhead light brightened a large foyer facing a staircase and hallway. The inside felt warm, considering Meg had said nobody lived here for the past two months.

She inhaled, catching a familiar scent. Coffee?

Rose shut the door and removed the dog's leash, dropping it on an old olive-green table with black scrolled decorative swirls, stationed against the foyer wall. Above the table hung a long mirror, a peacock etched in the glass taking up half the space.

Rose studied herself in the reflection, still shocked by the altered image. Circles under her eyes matched the tiredness taking over her body. Sleep had never sounded so good.

Thud!

Rose stopped, tilting her head toward the upstairs.

Thud!

A loud creak sounded from above. Her heartbeat picked up speed. Another creak. Footsteps? A light upstairs flashed on and cut a beam to the staircase wall. Bella's ears perked at the same moment the slow rise of panic crawled through Rose's veins.

Move. Move! Only she stood still, frozen in fear as her mind raced with images from vagrants to serial killers.

The dog emitted a guttural growl.

Slow creaks of the floorboards above magnified in the silent house. Rose stretched her trembling hand, snatched the leash off the table, and leaned over, just shy of snapping it on Bella so they could race like hell out the door.

Footsteps pounded. Fast and hard, they hit the staircase. Before she could grab the dog's collar, Bella bolted.

Owooooo-woo-woo-woo-woo!

Bella's howl echoed in the silent house. She stopped at the bottom step and stared fearlessly into the face of danger. Terror, however, had cemented Rose's feet in place.

A dark-haired man reached the bottom, gripping a baseball bat in a ready-to-launch position over his shoulder. "Don't move!" He stood at the last step, too close for her to make a quick dash out the door.

Rose's heart pounded against her ribs and her mouth went dry. She raised her hands in the air. "Please. Don't hurt me!"

The intruder blinked back at her through sleepy eyes. Thick tresses of messy hair jutted from his head. The rugged edges of an unshaven shadow highlighted his tight, angled jaw. Her gaze traveled past his wrinkled, loosely buttoned plaid shirt, his baggy sweatpants, and stopped at his bare feet.

Bella bared her teeth, glaring at him bravely as he towered over the short basset hound. Her nose lifted and she inhaled a sharp breath. *Owooooooooooooo! Owoooooooooo!*

The dog's war cry got the stranger's attention for a split second, but he quickly returned his narrowed gaze to Rose. "I don't know who you are, but you'd better have a damn good reason for breaking into my house."

* * * *

Leo Drake's head ached. He couldn't shake off his disorientation, certain he walked around in some awful dream.

"Your house?" Disbelief showed in the woman's rich blue eyes as they widened. Her gaze drifted to his arms. "Could you please lower the bat? I didn't break in. I have a key." She lifted a key on a plastic ring he didn't recognize.

Shit. He lowered the bat and took the last step down into the foyer. Goddamn Everett must've rented the place again.

She dropped her arms. "Wh-who are you?"

"This is *my* house. Who are you?"

"Emma. Emma Morris." She hesitated a brief second then jutted out her chin, her heart-shaped face shifting into a more confident pose. "I have papers showing I'm renting this place." She lifted a manila envelope off the table near the door. "For at least this month, possibly longer. Are you Everett?"

He clenched his jaw at the mention of his brother's name. "No. Leo Drake. My brother and I share ownership of the house. I'm sorry, but you'll have to find somewhere else to stay."

Her shoulders slumped. Uncertainty crossed her face as she reached up and tucked one side of her wispy, Lucille Ball–red hair behind her ear, highlighting a faded red stain on her neck near her lobe, perhaps from hair dye.

"Leave?" She shook her head. "No, I can't." She straightened her posture and a razor-sharp edge glistened in her determined eyes. "I signed a lease. My options are limited, so we'd better get this straightened out."

Leo took a step closer to her, his height a good head above hers. She didn't back away, only stared back with unyielding determination. Moxie when the going got tough always impressed him. A quality Camille had never possessed; his deceased wife had been so afraid of conflict she'd rather pretend to be happy. Even if it meant avoiding health concerns, from her mental health issues that had worsened over time, to allowing a cancer diagnosis to have its way. Further proof he was powerless to save those he loved.

He swept aside the wave of grief and studied the stranger from top to toe. Mickey Mouse struck his trademark kicked-back pose on her chest. Patterned pants lined her legs, looking more like they belonged on a clown or someone still in high school. Not this grown woman, whose age he guessed at over thirty and who spoke with more polish than her bad wardrobe taste would suggest.

She pulled out her cell phone from her windbreaker pocket. "Does Meg know you're staying here?"

"Who's Meg?"

"The real estate agent." She searched through an envelope and removed a business card. "I'm calling her."

"Well, it's pointless. Everett shouldn't have leased this place again."

She ignored him and dialed. He glanced at the dog, who threatened him with bloodshot eyes and a wagging tail. Some watchdog. He resisted the urge to bend over and pet the cute guy.

Leo lifted his gaze to the uninvited guest. "There's no way I'm leaving my own house."

"We'll see."

"Listen—" He paused, already forgetting the stranger's name. "You can't—"

She turned her back on him. "Hello, Meg…"

A renter. The last thing he needed. Returning to the Northbridge house to get work done had been Leo's last resort. Both his publisher and agent called him regularly, anxious to know about the book's progress. The deadline to turn it in neared, an ever-constant source of stress. The lake house stood amongst his favorite writing places. Back here, he expected to find his muse. God knows he couldn't find it anywhere else.

The return to this house was about more than work, although he'd never tell his brother. A desperate need to be alone ate away at him every day. He needed quiet. Peace. Surroundings completely different than everything he'd shared with Camille, with no reminders that their life together had been taken from him just when it seemed to be getting started.

Rage for his brother pulsed through his veins. Everett had better be armed for a good fight. Since childhood, Everett had won every battle the brothers ever shared. This time, though, Leo wasn't about to give in.

Chapter 2

"Co-owner of the house?" Meg's fiery glare aimed right at Leo, the strong stance undermined by a T-shirt with World's Greatest Mom splayed across her ample chest. "Oh, wait. I do remember a joint ownership, only the paperwork said Everett would be handling rental matters."

Rose stifled a yawn and stood quietly to the foyer's side to let the real estate agent take control of this mess. The long day had caught up with her during the wait for Meg. Leo Drake had disappeared upstairs during that time, leaving Rose in a formal living room with heavy drapes and antiques. Seated on a golden French provincial sofa made of threadbare but clean fabric, she'd twice almost drifted to sleep. The second the doorbell rang, Leo had returned with his hair brushed and eyes fully awake.

Meg pursed her full lips. "The problem is that Mr. Drake—the other one—never told me things had changed."

Rose gave the woman credit. She hadn't blown her cool, delivering all her concerns to him with the same sugar-coated sweetness she'd spoken to Rose with upon her arrival.

Leo shrugged, seemingly undeterred by her persistence "What can I say?" His deep voice carried a soft quality around the edges, but there was no mistaking the smidgeon of arrogance evident in both words and actions. "Everett never was the best communicator. It doesn't matter. I'm here now and this rental situation—"

"But I've always dealt with your brother and have to follow the paperwork unless he says otherwise. You see what I'm saying?" Meg nodded and the edges of her blunt cut moved stiffly.

Leo closed his eyes and pinched the bridge of his nose with his thick fingers. Rose almost felt sorry for him. Almost. She had her own problems, bigger than a sibling miscommunication.

"How'd you get in here, anyway?" Meg narrowed her eyes. "Do you have a key?"

He exhaled, removed his hand, and opened his eyes. "Of course. It's my house."

"Hmmm. So how long have you been here?"

"I arrived shortly after the last renter left." He shifted, discomfort a little too obvious. "I heard the house was vacant and decided to stay. I did tell Everett."

Rose almost let out a snort. Classic liar body language. How had she missed all the clues in her bastard of an ex-husband?

Meg tilted her head. "How do I even know you're who you say you are?"

"Oh, dear God." Leo rubbed his grainy cheek with his palm. "Hold on." He trudged up the staircase, scowling all the way.

Meg turned to Rose and dropped her voice. "I'm so sorry, Emma. I knew there was another brother besides Everett. They used to come here years ago. But since Mr. Drake Senior died, I haven't seen hide nor hair from this other son. Then he sneaks in here, unannounced."

Leo's footsteps on the old staircase signaled his return. Meg turned his way, her chin lifted high. He stopped in front of her and flipped open a black Hugo Boss wallet, the embossed logo visible on one side. Not a cheap wallet, but based on the size of this house, Rose figured there was family money. While he dealt with Meg, Rose inspected the rest of Leo, from his sweatpants carrying a coffee stain to his wrinkled shirt missing two buttons. A strange contrast to the costly wallet.

"Is a New York state driver's license enough proof?" Tight lines strained Leo's eyes, and his strong jawline went stiff.

Meg studied his ID, glancing up at him then back to the license. "I guess it's you. You need a shave." Leo raised a brow, but she didn't seem to notice. "Anywho, I left a message for your brother. He hasn't called back yet."

"Fine. We can deal with this tomorrow. There are a few hotels around the lake where she—"

"No way." Rose stepped forward. The quick escape plan was all she had to hold on to. Fear had pushed her to run and now nipped at her heals like a hungry wolf. "I'm exhausted and not going to a hotel. You seem to forget I signed a lease with your brother."

He tilted his head, considered her with something she almost deemed compassion for a fraction of second, and then tonelessly mumbled, "And we're back at square one."

"*You* could stay at one." Rose lifted a brow.

"Instead of my own house?"

She shrugged even though she knew the suggestion was a long shot. "It's not easy to find a place that'll take dogs."

He turned to Meg. "I assume you told this woman the reason we lost the last renter here. Plus, the rumors about the house?"

Rose cleared her throat. "My name is Emma."

The name still tasted wrong to her lips, even though she'd heard it often during her childhood. Emmaline Rose Holloway, adored child of celebrity parents. A persona that one day had vanished right off the face of the earth.

Leo arched a brow. "Okay, *Emma*." He studied her for a moment, eyes squinting as though he possessed the ability to see inside her mind. Slowly, he turned his attention back to Meg. "I hope you've been honest with Emma about this place."

Meg tilted her head, narrowed her eyes. "How do you know what happened? We kept it very quiet."

"Harry Gallagher next door told me. Seems he and the old tenant were friendly." Leo gave his full attention to Rose. For the first time since her arrival, a paper-thin smile traced his lips. "I hate to tell you, but you've been misled."

Rose glanced at Meg. "What's he talking about?"

"Don't listen to him." Meg waved her hand through the air. "It's silly."

"Not so silly at all. I'm sure if you knew the full story, you'd be happy to stay elsewhere."

"What is it?" Rose cut a glance between them both. "It can't be that bad."

Meg sighed and her shoulders wilted. "Well, the last tenant left because he claimed the house is haunted. I don't believe it's true, so I didn't want to alarm you."

"Haunted? Like how?"

"Strange noises, flickering lights." Bella walked up and sniffed at Meg's stark-white Keds. Meg smiled and patted Bella on top of the head.

Rose's parents had been screen actors. She'd grown up in the land of make-believe and watched horror movies made from behind the scenes. As a rule, she didn't believe in such stories and pretty much figured people were scaring themselves with runaway imaginations.

Leo raised a brow of overdone concern in Rose's direction. "I'm sure you wouldn't be comfortable here alone, especially once you learn about the murder. In fact, that's probably why a ghost lives in the house."

The hairs on the back of Rose's neck prickled at the word murder, but she did her best to hide it. She kept eye contact with Leo. "I don't believe in ghosts. But I am curious about a murder."

Meg winced.

"Go ahead, Meg," Leo said, his tone eerily reminiscent of the announcer for *The Twilight Zone*. "Tell her about the murder."

"The rumors about the place being haunted have been around since I was a kid." Meg spoke fast, her hands flying all over the place. "Shortly after this house was built in the 1930s, the man who built it shot his wife. To be honest, the tenant who was here last is the first time anybody has admitted to seeing anything paranormal."

"I hear things." Leo maintained a straight face.

Rose shook her head. "It's fine, Meg. Like I said, I don't believe in the supernatural."

Leo shrugged. "Can't say you haven't been warned."

Rose wasn't buying his staged indifference.

Bella wandered over to Leo and sniffed his still-bare feet. Her long, silky ears hit the ground. She lifted her pitiful eyes, swished her tail. Leo's expression remained stiff. Though he was a handsome man, the warmth missing from his personality diminished his good looks.

He lifted his gaze from the dog to Rose. "It's a moot point, anyway. You can't stay—"

"Wait!" Meg's faced brightened. "There might be only one way to skin a cat, but not when I'm on the case."

Leo scowled. "The expression is 'There's *more* than one way to skin a cat.' Not, well, whatever you said."

Meg glanced his way, her cheery expression persevering with no regard for his correction. "All I know is I've got a great idea."

Leo groaned.

"There's a separate in-law suite in the house where Emma could stay."

"Oh no," Leo said, an undercurrent of panic in his voice. "She's not—"

"It's got its own living room, bathroom, and a separate bedroom. Perfect!"

"It's not perfect. It's—"

"For *tonight*." Meg held up her index finger, pointed it in Leo's face. "We let Emma stay here tonight. Tomorrow morning, I'll talk to Mr. Drake—the other Mr. Drake—and we'll figure out the rest."

"Works for me." Rose crossed her arms and stared at Leo, trying not flinch at his frostier-than-ice glare. All she wanted right now was to get some rest.

The muscles in his thick neck tightened and he turned, heading for the stairs. "Do as you wish. I've got work to do."

* * * *

Leo bypassed his bedroom and went straight to the attic, but he couldn't get the new renter out of his head. When had he become so withdrawn he couldn't reach deep and be a little nicer to a stranger with a problem? Okay, so he'd never been the most outgoing guy in a crowded room. But people had always seemed drawn to his quiet and introspective personality. Since he'd lost his wife, though, friends teased him about being a little bit of a crank. Crusty but loveable, many of them said. It only got worse as the days passed. The grumpy side controlled him. He mulled over the change in himself, only it filled him with more regret.

Yes, he should've been nicer to that woman. Outside of her defiant exterior, he could've sworn he'd spotted fear, kicking in his—oh, what had his sister called it, his savior complex? His fist curled tight with anger at himself. After losing Camille, he'd vowed not to fall into his usual pattern of trying to fix everything for a woman. Since his first high-school girlfriend, he'd been drawn to damsels in distress like bees gravitate to honey. Never with the same sweet results. At this point, all his energy needed to go to finishing this damn book, not helping yet another damsel.

He climbed the steep staircase leading to his office, stomping out his anger on each step. Another roadblock to his productivity. At the top of the attic stairs, the unfinished knotty pine scent greeted him like an old friend, giving him a comfort most would find hard to understand.

When he was a young boy, he'd hide up here with his journal, recording his innermost thoughts. The decorating he'd done as a teenager remained on the walls: a Green Day poster and one from the Stephen King movie *Misery*. A sort of man-cave for an adolescent boy who wanted to escape reality and leave behind all the bad things that had already happened in his young life—all of them before he'd arrived in the Drake household.

He plopped into the worn leather chair near his desk, positioned to look out the window toward the backyard and lake. All he saw was darkness and lights from homes on the other side of the lake. He lifted his cell phone off the desk. Switzerland was either five or six hours ahead of Connecticut, meaning it was the middle of the night. He dialed his brother's number anyway.

It went straight into voice mail. "You've reached Everett Drake. Please leave a message."

Leo waited for the beep. "It's me. Shall I assume you never got my message two months ago saying I'd be staying at the Northbridge house? I know you have no interest in speaking to me, but I'd hoped you could at least respect my right to be here. When it comes to matters of joint ownership with this house, it seems we should make an effort to communicate better."

What had his father been thinking when he gave them shared ownership of this place?

"The real estate agent was just here. So is the woman you leased the house to. We need to get this straightened out."

He hung up and put the cap on a bottle of scotch he'd nursed this afternoon. Drinking wasn't usually his thing, but the dreary weather and inability to move forward on his manuscript were taking him to a worse place than a little booze.

Or was it the dream about Camille? She'd been on the fringes of his thoughts as he woke this morning, her image stirring such a bottomless sense of loss he'd struggled to get out of bed. Soreness inside his chest kept him down, an old bruise formed the day a social service worker told a five-year-old boy his mother had died. The news left Leo alone, scared, and wishing he had the power to help her. He'd buried the feelings beneath a brave front, but they were still part of his makeup. Each step into similar relationships always felt like walking on eggshells. The day Camille died, those shells cracked into a million pieces, leaving him with a hardened, miserable heart.

Creating a character mirroring her in this latest book had been a mistake. Leo had hoped *Street Views*—his agent had loved the title— would allow him to gain some clarity on his life. He'd tossed the proposal together quickly, only somewhat aware that the dynamics in the story were a means to work through his mistakes and the lingering guilt he had over Camille's bipolar disorder. A problem neither of them had taken seriously enough, until it was too late. The publisher had bit. Now Leo was stuck.

He'd been moving forward with the book at the start, only his progress stalled midway through. No matter how hard he thought about it, he couldn't figure out why.

Writing this book had forced Leo to admit something; nearly every relationship he'd had with a woman involved him trying to save them in some way. His success rate? Poor. The reason he'd sunk to the bottom of a pit and lost the will to climb out.

Three long years he'd been trying to let go of the lethal mix of sadness and resentment for his wife. She couldn't help the cancer diagnosis, but resisting treatment had been within her power. Camille always ignored unpleasant things. Part of her charm. Leo handled the full load of stress, a burden he'd carried without thinking.

His gaze landed on the 1952 Remington typewriter in front of him. The "Quiet-riter." If anything could aid him in getting this job done, it was this machine. An object facilitating the writer's blood pumping through his veins and motivating him to get words on paper.

He rested his fingers on the smooth metal keys. It had taken him through every first draft he'd ever written, including the book that won him the Pulitzer. The typewriter always worked for Leo.

At least it had.

Brutal reviews on the book he'd published after receiving the award had stolen the thunder of getting the esteemed prize at all. Logic and pep talks from his agent had barely boosted his morale. Writing a book so soon after losing his wife had been a mistake. One he paid for every day.

And now the current contract for another book hung over his head like an anvil on a fraying rope.

If only he could find his damn muse! His last hope had been to find it at the lake house. Now, instead of his muse, he got another renter.

He exhaled deeply and ran a hand through his hair. Something on the edges of his brain connected dots from the strange woman who'd arrived earlier to Camille, but he couldn't quite make out the finer details. Did it even matter? He wanted her gone.

Leo leaned on the desk and buried his face in his hands. He couldn't write worth a damn anymore. What good was glory when everything else that mattered in his life was gone?

* * * *

Rose pressed the phone to her ear as she laid Bella's big square bed near a corner of the living room area. While Joanne's number rang, Rose assessed her home for the night.

The apartment was cozier than the large house. Knotted pine floors finished with a dark mahogany stain contrasted with walls the color of clotted cream. A sofa and recliner covered in faded country-blue fabric and an old pine coffee table showed a few nicks in the honey-colored finish. Like the rest of the house—at least the part she'd seen—the pieces here possessed weary harmony.

Bella sniffed her bed, carefully stepped on top, and scratched a few times then plunked down.

"Wow, sleeping in the backseat today must've been exhausting."

Bella worked herself into a tight ball and shut her eyes.

On the fifth ring, a winded Joanne answered. "Thank God it's you. I couldn't find my phone. Are you at the house?"

"I am." Rose settled back into the sofa, immediately comforted by the sound of her close friend's voice. "Ran into traffic. Then we had a little issue when I got here."

She tucked her legs at her side and shared the details of her arrival in Northbridge.

"So he's there, right now?" Joanne asked.

"Yup. Upstairs."

Rose heard a loud clunk from the upper level. What could he be doing to make so much noise at this hour?

"He didn't recognize you, did he?"

"He was too mad to show it if he did. This guy doesn't strike me as the type to read an advice column in a women's magazine. And, if he's into politics, he might recognize John, but probably not me. Don't forget, I'm now a redhead with sort of a shitty haircut."

"It can't be that bad."

"I'm certain my regular hairdresser would have a stroke if she saw me."

"Least of your worries. How long do you think before John realizes you've left?"

"A week? Two?" And then what? Rose hadn't thought that far ahead. The pain of John's deceit stabbed at her heart. She willed it to disappear, just like the happier moments in their marriage before he ran for office.

"Did you hear again from the FBI?"

"No. I'm not sure if that's good or bad. All I keep thinking, though, is if they hadn't shown up at my door with their vague questions about campaign contributions going into my husband's account, I'd still be in the dark about my money."

The eye-opening visit from two special agents happened after John had agreed to a sticking point in their divorce settlement. For weeks they'd been at odds over the inheritance she'd received from her parents before entering the marriage.

The remaining funds were all she had left of their memory. Losing them at fourteen had been horrible, their murder-suicide a living nightmare. The Hollywood paparazzi had gone wild for the story, hounding a young Emmaline Rose whenever they could. At the age of eighteen, she'd had enough notoriety. Using the insurance money, she'd started a new life. She'd used it to get a Ph.D., escape from California with a new name, and eventually buy the beautiful house she'd shared with her husband. Nobody, except John, knew her past.

"Know what I mean?"

Joanne's question pulled her back to the conversation. "I'm sorry?"

"John's attachment to your money, it should've been a clue."

"I know. Something just didn't add up. The clause in our divorce agreement that I couldn't touch the money until after November was sly—a way to keep me from seeing the balance. I never would have thought he'd simply steal it." Rose let the depths of her naiveté sink in. "Was I was a fool to confront him? Maybe if I'd just shut up, I wouldn't be on the run."

"No regrets, Rose. At least you saw his true colors. Will the PI you contacted start work right away?"

"He says he will. Until then, I hope the FBI finds someone else to investigate besides me." She yawned away from the mouthpiece.

"You sound beat. Go to bed. Remember, if things don't work in Northbridge, you can always come here."

"I need to stay away from anyplace where John might easily find me, but thanks. So I'll see you tomorrow?"

"Be up around lunchtime."

She hung up and went inside the bathroom. After turning on the faucet to warm the water, she located her face cleanser and began to wash her face. The slow massage of her fingertip against her cheeks felt nice. She closed her eyes, but it didn't shut off her worries.

The FBI visit seemed like a lifetime ago, not three days ago. It had been the catalyst, kicking off a domino effect inside Rose's mind and hooking together events that revealed John's end game.

It had started with his insistence that she donate some of her inheritance to help with his initial campaign. He'd made the same request with his second bid. Then, as they sat in mediation, he'd demanded half the five hundred thousand dollars, citing marital property laws since no prenuptial agreement had been made.

As she'd pondered those facts after the agents had left, a loud click sounded inside her head. Months before kicking off his second campaign, John had said he wanted to safeguard all their account information. She'd willingly handed over her credit and bank account information, including passwords. She had no reason not to trust him at that time.

She'd been one step from calling the FBI agents back and mentioning John's access to her account. Before she did, though, she'd logged into the inheritance account. As her gaze fell to the balance, her mouth had gone dry. The account had been nearly emptied six months earlier.

Lies upon more lies. They couldn't be ignored. Confronting John had been a knee-jerk reaction. Fury drove her straight to his home office, where he'd been working. Accusations flew from her mouth like machine gun fire. Instead of denying it, John had laughed in her face. Not the sweet laugh that had helped him win his first term as senator for the state of North Carolina or the one that had charmed her on their first date. It was a callous snicker, followed by the words, "Honey, you *will* keep quiet about that money. Because I know things about you that you *don't* want leaked to the press."

The threat to spill her past and let the readers of her column, *Dr. Rose Says*, view her as a fraud had left her horrified. That her identity had formed out of self-preservation wouldn't even make the papers.

She'd gone off to bed, stunned that a man she'd once loved would resort to such despicable behavior for personal gains. Around two thirty, unable to sleep, she'd gone downstairs for a cup of chamomile. A beam of light had cut across the downstairs hallway near John's office door. She paused at hearing her name.

"Rose won't know what hit her." John had chuckled. "Hell, this'll kill two birds with one stone. But we need to do this fast. And listen, make sure he makes it look like a mugging, for God's sake. This way Rose won't get suspicious."

She'd stilled, holding her breath while he continued.

"Exactly. Suddenly I'll be *the* voice in Washington on behalf of gun legislation. Especially when I'm talking to the press about how gun violence killed her parents. Imagine what that'll do for votes."

Her parents…a mugging…gun legislation. Was John going to have her mugged and shot? All so he could use it for political leverage? Guns. Even the word made her muscles stiff from fear. They'd changed her life. Taken her small family away.

Fear mingled with a kind of surreal disbelief, a cloud of confusion. The cloud lifted when John's final words ripped her heart in two.

"Rose has been a thorn in my political career for too long. She's been a loose canon on the campaign trail. Once she's shot, it'll give her something else to worry about and put her out of the picture. Let's make sure the way we framed her when I withdrew the inheritance makes sense. If the FBI finds that paper trail, we want it to look like it was all her doing."

Rose had trembled as she hurried back upstairs, fearful for her safety mostly, but also the threat of arrest. Before the sun had risen, she'd come up with a plan to quietly leave this house and try to figure out what to do.

A day later, when John left their home in North Carolina for the resumed Senate session in DC, Rose had begun her escape. She'd skimmed what cash she could from joint bank accounts, purchased a used car from an unscrupulous car dealer, and left with Bella. The ten-year-old Ford didn't compare to her beloved Mazda Miata, but it was an untraceable getaway.

She washed away the soap with warm water, leaving her fresh and clean on the outside but her mind bogged down by the uncertainties that lie ahead.

With any luck, the private investigator she'd contacted from her hotel last night would get some answers. Answers to clear her name, get her inheritance back, and have enough information against John so she could safely return home.

Chapter 3

Cold seeped through Rose's thin socks as she walked across the black-and-white-checkered vinyl floor, popular in modern kitchens many decades ago. She parted frilly café curtains over the sink. A stream of morning sunlight bathed her in its warmth, but the view outside stole her breath. The backyard sloped down to a glimmering lake, surrounded like a fortress by gently rolling hills. A flock of geese descended over the water and landed. The tranquility wiped away her concerns, at least for a quick moment.

The rest of the spacious yard had garden beds in need of weeding, towering trees, Adirondack chairs, and a picnic table not far from a boat dock. Closer to the house stood a detached garage, right at the end of the dirt and gravel driveway. A cream-colored Mercedes was parked off to the side. Circa sixties or seventies, she'd guess. She hadn't seen it last night because she'd stopped near the front walkway. Spotting it could've saved her a few gray hairs.

In a corner of the kitchen, Bella munched on her kibbles. At least the dog seemed comfortable. Being in this unfamiliar house in a new town was so strange. It had only been three days since she left North Carolina, but it felt like a lifetime ago.

She turned away from the window and inspected the kitchen. Tired white cabinets were functional but sagging in a few places. She opened one and took stock of the contents: a package of Oreos, half-eaten bag of Doritos, and cellophane bag of miniature candy bars. Her stomach did a little flip. The processed foods she'd eaten while on the road weren't her norm. She longed for a healthy batch of steamed veggies with grilled chicken.

She shut the cabinets and scanned the rest of the room. A vinyl-topped kitchen table trimmed with a metal edge accompanied yellow, faux-leather-upholstered chairs. One seat back was sloppily repaired with electric tape. Her gaze drifted to a spot near the microwave where the linoleum curled slightly, like a cry to be replaced with something newer.

One thing was certain. This place had been vintage before vintage was cool.

She wandered across the room to a partially open door, passing heavily worn copper-bottom pots hanging on the wall near the stove. Nearby were mushroom-themed porcelain canisters on the counter, right next to an old radio with a dial. The door led to a pantry. Besides a few cans of tuna fish and canned chili, the checkerboard-lined shelves were empty. A classic car calendar from the nineties hung open to the month of August near a faded postcard of the lake secured by a partially rusted silver thumbtack. She took the postcard off the wall.

To Kat. Remember, a return here holds all the promise of a full moon. All my love, Phillip

She studied the beautiful penmanship, curious about both sender and recipient, then pinned it back to the spot. Now what could she do? Meg had promised to call by nine, two hours away. All Rose could do was wait and worry about how this rental disaster would end.

Since last night, she hadn't heard a peep from upstairs. A relief, since who knew what Leo's temperament would be like today.

Bella went to her other bowl and lapped at the water. Rose waited for her finish. "Come on, girl. Let's go for a walk."

Bella followed her back to the apartment. Rose slipped on never-worn-before gleaming white sneakers and her windbreaker then searched the main room for Bella's leash. Not on the coffee table or sofa. Not in the teeny alcove, where a small counter, sink, and dorm-sized refrigerator served as a mini-kitchen area. Not in the bathroom. She caught a glimpse of her choppy new style, run amok due to a restless night's sleep. After running a brush through it, she tried to pat down the few spots still sticking out. She missed her former style that could be tied into a ponytail with little fuss.

After removing her glasses from the vinyl top of the vanity, she slipped them on. A minute later she found the leash, in the bedroom on top of her luggage.

Bella gurgled a throaty sound and wagged her tail. Rose hunched down and stroked the dog's silky ears. All her love for the dog bubbled inside her chest. This journey would feel lonelier without her.

Almost two years ago, fate placed Rose at Bella's doorstep. At a place called C.A.W.S, also known as the Charlotte Animal Welfare Society. Their newly renovated facility, paid for with taxpayer dollars, had fallen second on John's list of political stops that day. He'd insisted Rose play the part of a good senator's wife and come along. She hated the role—one as fake as her Hollywood upbringing. A fact she'd made clear before he even ran for office.

Rose had attended, mostly in an effort to help their failing marriage. Afterward, they stood near the penned-up dogs as a local TV reporter interviewed John. Rose stood at his side and listened, nodding and smiling like a big phony. Her chest had ached, saddened by all the animals needing homes. John never wanted a pet, no matter how many times Rose had talked about getting one.

Her gaze drifted to a set of bloodshot eyes in a nearby pen. She'd tuned out the reporter and focused on a large basset hound, with drooping sable ears, stubby white paws, and a black, saddle-like patch on its long torso. Impulse had drawn her to the pen. She'd lowered herself to the ground and stuck her fingers through the bars. Bella had waddled closer, her tail wagging. Her wet nose nuzzled Rose's fingers, making her heart wrap around the animal in an instant. She wasn't sure how long she'd been there. When she finally glanced back, the cameraman had turned the camera on her while she played with the dog. Without missing a beat, she'd smiled at her husband. "Let's take this one home."

John's gleaming expression never cracked as he answered the reporter who asked how he felt about taking home a pet. Behind his positive façade, Rose delighted in catching a glimmer of his irritation.

Bella's happy burble pulled Rose from the moment. She stared into the same loving eyes that had caused her to defy her husband in public. She'd never once doubted the decision.

"Time for a walk." Rose patted her leg and Bella followed, unleashed for the moment.

They headed down the long hallway toward the kitchen, where the clank of food preparation meant Leo was up.

Bella's ears lifted. It took only a split second for her to kick it in gear and take off, baying her warning cry loudly.

Rose followed and entered the kitchen just in time to watch the dog slide across the linoleum floor and slam into Leo's bare calves while he stood at the sink filling an old metal carafe with water.

He shut his eyes and his jaw tightened.

Rose stilled, her tongue twisted in a knot at the sight before her. Besides Leo's pained expression, he wore only a pair of gray boxer-briefs. She tried not to gawk at his broad shoulders, tapered waist, long and toned legs. A swimmer's physique.

He opened his eyes, spearing her with his steely gaze for a few seconds before setting the metal pot on the counter and removing a can of coffee from an upper cabinet. Bella wiggled around his legs, tail wagging, but not getting any attention either. Rose breathed in the equally impressive backside of a man who seemed to hate her being there as much as she hated her husband. In sharp contrast to the way she felt about her husband, near-naked Leo made her insides crave a man's touch. It had been way too long.

He cleared his throat and turned around with the can in his hands. "Yes?"

"Nothing." She tried to gather her wits but was as giddy as a hormonal teenage girl. His gaze drifted from her throat to her breasts to her toes, making her cheeks burn. She willed herself back into control. Letting this unfriendly man make her feel this way was just wrong. "Come on, Bella. Time for a walk."

Bella happily followed, seeming unfazed by the stranger's disregard. Rose held her tongue. If she didn't need a pet-friendly place to stay so badly, she'd tell the arrogant grouch a thing or two.

She expelled a cleansing breath and snapped on the leash then hurried to the kitchen door, never happier to get away from anybody. She reached out and twisted the knob, but as a last thought turned to Leo and cleared her throat.

Leo glanced over his broad shoulder and raised his brows.

"Do you think, before I return, you could put on pants?"

The corner of his lip curled, and his toasty caramel eyes shimmered. "Sure." He returned to making his coffee.

Once outside, she inhaled the morning air to calm the wild beat of her heart. Flustered not out of fear, but because Leo made something else inside her crack.

* * * *

Leo stood at the sink, washing out a mug and waiting for the coffee to percolate. Idiot. He'd been half-asleep coming into the kitchen, forgetting all about the stranger living down the hall. What was her name again? She'd just called the dog Bella.

He stared outside. The morning sun outside the kitchen window made up for last night's storm. He reached into a cabinet for a glass and filled it with tap water, drinking it in one swoop to soothe his dry mouth. As he lowered it into the sink, he spotted the woman walking along the row of hedges separating his yard from Harry's property. The dog sniffed with excitement as her long ears dragged the ground. Leo smiled.

The woman's name, right on the tip of his tongue. It started with a T…no, an E.

She bent over and pointed at something. Despite her baggy gray sweatpants, the position she was in exposed the promise of a very nice behind. The shine in her eyes when he'd caught her staring at him in his underwear had shown some heat, or maybe it was only pure shock.

He examined her military-camouflage-patterned T-shirt, which clung closely to the curves of her hips and breasts, rounding out her petite frame. His urges hopped to life, his libido always begging for attention this time of day.

He closed his eyes, inhaled a deep breath. How long since he'd been with a woman? Three months? Four? Since he'd ended things with Susan, of course. Pleasant companionship, but nothing more. Around that time he'd become so absorbed in his book problems, he hadn't missed intimacy. In fact, not until now had he given it much thought. He groaned. *Come on, Leo. Control yourself. You want this woman out of here, not in your dirty fantasies.*

Yet he kept watching her. She'd surprised him with more than her arrival. She hadn't taken any guff from him when he'd tried to toss her out. A move like that deserved respect. When she'd asked him to put on pants earlier, he'd almost laughed, but the way she glared, he figured he'd pay a price for anything but a "Yes, ma'am."

Outside in the backyard, she continued a conversation with the dog and then she laughed, revealing a smile perfect as a crescent moon showcased on a face buried by those silly, oversized glasses. She should find a new optometrist. The haircut almost seemed hasty, the hair color possibly new given the dot of hair dye near her earlobe, and the clothes more suitable for a high school student—not someone who he'd guessed was over thirty. And yet, he couldn't tear his gaze away from the symmetry of her heart-shaped face or those sharp blue eyes.

Had he closed himself up so tight that he'd forgotten what he found attractive in a woman? Forgotten what made him fall in love with Camille?

A raw ache seized his chest, the same ache that stole a little piece of his life every time he thought about his wife.

He breathed in the scent of coffee and waited for it to replace his pain. The scent of waking. Starting a new day. A reminder he was alive and not as dead as he sometimes felt inside. He turned off the burner and got out two mugs, cream, and set the items near the sugar bowl.

The wall phone rang and he walked over and answered. "Hello."

"Mr. Drake? It's Meg, from the real estate office. Good news! I just heard from your brother. He's asked me to draw up a new agreement to allow your tenant to stay in the guest quarters."

"Good news for who?" Leo mumbled.

"What? You think it's good news, too? I hope so, because I have some papers that I'll bring over for you and Emma to sign."

The dog trotted toward the house, his owner in tow. "Come by when you're ready. Thank you."

He hung up and headed for the staircase. Probably better to tell his tenant the so-called good news with his pants on.

How would he ever get this book written with all this activity around him?

God damn his brother! Leo went upstairs. Everett renting the house without telling him once was bad enough, but this second time was deliberate and crossed a...

Leo stopped at the top landing. His anger withered with the realization he did have some power. He'd managed to get one tenant out using this technique. Sure, it was childish, but the last renter had fallen for it rather quickly. And desperation forced extreme measures. Didn't it?

He weighed the foolishness of committing another fake haunting. The first time he'd done it, he'd been surprised the tenant actually fell for it. Considering the idea again reached an all-time low. Once, he never would have considered the act. But he'd never been faced with an unreachable deadline or horrible reviews from his last release. He could do it one last time, then get the lawyers to write up some paperwork stating Everett could no longer rent without Leo's approval.

Decision made. More than anything, he wanted to be alone, and right now he'd stop at nothing—no matter how foolish—to make it happen.

* * * *

"Okay, Emma. Put your John Hancock right here." Meg pointed to a line on the contract lying on the kitchen table.

Rose leaned over and carefully read the reworded document. She made sure it said the dog could stay and the rent was reduced for the smaller living space. Everything seemed in order, so she scribbled her signature, taking care to sign the name Emma Morris. Signing a contract with a fake name probably broke some laws, but she'd pay on time so there were no issues.

She sensed Leo's stare. Lifting her gaze from the document, she found him watching her from his perch at the threshold. He leaned on the trim, his arms crossed and a scowl on his face.

She pushed the contract toward Meg. "All signed."

"Bet you know all about John Hancock." Meg winked at Rose.

"Beg your pardon?"

"Being from Boston and all."

"Oh, yes. Of course, John Hancock is quite popular amongst his fellow Bostonians."

"You don't sound like you come from Boston." Leo pushed himself away from the door and took a step closer, his dark eyes assessing her.

His interest made Rose uneasy. "I was a transplant to the area. Just because I don't *pahk my cah at Hahvad Yahd*, doesn't mean I didn't live there." She turned to Meg. "Is that all?"

"I'll need yours, too, Leo. Your brother suggested you sign this time, so everyone is clear on the arrangement."

He pulled a sour face. On his way over, he took a pair of glasses off the counter and slipped them on. After a quick scan of the agreement, he scribbled an illegible signature. Over the tops of the half-framed reading glasses, he looked at Rose.

"Okay, Eileen. As—"

"Emma," Rose corrected. "It's Emma."

He stared for a long second then removed his glasses. "As a tenant here, there are a few rules. Use what you need from the kitchen; use half the fridge. Keep your dog inside your apartment. And most important, the second level and attic are off limits." He curled his lips into a near-smile. "We wouldn't want another incident like this morning's. Right?"

The image of him at the sink sent a wave of heat to her cheeks. "And you'll stay out of my apartment, too?"

He snorted and shook his head. "If you'll both excuse me, I have work to do and hope it stays quiet enough for me to get some done."

Meg and Rose watched him walk out of the kitchen. The second the stairs squeaked from his footsteps, Meg lowered her voice. "What happened this morning?"

"Oh, nothing really." Rose mentally rehashed every well-muscled, manly inch of detail she'd stumbled upon. "He wasn't dressed properly for a houseguest, that's all."

Meg's eyes widened and a wicked grin crossed her ruby lips. "Lucky you. I've seen pictures of him on the Internet and...well, my-oh-my. He's dated some real beauties. But I had no idea he's such a grump."

"On the Internet? Is he famous?"

"He's a writer. His books are big bestsellers. What is it you do for a living, hon?"

"I'm a travel agent." Rose hoped she sounded nonchalant. "I work from my computer at home, too. I'll be sure to stay out of his way."

"Probably not a bad idea." Meg gathered her papers and stuffed them into her leather tote. "Don't forget. You have a map of town, but it's pretty easy to find your way to things. Call me if you need anything at all. Oh, and I hope you're not worried about those silly ghost rumors and the murder Leo mentioned last night."

Rose laughed, but it didn't stop a tremor inside her belly. "Trust me. Haven't given them a second thought."

Another lie, tossed out like it was a useless penny. Every single time Rose heard a story about a spouse killing the other, her parents flashed in her mind's eye. She stood and followed Meg to the door, working hard to erase the memory. "Thanks for all your help. My ex, he's kind of been stalking me lately."

Meg touched Rose's arm. "You poor dear."

"Yeah, well, I'm done with him now. If anybody comes to town looking for me, can you keep my location quiet?"

"I sure will." She shook her head. "You know, my husband left me last year." Meg's cheery disposition faded. "For another woman. Younger, of course."

"I'm so sorry, Meg. It must be hard."

Meg nodded. Her eyes watered as she launched into a story about how her high school sweetheart had turned into a womanizing bum. "But every day I get up and put a step forward. I refuse to let him ruin my life."

"Sounds like you are doing all the right things to get your life back on track." Rose slipped into psychologist mode automatically. "That's what's important."

"I'm sure trying." Meg sniffled. "Jumping right back on the horse's back."

"Back in the saddle is a great place to be." Rose smiled and winked. "Just don't pressure yourself to drive too fast."

Meg laughed. "I won't. I'll touch base in a few days. See how you're doing. And I hope that ex of yours doesn't show up."

"Me too. And thanks."

As Meg left, a creak sounded on the stairs, followed by footsteps treading on the second level. Rose made a mental note to watch what she said around this place. Leo seemed to be working hard to figure her out, and she didn't like it one bit.

Chapter 4

Bella's wild howl sent Rose dashing from her bathroom and into the main room. The apartment door leading to the rest of the house had somehow become wide open and the dog was nowhere in sight. Already she'd broken Leo's house rules.

Bella let out another distant wail. Rose followed the sounds and found her at the kitchen door, sniffing at the crack near the floor. She peeked outside and spotted Joanne's black Audi next to Rose's used car. A second later, Joanne stepped out, bringing Rose relief at the sight of the first familiar face in days.

"No more howling, Bella. You're going to get me evicted." Rose gripped the dog's collar and opened the door. "Hey! Welcome."

"Boy, am I glad to see you." Joanne draped a vibrant, patterned scarf over her shoulders and reached into the car, removing a red fedora. She tossed the hat on top of her thick sable hair and headed toward the house.

"Holy altered appearance, Batman!" She took the short flight of steps. "That is you, right?"

Rose let go of Bella and reached for Joanne, hugging her college friend tightly. "Yes. It's me." Rose leaned back and lowered her voice. "It's my disguise."

Joanne eyed her from top to bottom. "A far cry from the woman I used to know." Bella squeezed between them and Joanne glanced down. "Well hello there, Bella. I've only seen pictures of you." She patted the dog's head, all the acknowledgment Bella needed before walking away to check out her water bowl.

Rose motioned Joanne into the kitchen and shut the door behind them. "I don't know how I would've gotten away from John without your help."

Joanne flipped her hand with a dismissive wave. "You, my dear, are a fighter. You'd have been fine." She removed her hat, which was crooked from the hug. "First things first...I need a bathroom. There wasn't a single rest stop on these country roads."

"It's definitely quiet up here. Far from the crowds. Just what I asked you to help me find." Rose pointed to the alcove near the kitchen entrance. "The door on the right."

Rose stared out the window over the sink while she waited. Seeing Joanne brought some relief. As freshmen at a small private school in North Carolina, they'd formed a sisterly bond. Rose had even told Joanne that her parents died, leaving out details like who they were and where she'd come from.

Nobody except John knew that on the day after her eighteenth birthday, Emmaline had legally changed her name to Rose Morris, a combination of her own middle name and mother's maiden name. She'd registered at a college on the east coast. She'd thanked her aunt for taking care of her the past four years, then split California for the furthest coastline possible.

A switch inside her had flipped that day, shutting off all sentiment for her past. She'd always felt like just another prop in the stage lives of two celebrities with stadium-sized egos. Destroying what they'd created—Emmaline—had been the only way Rose could stop her childhood from guiding her adulthood.

Silence about where she came from had been a necessary choice at first. Years later, there were days she'd wondered if her new friends would care that her parents had regularly appeared on magazine covers and starred in films. Would they judge the not-so-movielike ending that had left Rose orphaned at the age of fourteen? Answers eluded her. Confession carried risk, and fear had driven her to complete silence.

A creak in the house snapped her to attention, but then silence followed. Was Leo around? The bathroom door opened and Joanne swept into the kitchen.

"I still can't get over how different you look. That hair color, will it come out easily?"

"It says it's a temporary rinse, so I hope so."

"Those glasses are, uh, interesting. And when did you start wearing camouflage patterns? Dear God, Rose. Please tell me you haven't taken up hunting since I last saw you a year ago."

Rose laughed. "No hunting, I swear."

"Well, I wouldn't recognize you if I passed you on the street."

"That's the idea. And a reminder not to use my name. Here they know me as Emma."

"Sorry!" Joanne's hand flew to her mouth as she gasped, her well-shaped eyebrows lifting upward. "I'll be more careful. I still can't believe this is happening."

"Me either. I was so stupid."

"You're not stupid. What John did was wrong."

Hurt over his actions again took a nasty swipe, but Rose gathered the strength inside that always allowed her to persevere in the face of disaster. "I know. To think he'd hurt me, then allow me to go to prison for something he did. I'll be damned if I go without a fight."

"You know I'm here to help you." Joanne glanced around. "Where's the guy who lives here?"

"Not sure. Maybe upstairs."

"Why did they rent it if someone already lives here?"

"The home is owned by two brothers. One rented the place to me but didn't know the other one was already living here."

"I see. Well, remember. My offer to come to my place always stands if this gets to be too much."

"I'll keep it in mind. It's more remote here and nobody knows me." Sadness and disappointment over having to leave her life behind rolled at her like an unexpected wave. More quietly, she added, "The real me."

"Won't being here with a stranger be awkward?"

"Probably. I think he hates me. Oh, he's a writer, like you."

"What's his name?"

"Leo Drake."

"*The* Leo Drake? Pulitzer prize-winning Leo Drake?"

"Could be. My real estate agent said he writes bestsellers."

"Must be the same guy. I'd kill for his sales. Although I don't think his most recent did too well—at least with the critics."

"Explains why he's so miserable."

Joanne laughed. "I've heard he can be the brooding literary type."

"Just my luck."

"Do you think it's safe for you to head into town for lunch?"

"Sure. So far, this disguise is working."

"Great. I'm starving. You can show me around. This place has some interesting history. Did you know its original Native American name for the lake was twenty-two letters long?"

"No. What was the name?"

"Puttacaw—something or other. Not a word you see every day. Let's get going and I'll fill you in on everything else I learned about your temporary home. I think you'll like it here."

"I hope so." She might like it, but she'd never get attached. No place she'd ever lived had settled in her heart as a real home. Lately, though, she could admit something inside of her was the problem. "Let me put Bella in the apartment. My new landlord doesn't appear to be a fan of dogs or desperate women. In fact he's kind of grouchy."

Joanne chuckled. "I'll meet you outside."

She left. Rose returned Bella to the apartment, made sure the water bowl was filled, and closed the door tight on her way out. She wished the living quarters had an outside lock. She'd ask Meg about it later today.

Rose neared the car and realized she'd forgotten money. She hurried back inside and was surprised to find Leo standing in the kitchen, staring into one of the cabinets.

"Hello," she said.

He nodded and went to the refrigerator without a single word.

Rose hurried to her apartment, curious if Leo had overheard any of her conversation with Joanne. She needed to be more careful.

Bella waited on the other side of the door, her tail wagging full force. "Sorry, Bella-bug. I forgot something."

She started toward the bedroom to her money stash: a manila envelope hidden inside her luggage. On her way there, she spotted the change from a fifty broken for groceries last night sitting on the coffee table. She grabbed that instead.

"Back soon," she said to the dog, a twinge of guilt over leaving her alone hitting hard. She shut the door quickly while stuffing the cash in her purse.

On her way through the kitchen, Leo glanced her way as he opened the pantry door. "Leaving?" He raised a brow, a little too much hope in his expression.

"Yup." She hurried to the door. "But I'll be back." She peeked over her shoulder, just in time to catch Leo's optimism wither into a grimace.

* * * *

The brooding literary type?

Leo bristled over the remark and peered out the kitchen door. The visitor's car pulled away, his new tenant riding shotgun. Connecticut plates. So her friend was a fellow author, living in the state. His attention drifted back to the comments the women made. Who'd called him brooding? A thinker perhaps, not exactly extrovert, but brooding?

This was the very reason he needed her gone. Too many people. Too much noise. All equaling less concentration on his writing.

Guilt over eavesdropping gave him a not-so-friendly swat. He hadn't intended to snoop on Emily's…Eileen's…God, why couldn't he remember her name? No matter. With her gone, the book would be done in no time.

He turned away from the door armed with new information about the stranger. From the tidbits he'd caught this morning from the top of the stairs, she played the part of a travel agent on the run from her ex-husband. Did that explain the changed appearance her friend had talked about? Or the name change?

His head pounded while he tried to retrieve the name she'd asked her friend to call her. Argh, what the hell was it? Emma! That's it! He'd been friendly with an Emma back in college so mentally thumbtacked the connection to the name in his brain.

He opened the refrigerator and removed the half-grinder left over from yesterday's lunch as his mind drifted to the conversation about the lake's original name. He remembered the summer he'd learned how to pronounce Puttacawmaumschuckmaug Lake—no easy feat. For a brief few seconds, the irritation weighing him down subsided with fond memories of the cute local girl who'd taught him. Only as he grabbed a Coke and sat at the table to face his lunch, the nasty comments he'd just heard returned.

His appetite shriveled with thoughts of the visitor's description of his writing career. To state that the book he'd written after his Pulitzer Prize-winning novel "didn't do well" was a severe understatement. Try bombed, at least from the critics' perspectives. Fans had received it fairly well, but it wasn't a blockbuster like his Pulitzer Prize winner, or even the bestselling novels before it.

And what right did Emma have to call him grouchy? The night she arrived, he wasn't quite himself. Well, okay. So maybe she had grounds. But not being able to write made him irritable! Fury swelled, rushing in angry streaks to the tips of his fingers. He clenched his fist. Writer's block. Something he'd read about, heard other authors discuss. Not once in a lifetime of writing had he suffered. Only now, it owned him.

He banged the table. The dog whined from the other room, but caught up in his situation, he ignored the cries and took a long sip of his soda.

Finished beating himself up, he turned to the newly discovered facts about his "roommate." The friend had shown surprise at Emma's altered appearance. So what had she changed? He tried to imagine her with black or brown hair, or clothes more suitable for someone old enough to drink legally. Plus, those glasses that didn't fit had to be fake. And who was John? What had he done that might send her to prison?

The dog woofed then let out a long whimper. A little ache singed Leo's heart. The second he saw the basset hound on the night of Emma's arrival, it had reminded him how much he loved having a pet. Camille had never wanted one, despite Leo's stories about his memorable first dog, Max.

A psychologist had recommended the Drakes get Leo a dog shortly after he'd been adopted. His mother's death from an overdose and his subsequent placement in foster care had left Leo distrusting, even of a family trying to do good things for him. Philip Drake, his newly adoptive father, had taken him to the kennel and pointed to a purebred collie recently turned in after the owner passed away.

Instead they'd left with Max, the sandy-colored mixed breed in the next cage with a fanlike tail and floppy ears.

A mutt. A dog whose heritage nobody really knew. Like Leo, who'd never known his father or his mother's family. Each time he'd asked her for answers, she'd concocted another story. Fiction had become a part of Leo's reality long before he started writing and loss had become just another part of living.

The basset hound whined again and, this time, scratched at the door. Leo swallowed back the pain of losing his close canine companion right before he went off to Princeton.

Another scratch to the door, followed by the fast click of paws on hallway hardwood floors. Leo suddenly remembered how the door latch in the apartment sometimes didn't click tight. Bella rushed to the table and danced around his legs while grunting throaty noises of excitement.

"Okay. Okay. Relax." Leo leaned over and rubbed her chest. She stretched her chin upward, taking in the ecstasy of a good scratch, then dropped to the ground and rolled onto her back. He rubbed her belly and calm flowed over his body. "Sorry I've been ignoring you. You're a good doggy, aren't you?"

He stopped and reluctantly stood. Attachment wouldn't be good. "Let's get you back where you belong."

When he called the dog's name, she followed him down the hallway and walked straight back into the apartment. He closed the door, giving it an extra tug until the latch clicked tight.

As he returned to his lunch, Bella howled from behind the closed door for at least a solid minute or two. Leo got up and turned on the counter radio, but the dog seemed to bark even louder. He ate, read his book, and tried to ignore the poor basset's pleas for release. Each second of the dog's sadness became his own.

She finally stopped, and he felt oddly relieved.

Leo finished his meal, enjoying the quiet. He put down the book and lowered the radio. Nope, not a peep from the dog. In fact, it was strange she'd stopped barking so suddenly. A friend of Leo's had lost a black lab while away at the office. The dog had found a smaller ball meant for his cocker spaniel and swallowed it whole. It had become lodged in the lab's throat and she'd died.

Worry took hold of Leo. Had Emma dog-proofed the apartment? He had no idea what could be lying around in there. What if something happened to her pet and she blamed him?

He walked down the hallway, waiting to hear Bella's bark or a scratch at the door. Nothing. He opened the door. "Bella?"

She didn't come. Glancing around, he didn't see her anywhere in the main living area. He stepped inside and peeked into the bedroom. Bella lay on the large bed, spread out like a queen and sound asleep.

"There you are!" Leo had never been more relieved to see an animal.

Bella's eyes flashed open and her tail thumped on the mattress. She scrambled off the bed and rushed Leo. He squatted to pet her and she jumped up, put her paws on his knees, and dragged a wet tongue across his cheek, throwing him off balance.

Leo laughed and plunked onto the floor. Bella sat, too. Leaning against his side, she flipped back her head and gazed at him with bloodshot adoration. Leo ran his hand along her neck. "What's your owner up to, huh, girl? I wish you could talk."

Leo sat that way for a long minute, aware of sense of pure peace settling over him, a weight lessening in his usually stiff limbs. Tight for too long with worries about this book and a general sense of anger about life that had consumed him since losing his wife.

Yet at this exact moment, all the resentment driving him had disappeared. Why couldn't he work harder to feel this good around people? He hadn't always felt so distant from others, so uninterested in being a decent guy.

He stood and glanced around the bedroom. The last time he'd been in here was when his adoptive mother's cancer had worsened and made it hard for her to use the stairs during a family stay. Now a stranger occupied the space.

The double closet held some clothes. Shirts, sweaters, pants, most still carrying tags. A receipt on the dresser caught his attention, so he went over and lifted it. He squinted, his glasses left behind in the kitchen. Target?

Three hundred and fifty dollars? Mostly clothes and toiletries. Roanoke, Virginia? Her Escort had Massachusetts plates and she'd made a point of defending her address when they'd signed the lease. He lowered the suspicious receipt.

A suitcase placed on a walnut luggage rack near the dresser sat open. Only a few items remained inside, and when he caught a glimpse of silk and lace, he immediately turned away.

Woof!

The dog stood looking up at him, a plastic toy chirping inside her mouth each time she bit down. "You want to play, huh?"

A healthy tug of war ensued. Leo won.

He ignored the slobber on his hand and tossed the toy outside of the room. "Go get it!"

As the dog rushed off, Leo laughed. On his way out, he caught his reflection in the mirror above the dresser. A smile. Pure joy, so evident his eyes shined. A rare sight, at least these past years. The smile vanished.

He wandered out of the room, making a quick stop to rinse his hands off in the bathroom. Next to a travel toiletry bag was a box of hair rinse, the shade pretty close to the brassy reddish-orange of his tenant. He tried to imagine her with different colored hair, or in a wardrobe she may have left behind.

He walked into the main living area and spotted a leather attaché leaning upright in the corner of the sofa. Moving closer, he examined the high-quality bag. Something like this would run several hundred dollars. Compared to the used car she'd arrived in, this seemed like a luxury.

Psychology journals lay scattered on the sofa cushions. Odd pleasure reading for someone in the travel business. He peered at the unzipped briefcase where papers stuck out, but quickly discarded any notions about searching inside. Doing so *would* cross a line, further than he'd crossed by entering the apartment.

A picture on an end table caught his eye. A photo of his entire family, taken down at the dock on Blue Moon Lake one summer as they readied themselves for a ride on the motorboat. For a second he wallowed in sadness over losing his adoptive parents, but he shook off the dark cloud as fast as it had rolled in.

The photo gave him an idea for another tool he could use in his plan to scare Emma from the house, as he'd done to the last tenant. He turned it facedown on the end table. This subtle tactic might not get her to leave, but it would make her pause after the picture moved a few more times on its own. That plus a few other tricks far worse than this one he would pull out of his magician's hat.

The last tenant had been easy to get rid of. Over the course of several days, Leo had let himself in with his key each time the man went to work. Staging a haunting wasn't hard. Either that, or the guy spooked easily.

As he stood looking at the overturned photo, part of him felt utterly ridiculous considering the scheme again. But Everett had shut him out, refused to listen when Leo said he needed this house to work. Everett loved control. And since their current problems had developed, he loved tormenting Leo. They needed a long talk, but with Leo's deadline looming, he didn't have the luxury of time.

He'd try this silly haunting thing one more time. It could end up making him look like a fool. Plus, he almost felt bad for Emma. The night of her arrival, a bit of vulnerability showed in her eyes in spite of the brave demands to stay. The idea Emma required help tickled the part of him that couldn't stop caring. A danger zone that he needed to veer as far away from as possible.

Time to think about his own needs. Yes…a second haunting might make this new tenant reconsider living here. He couldn't worry if Emma ran from this place with her tail between her legs because he had a job to do.

But he might miss Bella.

Chapter 5

Only a few days earlier, Rose had enjoyed dinner in her beautiful country kitchen while looking out to the gardens in the backyard. Now, she balanced her salad and chicken in one hand, a glass of wine in the other, and was headed for the teeny apartment she called home. A better choice than sitting at Leo Drake's table. He made her so uneasy she'd probably need an antacid for dessert if she had to eat near him.

Bella had emptied her food bowl but disappeared.

"Bella?" Rose peeked around the corner into a formal dining room with a Queen Anne table and ugly goldenrod curtains. The dog sat near sliding glass doors, her nose pressed to the window. "Come on, pretty girl. My turn to eat."

The hound did a double take at the plate and followed Rose.

Once inside her apartment, she put down her food and slipped on ankle-cropped yoga pants. Fishing through the closet, she found a two-dollar, bargain-rack, white lace T-shirt with a stitched-in black tube top. Probably had been hanging in the store since Madonna arrived on the scene. Rose wasn't leaving this room tonight, so she put it on.

The home's quiet made her wonder if Leo was even home. When she and Joanne had returned from lunch, Joanne had wanted to meet the famous author. Only he wasn't downstairs and going upstairs violated his house rules. Instead, they'd returned to Rose's apartment and done an Internet search on the Drake clan.

They'd found out his parents, Philip and Katherine Drake, had been big into philanthropy, well liked, and both had died before hitting seventy. Mr. Drake had been president of a large firm in Manhattan. Besides the family home on the lake, they owned a place in Manhattan where they'd lived most of the year. Rose recalled the postcard in the pantry and the names took on more meaning.

She sank into the sofa and unzipped her briefcase to remove a study given to her three weeks ago by her editor. Running away or not, she still had deadlines.

She also removed notes she'd started a few weeks ago for the next column of *Dr. Rose Says*. The column always started with a quick line of advice then three or four letters related to the advice theme. The topic choice for the upcoming issue hit too close to home.

Dr. Rose Says: A strong relationship always has trust.

Anger for John shot through her veins like a hot coil. She'd trusted him, perhaps naively so. She no longer loved him, but had she ever? Maybe all John ever represented was the illusion of a "normal" home, not the tender, hard-to-describe emotion people felt for each other.

At the cocktail party where they'd met, he'd charmed her with his intellect, good humor, and charismatic brown eyes that matched his hair, gone slightly gray at the temples. He worked as a partner in a large Charlotte law firm and carried himself with confidence and grace. John was older and wiser than the other men she'd gone out with and his attention disarmed her usual caution.

The longer they dated, she'd found herself confiding small things to him. Like how she'd been orphaned, that she'd been left a sizable inheritance, and, eventually, the truth about her famous parents. When he'd proposed six months after their first date and suggested they run off to Vegas and get married, she'd been ecstatic. The quiet family existence of her dreams had seemed a reality. Second thoughts came three months later.

While dining in the dramatic dim light of Del Frisco's with two other partners and their spouses, John had surprised her by announcing he planned to run for the Senate. As his coworkers shook his hand and vowed to work to get him elected, Rose had sat with a frozen smile that belied the turmoil raging inside her.

Public attention of that type terrified her. Right away, she'd worried the press might uncover details about her old life and her parents' deaths, even though she had thought she'd buried her tracks. Later that night, when alone, he'd asked about using her parents' inheritance for his campaign. She'd said no, suggesting they save it for their children's college. Yet the day he asked for her account numbers and passwords to keep them in a secure place, she'd handed over her PIN without giving the matter any thought. Because she'd trusted him…

What a stupid mistake. She put the pad down and turned to her dinner, spearing a piece of chicken off her plate. Once the PI provided answers about how John had managed to make illegal campaign contributions in *her* name, she'd have to decide how and when to step forward. Only when she could fully prove her innocence. She wished she could prove to the authorities that he intended to hurt her, but she didn't even know who he'd discussed doing so with on the phone.

She swallowed the suddenly tasteless food and reached for her wine glass. The stem clinked, caught on a picture frame turned face down. She flipped it upright. Leo as a teenager stood with people she assumed were his family, a boyish version of the man he'd become. The Waspy, blond features of his parents and siblings made Leo stand out as different. Where had the dark hair, lanky build, and intense gaze come from?

She returned to her work, ignoring the column and focusing on the feature article her editor had asked her to write. "Find a new take on this," her editor had said, giving Rose a study by a psychologist who claimed he could make people fall in love.

Rose had cringed, reminded that her boss didn't realize she was a grade-A phony. Writing a column on relationships didn't make her an expert on love. Nor did her doctorate in psychology.

She spent the next forty minutes reading over the study. The premise: human subjects who'd never met, simply asking each other a series of questions and supposedly falling for each other.

Sure they did. What a ridiculous notion, but this could make a great article. A specific angle eluded her, though if she found some real life guinea pigs and put them to the test, a story idea might evolve.

She rummaged inside her briefcase for her planner to jot down a brief outline. The planner wasn't there, so she went into the bedroom and straight to the luggage. Last she'd seen the planner, it had been next to her money inside one of the pockets.

Rose easily found the planner, but with a further look around, she realized her money wasn't there. She patted the main compartment, pushed aside a few items she hadn't unpacked. Still no money.

The slow heat of panic rippled through her chest, but she took a deep breath. Maybe she'd unpacked it. She yanked open every dresser drawer, checked behind and underneath the furniture. Once she'd searched every cranny of the room, she pulled apart the bathroom and living room. Nothing.

She took a steadying breath and grabbed her car keys. In the dark driveway, she used the flashlight from the glove compartment to search the car but came up empty-handed.

Tears burned at the back of her eyes as she returned to the house. How could she have been so careless? She entered the kitchen and canvassed the counters, although she didn't recall ever having the money in here.

She'd given Meg the rent money. Then there was the grocery store visit. The moment she'd come inside before her lunch with Joanne, she'd grabbed change from the fifty off the table. So where could the rest be?

A slow awareness of Leo standing in this very location at that moment made her blood boil. Her unlocked apartment while she'd stepped out for lunch provided a perfect opportunity for someone to enter her room.

Rose stormed down the hallway to the staircase and flipped on the light switch. She paused for a second, remembering his rules. House rules be damned!

At the top, a long hallway greeted her with several aged, brown-stained doors, all closed but one. One at the far end faced her. Light peeked out from beneath the lower edge and jazz music drifted from overhead.

She headed toward it, pausing near a room with an unmade four-poster bed, heavy blue curtains, and oriental-patterned rug. Leo's bedroom. She continued to the door she hoped was his office, inhaled a deep breath, and banged on the raised panel.

Nothing. Rose jiggled the glass doorknob. "I need to talk to you!"

A chair scraped; the music lowered. The heavy tread of footsteps pounded, like someone walking down stairs.

The door flew open. Leo stared back, his gaze hard as granite. He wore sweatpants and a Princeton sweatshirt, the sleeves pushed to his elbows. He took a slow sweep of her from top to toe; then his eyes met hers. "Didn't I ask that you not come up here? I'm working."

"You did. I have a problem." She glanced over his shoulder at a staircase, presumably leading to the attic.

He crossed his arms across his broad chest and shifted, blocking her view. "Which is?"

"I left today and…well…" She swallowed, not having really thought through exactly how to say this. "Were you in my apartment?"

His lips twitched and shadowed jaw clenched. "Why would you ask that?"

"My money is missing. It was in an envelope and now I can't find it. I even checked the car. Since there's only the two of us in this house—"

"I'm sorry it's missing, but I did not take your money." He unfolded his arms and ran a hand through his hair, making the pieces shift into a perfect mess. "Anything else?"

"How can you explain that it's missing? Who could have—"

"Do I seem like a man who has to steal to survive?" he asked tightly.

He didn't, but she shrugged. "What else can I assume?"

"Well, I don't need to steal to pay for groceries or other overheads." He arched a dark brow. "In fact, when I'm not being interrupted, I work and actually get paid. There are some ATMs in town. Hopefully, what's missing will turn up." He reached for the edge of the door. "Unless you have something else to ask me…"

"No, but I—"

The door closed. Rose fumed. This guy was lying. Maybe not about stealing her money, but guilt of some type was written all over his unfortunately handsome face.

* * * *

Leo pulled into Litchfield Hill Farm and Vineyards. He passed Jay Moore's colonial at the entrance and continued to the barn-turned-tasting-room. Bright lights illuminated the building against the dark fields.

Leo drove straight up the hill and parked in front. He sat inside the dark car, early for his meeting with the Jay. Emma's accusation that Leo took her money had taken him by surprise. Chalk up another encounter with her where he'd reacted poorly. Not the man he once was, but some angry shell of himself. So what if she'd ruined his ability to concentrate? Concentrate on what? A half-finished novel missing something critical he couldn't identify?

Without a doubt, he could've been more sympathetic. Hindsight, a useful tool for insight and nothing more. Rather than let the regret take him down, he opened the car door and hoped Jay didn't mind if he was early.

Leo walked to the side entrance, to the room where wine production took place. He could only hope his creative skills didn't fail him tonight. Helping come up with names for the winery's two new creations had sounded like fun.

It surprised Leo he'd found a friend in Jay. Socializing wasn't his thing. On his second day back in town, while Leo sat at the Sunny Side Up counter having a quiet lunch with his book, a tall man two seats away with blond hair fading to silver pulled back in a short ponytail turned to him.

"New in town?"

Leo turned, surprised by the interruption. The stranger wore a beige cap that said *Litchfield Hills Vineyard.*

"Sort of." Leo hadn't been in the mood to go into details, but a vineyard held interest. "Is that winery on your cap nearby?"

Jay talked for the next ten minutes, his love for the vineyard property drawing Leo right in. Before Leo knew it, he'd agreed to stop by that afternoon to take a look around. By that night, he'd found a comrade. A man who—like Leo—enjoyed the simpler things in life, had little tolerance for things that didn't sit right, and, to Leo's surprise, was widowed like him. Not that either ever discussed the aftereffects of their tragedies. Only surface chat about Jay's wife's car accident this past year, Camille's cancer, and how Jay found single parenthood tough.

Leo pulled open the door and stepped onto the polished concrete floor. Passing a lineup of stainless steel vats and a crate filled with empty wine bottles near a machine used for bottling, he entered the tasting room.

"Jay?" Leo's voice reverberated in the quiet space. He spotted a light on in one of the upper-level offices overlooking the rustic tasting room.

"Be right down."

Leo stood for less than a minute and Jay appeared at the top landing, looking down. "Hey, buddy. You're early." He walked down the stairs. "Thanks for helping out with this." Jay smiled, but circles under his eyes suggested he hadn't slept well.

Leo had had countless bad nights' sleep the first year without Camille. "Glad to be of service. Never did I dream I could mix my love of both writing and drinking."

Jay softly smiled as he went behind the bar, removed two stemmed goblets from a rack hanging overhead, and put them on the bar top. "First, you've met Trent, right? Our marketing manager?"

Leo nodded. "I have. The musician."

"Yup. He came up with what I thought were great names for the new additions to our collection. Sophie didn't like them and Duncan was on the fence. When I told them we had a new customer with a palette for wine tasting and a Pulitzer Prize in fiction, Duncan sarcastically suggested we ask you to do it. Figured it wasn't a bad idea."

"Your call this afternoon was a welcome distraction."

"Bad day?"

"Bad couple of days. The never-ending saga with my brother." Leo had complained to Jay about Everett renting to the last guy at the house.

"Siblings. It's never easy. Sophie and I still have our share of disagreements." Jay tugged out the cork. "But overall we get along."

"Unfortunately, the bullshit with my brother has gone on for years. Everett makes the Hatfields and McCoys look like they haven't a care in the world."

Jay winced and poured a little bit into each of their wine glasses. "Sounds stressful."

"It is. It really is. Thank God for my sister. If I couldn't vent to her, I'd be lost." Leo chuckled. "Now if she'd only stop with the blind dates."

Jay eyes widened. "Don't mention that around Sophie. Don't want to give her any ideas." He re-corked the bottle, his thoughts elsewhere, before he glanced up. "Mind if I ask you a question?"

"Not at all."

"How soon before you started dating again?" Jay's tone shifted, less conversational and softer. "I mean, after losing your wife."

"I guess it was around the year mark. My sister fixed me up with a woman she played tennis with."

"Were you ready for it?"

"No. Not even close. Much as I hate to admit it, it was a good first step. My sister made me change my shirt twice and talked nervously through the entire meal, barely giving me chance to get to know her friend."

And where was he now, though? A handful of dates past that moment with one attempt at a relationship, ended because it hadn't felt right. Now he'd run from the urban environment where he'd at least occasionally meet people. Northbridge took him further into a retreat. Jay's question was a good one. Maybe Leo hadn't been ready before. Was he even ready now?

"Must be a good memory."

Leo drew his attention back to Jay, whose expression was filled with curiosity. "Sorry. Neither good nor bad. Just remembering those first few times. They were tough. Why? Something come up?"

"A few hints from friends. Just trying to decide when it's right to move forward."

"You're probably asking the wrong guy. I'm still sorting things out. Guess we'll both know when it's right."

Jay reached out and patted Leo's shoulder. "Glad to know I'm not alone." He pushed one of the filled glasses in front of Leo. "Now let's name some wine."

* * * *

Beethoven's "Ode to Joy" mingled with the smell of coffee. Rose opened her eyes and processed the strange surroundings. Oh, right. Her hideout.

Her phone continued to ring the musical masterpiece. She used her elbows to sit up and reached for it. Her mouth was thick and dry, but she licked her lips and said, "Hello."

"Emma?"

Rose took a second to process both the voice and name. "Meg?"

"Yes. Oh, I'm sorry. Did I wake you?"

"It's fine. I needed to get up soon." Rose shifted to her bottom and pushed the pillows behind her back. She glanced at the clock. 9:00. She never slept this late.

"Just checking in. I hoped everything was going all right with Mr. Drake…Leo. I'm worried about you, that's all."

"Aw, thank you, Meg. You're very sweet. Leo was fine. I have a little problem, though." Rose considered her words, because she couldn't blurt out the truth. "I was going to open a bank account in town today, but now I can't find the cash I'd brought with me. It's left me with not much money in my pocket."

"Oh dear." Meg was quiet for a moment. "I've got an idea. Because you paid me for the original full month rent, I was just going to apply the overage to the next month, at the new rate. How about I return the second month to you?"

"Thank you. That would be a start."

"I know you work at home, the travel agent thing, but any interest in a weekend job to make a little extra?"

"Doing what?"

"Two days ago, my friend who owns a vineyard said she needed someone part-time on the weekends. It's the vineyard you passed coming from town to your place."

Working outside of this house while in hiding didn't seem practical, but how many people could there be visiting vineyards in remote rural towns? "I'm not sure I'm qualified."

"Why not let them decide?"

At least it would give her more cash. She'd keep searching for the envelope in the meantime. "Okay. So how do I apply?"

"Let me call Sophie, the owner. If she's around, can you stop by today?"

"Sure."

"I'll call you back."

"Thanks, Meg. I truly appreciate the help."

"Anytime, hon. We gals gotta stick together. God knows we can't count on the men."

"No kidding."

Rose hung up and swung her feet over the side of the bed. Bella lay flat on her back on the floor, her front paws limp and back legs wide open.

"That's not a very ladylike pose."

The dog blinked back but stayed that way. Rose showered then tossed on her stretchy pants and a baggy UConn Huskies sweatshirt purchased at a rest area. She tugged the price tag off the sleeve and slipped on a pair of socks decorated with cartoon dogs. Not a normal wardrobe choice, but something she planned to wear even after this ordeal ended.

After running a brush through her wet hair, she put on her glasses and headed to the kitchen. Leo sat at the table, the paper open in front of him and a mug in one hand. Instead of his usual gray sweatpants, he wore faded jeans, a slight tear in one knee, and a wrinkled *House of Blue's— Chicago* T-shirt.

His gaze focused on the paper behind a pair of wire-framed glasses she hadn't seen before. He didn't look up. "Good morning. I made a big pot of coffee. Help yourself."

"Thank you."

She walked over to an old-fashioned stove percolator, wondering if she'd traveled back in time instead of across several state borders. The tin object had a few dents in its armor from decades of use. Near it sat a white coffee mug decorated with bright flowers and a cracked glaze interior.

"The mug is for you." Leo turned the page but still didn't look her way.

"Thank you."

She filled it and added cream. Yesterday he'd left the coffee fixings out, too. A nice gesture, in spite of his aloof behavior the rest of the day.

Bella wasn't hovering around for her breakfast, so Rose tossed an English muffin into the toaster for herself. Keeping her back to Leo, she waited and looked out into the backyard. A minute later, Bella's nails clicked on the floor. Rose opened the container of food and filled the bowl with kibbles. She looked down, surprised Bella wasn't doing the I'm-gonna-eat wiggle around her legs.

She glanced over her shoulder. Leo had lowered the newspaper and pushed the glasses to the top of his head. Leaning over, he scratched under the dog's chin, the distant, angry expression he usually wore replaced by softer lines.

In a low voice, he whispered, "How's sweet Bella today?"

Good to know the man who stole her money wasn't a completely heartless ass. "Okay, Bella. Breakfast."

Leo jerked his hand away and scrambled for the paper.

Rose lowered the bowl to the floor and caught Leo watching her. "Mind if I leave the dog in here with you while I dry my hair before taking her out?"

"It's fine." He continued reading.

She started down the hallway.

"Oh, Emma?"

She turned. "Yes?"

"About your lost money. I understand paying the rent may be tough." The corner of his lip lifted slightly against the shadowed grain of his cheeks. "I'd be happy to let you out of the lease we just signed."

She narrowed her eyes. As she suspected, he had *every* reason for making her funds disappear. Her gut trembled, but she forced a smile. "Lucky for you, I'm paid through the month. Besides, I may have a job interview in town."

Leo watched her with raised brows and a smug twitch of his lips.

"FYI. If you think a little thing like stealing my money will change my plans, you, sir, are sorely mistaken."

She straightened her back, lifted her chin, and stalked down the hallway, the burn of his gaze searing her back.

Seemed he was still an ass, after all.

* * * *

Leo drank in the angry flash of Emma's eyes, icy as an arctic blast. Not cold enough to dismantle his appreciation of her backside as she left. With each step, her fitted pants showed off her swaying curves. The dog socks were an interesting touch. He smiled, in spite of his better judgment.

As she disappeared into her doorway, the quick glimpse of the silky garments from her luggage popped into his thoughts. He shifted in his seat, bothered by both his desires and the idea she could cause this reaction. Her determination at his door last night had been annoying, yet everything about her pushed the buttons of his curiosity.

Or could it be the lies she told? There were lies, and then there were *lies*. He sensed hers stemmed from the glimmer of sadness he'd often catch in her eyes. The type of lies not meant to hurt anybody. If he didn't have his own problems right now, he'd almost feel bad for her.

Last night's accusation about the money still nagged at him. He'd been caught off guard when she accused him of going into her apartment. Right away, he figured she'd learned about his snooping around.

The dog finished eating and waddled over.

"Hey, Bella. My new friend." He leaned over, patted her side, and whispered, "Remember, my visit is our little secret." Bella offered a compliant tail wag.

Leo removed his glasses from his head and put them on the table. He went to the stove to pour a second cup of coffee. With any luck, this tenant of his might not want to stay here much longer. Moving the picture was only a start. Tomorrow night he'd take it a step further. Nothing overly terrifying, but he'd once read about the psychology behind paranormal belief. How the mere suggestion of supernatural elements often made people buy into the idea that what they'd witnessed was ghostly—not explained by natural forces. People believed what they wanted to believe. Hopefully he wouldn't frighten her too much.

What if he did terrify her, though? A sensation inside of him shifted, almost like...no. Guilt? He couldn't back down now. Otherwise, he might be stuck with her for months. Or longer.

He shook it off, with better thoughts of a bike ride this morning. For the first time in ages, he'd woken with an urge to move his body, breathe in the fresh air. It might help stimulate some progress once he got back to his office.

He stood and patted his side. Bella followed him to the apartment door left partially open. From here, he could see Emma at the living room window, staring outside with deep concentration, the sunlight picking up highlights of rich copper in her dried hair. A woman with problems, for sure. The desire to understand why swept through him. As quickly as it hit, he pushed it aside. He had his own problems.

He cleared his throat. "Emma?"

She turned and her worried expression vanished.

"The dog's done eating. I'm going upstairs."

She came toward the door and motioned for Bella to go inside. "Thank you."

He stopped himself before saying "Anytime." "Tomorrow I'll be heading out of town for the night. Please make sure you lock up if you leave."

"I will."

He drained his coffee and headed upstairs to change. At the base of the staircase, he stopped and leaned over. A silky pair of bikini underpants lay on the hardwood floor. Where the hell did those come from?

Great. Now she was carelessly leaving her things around the house. Why was she even near the stairs? He'd asked her to stay away from the second floor. The usual irritation lassoed him. More distractions. This one a disturbance of the worst kind: a reminder of the opposite sex and all the great things that came with them. Another reason why he didn't want a stranger lurking around.

He picked them up and headed back toward the kitchen, guided by his irritation and ready to remind her about his house rules. Halfway to her apartment he paused. What was he going to do? Knock on her door and hand them off, as if that wouldn't come with its own embarrassment? He turned around. Next time she left the house, he'd slip them back inside her room.

He hurried upstairs to the attic, tossed the panties in the bottom drawer of his file cabinet, and sent off a quick email to his assistant about getting together. After shutting off the computer, he went to his room to get changed for his ride.

On his way downstairs, he brainstormed ideas about his manmade paranormal encounter. Then another idea hit him. Before going through all the trouble of staging a haunting, he might try to appeal to Emma's reasonable side. Surely she had one. After all, a gentlemanly part of him hated to scare her if he didn't have to. If she knew the truth about his contract commitments and trouble writing, she just might reconsider living here.

And if reason didn't work, surely after one scary night, Emma would beg the real estate agent to find her a new place.

Chapter 6

Rose crinkled her nose as she stared into the refrigerator. She pushed aside Leo's leftover slice of pizza—sitting unwrapped on a plate—a half-used can of Hormel chili, and two six packs of Coke. Behind them, she took stock of her own remaining food: two apples, a container of baby romaine leaves, and a half wedge of cheddar. Her stomach growled. She'd have been to the grocery store and back with food for lunch if she hadn't gotten sidetracked searching for her missing cash.

She wished Leo were leaving for his overnight today, not tomorrow. Earlier, Meg had dropped off the other half of the rent money. Rose had half considered getting some takeout for a festive dinner tonight; after all, having some cash in her hands deserved a celebration. The idea of eating alone in her apartment, though, didn't have the same appeal as sitting at a nicely set table—something she couldn't do with him home. Plus, the found money shouldn't be wasted. She hoped this afternoon's interview at the vineyard could solve her money woes.

Leo walked into the room, came up behind her, and peered into the refrigerator. His warmth radiated against her back. Pretty cozy for a guy who'd stolen her money. She pulled her thin cardigan tight against the haltered maxi-dress top. Not the strangest article of clothing in her new apparel, but worn with black Keds instead of pretty sandals, she hoped it sent a very unlike–Dr. Rose message.

She glanced over her shoulder and his smoldering caramel eyes met hers. Why couldn't she have landed in the home of an unattractive writer, with bloodshot eyes and a wart on his nose? Her glasses slipped a notch and she pushed them back up. "Am I in your way?"

"Nope." He reached past her and removed the slice of pizza. Then he smiled. A little too nicely.

She almost asked where he planned on going tomorrow. Instead, she shut her mouth. The less she knew about him, the better. With one last sweep of the refrigerator, she closed the door and turned around.

Leo's back was to her as he opened the microwave door and put in the plate. "I wanted to apologize to you."

"For taking my money?"

"No." He sighed and shook his head. "To say I'm sorry about how I acted the night you arrived. I wasn't showing my best side." He closed the door, pushed a few buttons on the keypad before facing her again. "But I'd like to explain why."

She crossed her arms and leaned against the counter, quite curious where this was headed. "Go on."

"When I write, I need solitude to make progress on my work."

"That's understandable."

The corners of his mouth turned up, one step from a full smile. It warmed his face and showed he was really quite handsome when not scowling.

"The reason I asked you to find somewhere else to live is because I'm running the risk of not meeting the deadline on my book. I returned to this house to get it done. It's where I spent time growing up, and where I often do my best work."

Rose nodded and waited.

"This house, the lake, it's always been one of my favorite places since I was a kid. It's where I've penned a few of my more successful novels, and I guess I simply write better when I'm here. And it's quieter with nobody else around."

"The place sounds special to you. But I can't imagine Bella and I are creating that much noise."

"Having others in the house, it's a distraction."

"I see. Well, thank you for explaining. I promise we'll be quiet." Had she misread him? Maybe he wasn't such a bad guy after all. "I'm heading to Bellantoni's to pick up a few things. Do you need anything? Maybe some plastic wrap for your unused food?"

"No, but thanks." He paused and studied her for a moment. "In light of what I shared, I hoped you might reconsider your plans to stay here."

"Oh." Leo, with sleight of hand, had played the honesty card. "So, me leaving would help you get your book done?"

He smiled more comfortably. "Exactly. It would go a long way to restoring my preferred work environment."

The microwave dinged. He removed his food, set it on the table, and sat down in front of it, watching her with an expectant expression.

"May I ask you a question?"

"Sure." He reached across the table for a napkin.

She pulled out the chair across from him. "In the time you were here before I arrived, how was your writing coming along?"

"Fair." He avoided her eyes.

"Perhaps the writing issues you're having are about more than me being in the house. I mean, if progress was fair before my arrival, the problem might not be me."

He lifted the pizza. "It's a bit more complicated. However, rest assured, your presence *is* a distraction."

Leo's incessant need to get rid of her hurt, deep in a place Rose always guarded carefully. Silly she'd let it bother her, but John's lack of love these past years had her almost believing she was neither likeable or loveable to the opposite sex.

Rather than let the feeling own her, she took a clinical approach. "You know, I may be able to help you."

He'd been about to bite into the slice, but lowered it and raised his dark brows. "By leaving?"

"No." She couldn't tell him she wrote a self-help column for a magazine, but another little lie couldn't hurt. "I'm getting a graduate degree in psychology. Even taking some online classes right now." Not so far from the truth. She just happened to already have the degree. "You should go back to when you first started having trouble with your writing, to pinpoint the real issue."

"Look." He straightened his back, returned the food to the plate, and scrubbed his unshaven cheek with his palm. "I need it quiet. I know my process."

She waited. Silence. A tried and true way to get her patients to talk. Leo stared back, his brown eyes clouded.

When enough time passed she said, "I read a case study about a painter. Whenever his relationships started, it inspired his artwork. Probably from that rush we all get when we're in love."

Leo rolled his eyes.

She continued anyway. "Whenever a relationship ended, he couldn't paint at all. The same type of thing might be going on with you. Like the problems you appear to have with your brother, or—"

Leo shot to his feet and his chair scraped against the vinyl floor. "I thought if I explained this to you, you might be more understanding. And I don't recall asking for a therapy session."

He went to the refrigerator and removed a can of Coke.

"Fair enough. I'm sorry." John had always hated when she got scientific, too. Being clinical made her feel safe and restored order to things that otherwise left her sad, even confused. But others didn't have the same need. "Listen, I'm only trying to help. For instance, a healthier drink choice might be water, or even seltzer. Maybe caffeine has your mind so wired you can't work." She grinned, hoping a little humor could steer this conversation in a better direction.

He paused and considered her with furrowed brows for a long second, then returned to his seat and yanked off the top tab. "I don't need anybody's help. With my drink choices or why I'm stuck on my work."

Rose doubted it, but she kept quiet. Her cell phone vibrated on the kitchen table. The name of the PI she'd hired flashed across the caller ID. She grabbed the phone and got up. "Excuse me. I need to take this."

She hurried down the hallway, shutting the door, and quickly answered. "Hi, Dan. Any news?"

"Just an update, like I promised." Dan Montgomery's gentle voice held a quality that reassured and calmed, one reason Rose had hired him to investigate John's deceptions. "Are you okay?"

"Hanging in there."

"Good. Here's the latest. An investigator has been following your husband since yesterday. We may need to get access to his personal computer to get to the bottom of this. My top guys are on it, though. If John's done what you think, we're hoping we'll be able to prove *he* siphoned money from your accounts and disbursed those funds into his campaign—not you. Anything to show the Justice Department you're not behind those contributions is our goal. Hopefully we can get something before they catch on. Give me a week, ten days tops."

Accessing John's personal computer? It almost sounded as if Dan might be doing something illegal to find out the truth. Could she get in trouble for that, too? The weights of justice teetered evenly, one bad thing versus another. Ultimately, though, her only choice was to overlook the PI's actions. Evidence pointing to John could mean the difference between her going or not going to jail.

"Thank you. Call the second you learn anything."

Rose hung up and searched the apartment for Bella. Shoot. She'd left her in the kitchen with Leo.

Damn him! Did he really think she'd leave simply because he couldn't write his book? Given his bad relationship with his brother, he clearly had problems before her arrival.

She'd tolerate Leo and his rudeness for now. If Dan's progress went well, she might be out of here in less than a month. Assuming nothing else went wrong.

* * * *

"Aaarrrggghhh!" Leo ripped the paper from the typewriter, crushed it into a ball, and threw it into the corner. It landed on the floor, about a foot from the trashcan near the other crumpled paper balls.

He inhaled a deep breath, blew it out, and his shoulders relaxed. Maybe his sister was right. If he used a computer, like the rest of the civilized world, he might save a rainforest or two. He lifted the yellow legal pad where he'd sketched out a loose outline. He still couldn't figure out what was missing from one of his characters, one that he wanted to have a strong point of view, yet every time he tried to hone in on what motivated her, he came up empty.

Let's face it. He'd been useless since returning to work after lunch.

Emma's cute quip about caffeine had surprised him. The mysterious phone call that sent her scurrying down the hall had left him far too curious. And worse, his honesty had backfired. The conversation hadn't gone as planned. In his head, it would have played out more genuine and heartfelt. The way he used to have conversations with people. He worried stress and irritation over his deadline had made his words sound disingenuous.

For a brief moment, she'd seemed to hear his deadline concerns. Then, without warning, the conversation switched to a quick round of psychoanalysis. On him! Instead of taking the bait, she'd unleashed annoying reminders of why his muse had probably disappeared in the first place. She had no business giving him advice; she seemed to have her own problems.

Plan B—being reasonable—was out. Pressure to meet his book deadline loomed. Hope to finish the book rested in the idea he could restore quiet to his household. The jumbled mess of limited choices that might get her to leave pounded inside his head. All roads returned to those ridiculous scare tactics, mainly because it had worked on the last tenant.

A voice from outside carried through the open attic window. He stood, stretched his arms over his head to work out the kinks, and made his way over. The quiet lake rippled and trees were now in full bloom, hiding homes on the hillside and changing the entire landscape from when he'd arrived two months ago.

"Go get it, Bella-bug!"

On the lawn, not far from his boat dock, Emma tossed a neon tennis ball. Bella's ears flopped as she raced to the rolling ball. She picked it up then happily trotted back to Emma, dropping it at her feet. Emma threw the ball again and the dog went wild in pursuit. On the third toss, Bella walked in the opposite direction of the ball. A gentle breeze molded the fabric of Emma's long skirt to her body, outlining every soft curve of her hips and thighs for him to view.

Emma tossed back her head and laughed, hearty and genuine. "Aw, come on!"

The dog sniffed the grass and ignored her, obviously on the trail of a good scent. A scent better than a ball.

Emma hurried over to the ball. As she ran, her boyish sneakers peeked out from beneath the dress hem. She picked up the ball, talking to Bella the whole time. When Emma rolled it directly to the dog, the canine sniffed it once then plunked her chunky body down on the ground, no longer interested.

Emma's runaway strands of shiny red hair shimmered from the sunlight, and her joyful laugh filled the air, carrying up to his window. A peaceful sensation rolled over him and a smile crept along Leo's lips, catching him by surprise.

Everything missing since he'd arrived at the house became clear. This stranger and her dog brought energy here. Camille's energy. So contagious even a sworn loner like him wasn't immune to her power.

Emma probably thought him a grouchy ogre. Exactly what his wife had thought when they'd first met—at a family gathering—right after Leo graduated from college. When she'd been dating his brother.

When Everett introduced Camille, Leo had pegged her as another blue-blooded and entitled wealthy gal, the type his brother always dated. It wasn't until years later, long after Everett and Camille had ended things, that Leo ran into her again in a Manhattan restaurant.

An innocent cup of coffee the next day had led to dinner two nights later. Camille was nothing like he'd assumed. Her presence had brought Leo a measure of peace he rarely felt. They'd become inseparable. At that time, Camille confessed her ogre opinion of Leo from that first family gathering. She'd also said she was glad she'd dug deeper, because he hid all his good parts from others. It made Leo love her all the more.

A month later, Leo had finally found the courage to call his brother and tell him about the chance meeting with his ex-girlfriend and their dating. Everett had been silently polite. The fury had come during their first family get together as a couple. Everett had refused to speak to either of them.

It hadn't taken much to figure out why. Winning drove Everett. Not only during childhood when the kids played games, but proven by his success in the corporate world as an adult. Leo's relationship with Camille fell under Everett's loss column.

Bella howled as a duck landed on the dock, jarring Leo back to the view from the attic window. Thinking about Everett's competitiveness drew another reality about his relationship with Camille to light. One making Leo queasy with a truth he'd never seen before. Were his goals in pursuing Camille back then pure, or had Leo found a teeny piece of satisfaction in the idea that he had secured the love of a woman who wouldn't give it to his brother? A brother who'd shoved every win in Leo's face. Like Leo's start in life didn't leave him feeling inferior enough.

His cell phone rang. He checked the display. Shit. Seth. Leo hesitated for a second then answered. "Hey. I've been meaning to call you."

"Oh? Good news?"

"You need news? I can't just reach out to a friend?"

Seth laughed. "Hey, an agent can hope. Two things…first, good luck at your interview in Boston this week. The producers appreciate you doing some promo for the movie."

"I'm happy to do it," he lied. Promotion was his least favorite part of writing. Movie rights for *The Wolfe Wars* had sold right before the novel won the Pulitzer. The complex examination of class struggles took the success of all his novels to unimaginable heights, but scrambling to stay there was prudent. This interview was necessary.

"Good. I'm heading to Vermont this weekend. A firm retreat. One of the other agents has a house up there."

"Sounds fun."

"Not really. But sometimes duty calls. I pretty much drive straight past your lake house. Up for some company and an overnight guest? Assuming you're coming back home after the interview."

Leo hesitated, knowing full well this was more about a face-to-face talk than the book. It could help, though. "I'll be back by then. Sure. Come on up."

"Susan might drive up with me. Do you mind if she stays, too? She said you two were still friends."

Susan, Seth's co-worker who Leo had dated last year, possessed a quality Leo couldn't resist. Quiet desperation. Her needs were hidden beneath a likeable persona, but the first time they'd talked, Leo had learned about her unhappiness after a difficult divorce. His "fix-it" desires wanted Susan to feel happier. Only this time, a few months into dating her, Leo woke to the reason why he chose this type of women: he'd seen enough of his mother's addiction issues as a kid to wish he'd been able to fix her, too. He'd ended things with Susan before they got too serious.

"Of course we're still friends. Let her know she's welcome."

"Great. Glad to see you're not going all J.D. Salinger on us."

Leo chuckled, even though his efforts to be alone continued to unravel with more visitors. "No. I told you where I was. I'd love some company."

"Try to find a decent place for us to go out Friday night. Preferably where I don't need a flannel shirt."

"Bring one along, just in case."

"See you Friday around dinner time."

As Leo hung up, a car engine outside the window sputtered to life. He went to the window in time to see Emma's car disappearing down the driveway.

He headed out his door and down the stairs. Time for a break. Besides, if Bella was alone down there, she might like some company.

* * * *

"The lake view from here is spectacular." Meg pointed across the field.

Rose turned and squinted into the sun. From this vantage point, the lake opened up, showing more of the nooks and crannies of the shoreline than were visible from Leo's house. Besides the perfect view and lines of leafy vines along the hillside of Litchfield Hill Vineyards, goats bleated in a pen near the barn and hens clucked.

"Such a beautiful lake. And this vineyard and farm…it's so peaceful around here."

Meg nodded. Dressed in jeans and a flannel shirt, not her real estate attire, she looked like a downhome country gal. "A few years back, this place was a dump. My friend Sophie, her husband, and her brother worked magic. Let's go inside and see if Sophie's free."

They entered a warm and welcoming room with rustic beamed ceilings and terracotta tiled floors. A woman glanced up from stacking wine bottles.

"Hi. You must be Emma." She lowered the box to the floor and came out from behind the bar, her hand extended. Her dark eyes matched her chocolate hair and she'd dressed in barnyard casual, like Meg. "I'm Sophie Jamieson. Nice to meet you."

"You, too." Rose suddenly wished for her old appearance. The cheap glasses to disguise her face got a little looser every day and she desperately needed a better haircut. "This is a beautiful place you've got here."

"Thanks. It's been a lot of work, but worth every second."

"A real dream come true, right, Soph?" Meg piped in.

A tall man entered through a doorway wiping his hands on a dirty rag. Worn jeans hung on his hips, kept in place by a thick leather belt that also secured his chambray shirt.

"Hello there, ladies." He winked at Meg. "I thought I heard you."

Meg's fair skin turned pink. "Hi, Charlie."

"Emma"—Sophie put her hand on the man's shoulder—"this is Charlie Van Patten. He joined us three months ago to give Jay, my brother, a hand with our wine making. We don't know how we got by without him."

"Thanks, Sophie." He tipped his head at Rose. "Nice to meet you." He quickly returned his steadfast gaze to Meg. "I'm glad you're here. Got a second? I need an opinion."

Meg's sweet face brightened. "Me? Of course I've got time for you."

Charlie grinned, and they disappeared through the curtained doorway.

Sophie turned to Rose. "Poor Meg. Her husband left her last year. She was so loyal to him, but he…" Sophie shook her head. "Well, he wasn't as good to her. I'm thrilled to see this thing brewing with Charlie. He's a great guy."

"That's sweet." Sadness niggled at Rose. She wanted a great guy. Not a man who used her, like John. "Meg has made me feel at home here."

Sophie motioned to a table and pulled out a chair. "Meg's the best. Why don't you take a seat? Can I get you something to drink?"

"I'm good." Rose sat down opposite her. "Thank you for seeing me today."

"The timing is perfect. Someone just quit and then Meg told me about you. What brings you to Northbridge?"

Rose inhaled and hoped the line she'd rehearsed came out as believable as it sounded in her mind. "I'm dealing with the aftermath of a bad divorce. My husband just won't let it go." She folded her hands on the tiled tabletop, hoping it made her seem more composed than she felt inside. "I saw the ad for a rental space on the lake and figured it would be peaceful and far from him, you know?"

"Yes, the Drake estate is secluded. I heard the renter there before you left pretty quickly."

Rose laughed. "Guess he thought the house was haunted."

"And you're not afraid?"

"Trust me; I don't scare easily."

"We need someone with that kind of attitude around here. The job involves working in our tasting room. Do you like wine?"

"Are you kidding?" Rose grinned. "But, to be honest, I'm not sure I could talk about it like a pro."

"We'll train you. My brother-in-law and brother have come up with blurbs on each wine. All you need to do is memorize them. We keep little cheat cards nearby when you first start."

"Sounds easy enough."

"We need someone Friday nights from five to nine. Saturday hours will vary, but definitely the afternoon from noon to five. We sometimes run night events, so those nights you can pick up another shift. Then Sunday afternoon for a few hours."

"What's the job entail?"

"Talking up our wines to visitors, stocking things, cleaning up. This'll be our second year in business, so our selection and stock is building. And of course, talking to our guests. People love to talk about themselves, hear about what we do here, even hear about the town. What's your background?"

"I worked in customer service." Wasn't her experience as a counselor and advice columnist doing a service for some?

"Then you're perfect. If you can deal with people, you've got half the job battled. Emma, you're hired." Sophie scribbled down a number on a business card and handed it to Rose. "If this hourly rate works, can you start tomorrow for training? Friday will be your first day working."

Rose noted the halfway decent rate. "I'd love to take the job, but I have a favor to ask. Any chance you could pay this off the books? With everything going on with my ex-husband, it would just be easier."

Sophie considered it for a moment then extended her hand. "Sure. Welcome to the vineyard."

"I can't wait to get started."

On the way to her car, Rose exhaled her relief and the tenseness in her shoulders lightened. The paycheck would help her get by. Not enough to pay the PI, though. If she got lucky, by the time Dan delivered a bill, her landlord would have the decency to return the envelope he'd taken.

At least, she could only hope.

Chapter 7

"Come on. You can hang with me for a while." Leo held open the door and Bella moseyed out of the apartment with a rawhide chew dangling from her mouth.

Emma had gone out again today. For someone new to town, she sure had a busy social life. Both times she'd left, he'd heard the dog whining and let her out so she'd have some company.

The dog followed him to the far end of the hall. Leo turned into the alcove and crouched in the corner near the dryer, never having felt more ridiculous. He took out the recently purchased recording device from his pocket and put it on the floor while removing a previously cut out section of Sheetrock. He made an adjustment to the timer on the electronic device and laid it inside the wall. Every fiber of his being tried to ignore the foolishness of the act and instead concentrate on the reasons he wanted the house back to himself.

As he pushed the square of Sheetrock back into place, Bella stood close, bumping Leo's shoulder with the rawhide chew.

"Ever heard of personal space?" he asked, chuckling and gently encouraging the dog to back up while he crawled out from the corner. Rolling back on his heels, Leo stood upright. The replaced Sheetrock piece, located on the same wall as the guest apartment bedroom, blended in perfectly.

The summer before he'd entered second grade, he and his siblings had discovered this opening in the wall during a rainy-day game of hide and seek. In their younger years, they'd used it occasionally to eavesdrop on weekend guests who stayed in the downstairs living quarters. Later, when teenagers, it had provided a great hiding spot for cigarettes and pot. Once they'd even used it to scare Aunt Harriet with a tape-recorded message in the middle of the night. Leo had never forgotten how his aunt came down to breakfast saying she was leaving early.

The childhood shenanigan had prompted Leo to try this with the last tenant, when Everett had rented the place without telling Leo. Feeling ridiculous but desperate, he'd combed the Internet until he found a recording device with a timer. A little further digging uncovered a CD of authentic haunting sounds. Leo easily transferred them to the small recorder. When the tenant had gone to work one morning, Leo let himself into the house and left the recorder in the attic, right above the guy's bedroom. Two days later, Leo had watched the man move out.

The timing of this visit to his sister's worked out well. Emma would be alone here tonight. If he could scare her out, and somehow get through the Friday night visit from Seth, he might soon have the solitude he craved.

Bella lifted her sad eyes while the half-eaten rawhide dangled from her mouth. A cry for attention if there ever was one.

"You wanna play?" Leo shifted to the silly voice he'd found himself using around her. "I'm gonna get your toy."

Bella's entire body swayed with happiness and she emitted a low, throaty growl. Leo grabbed the tip of the damp toy and tugged. Bella gave him a good fight, but Leo won. Stepping into the hallway, he tossed the rawhide into the kitchen and laughed as Bella slid past it before she could stop.

The dog suddenly ignored the toy and gave a clipped bark as she ran to the door. Leo followed and peered outside. Emma's slightly rusted Escort pulled into a space near the detached garage and the driver's side door opened.

He rushed the dog into the apartment and tossed the toy on living room floor.

A glance at the end table showed the photograph he'd turned upside down was now upright. He rushed over, turned it face down again, scratched Bella on the head, and hurried from the room. He reached the staircase at the same second the back door opened.

Once upstairs, he packed his overnight bag. When finished, he called Mallory. At the fourth ring his sister answered.

"On your way?" she asked, her voice always bright as a sunny day.

"Running a little late but wanted to let you know."

"Always the more considerate brother."

Mallory had buffered the problems between Leo and Everett over the years. Especially when Leo had arrived at their home as a foster child and

Everett hadn't even tried to hide his contempt. His heart warmed for his sister, probably his best friend.

"As much as I'd like to agree, we both know I've had my moments, too."

She laughed. "We won't talk about those. I made a dinner reservation, but we should be fine unless you hit traffic."

"I'll call if I do. See you in a couple of hours."

He grabbed his bag and went downstairs, heading straight for Emma's door and knocking.

Bella howled. He waited. Nobody answered, so he knocked again and the dog barked.

The door's handle jiggled, followed by Emma's muffled voice. "Shhh. Come on, move back." The door opened halfway and she peeked out, clutching a tartan plaid robe near her chest.

Dripping ringlets of hair clung to her slim neck. With those horrible glasses removed, her large blue eyes showed a deceiving innocence. The shape of her face was so heart-like Cupid would smile. He dropped his gaze to her lips, which were a little too small for her face, but a luscious shade of pink. Quite desir—

"Yes?"

Her voice jarred him. Bella whimpered and pushed at Emma's human blockade. Her slender thigh bent to keep the dog inside, giving Leo a perfect view of her ivory-smooth skin peeking from the robe's slit. Leo's tongue twisted into a knot.

His gaze took a slow trail along her thigh, past the knot of her bathrobe at her waist, paused at the glistening water near her chest at the "V" where her bathrobe joined, and stopped at her piercing gaze.

She cocked a brow. "Can I help you?"

A warm sensation hit the center of his heart. The same one he'd felt yesterday, while watching her play with the dog from his attic window.

"Leo?"

"Yes. Sorry." *Get a grip, man!* "I just stopped by to remind you I'll be gone overnight."

She watched him, her crystal eyes flickering as she studied his face. "Okay. Did you want me to do something here while you're away?"

"No."

Behind her strong gaze rested a glimpse of vulnerability. A chivalrous gene in him wanted to learn why. Did it matter? An hour ago he was setting the stage for some good old-fashioned psychological fear.

He refocused on his original goal. "No. Only to let you know you're here alone and to make sure you lock up before bed."

"Right, I'll lock up. Have a good trip."

Bella's head appeared near Emma's shin. When she shifted, the dog broke through and went to Leo, jumping up and planting her paws on his knees.

He stroked her silky ears and cooed a few sweet nothings but sensed Emma's watchful gaze.

"I'm sorry about her." She stepped out, still clutching her bathrobe, and gently coaxed the dog down.

Their gazes met. A sensation inside his chest stirred, one he rarely felt. Since the night she'd arrived, Emma Morris—with her odd clothes and made-up life story and cartoonish dog—had penetrated a fortress he'd hid behind since losing his wife.

"No problem," he finally managed.

She closed the door. Before it clicked tight, he swore he heard her say "traitor," presumably to the dog.

He walked away, his head in a fog over the brief conversation. What the hell just happened?

* * * *

"This merlot was a silver medal winner at a competition in the Finger Lakes last year." Sophie poured from a bottle labeled *Jay's Joy*. "From the name, you can tell my brother is quite proud of this one."

Rose listened from her place on a stool at the bar, literally drinking in her vineyard training. Good thing she'd had lunch before coming. While she took the job out of necessity, learning about the various wines was fascinating. "Jay should be proud. A silver medal is notable."

"Damn straight." Jay came out of the backroom and winked. Heading for the staircase to the offices, he glanced back over his shoulder. "Going for the gold next time."

Sophie shook her head. "He's got a serious competitive streak."

They continued the lesson. Rose swirl, sniffed, and tasted.

After a few rounds, Sophie poured one last glass. "Okay, let's see what you've learned."

Rose took a sip, swished the contents inside her mouth. This job was better than any she'd ever had. "Medium bodied?"

Sophie nodded.

Rose took a second sip and let it settle on her taste buds. "Cherry, with a hint of butter."

"Pretty close to the blurb on the card. I think you missed your calling."

Sophie's husband, Duncan, walked in for the second time during their training, this time holding a box pressed to his broad chest. His sandy hair and rugged face could sell wine on looks alone.

"Where do you want 'em, babe?"

"Leave them behind the bar. I'll put them away."

He lowered the box and walked over to his wife, casually slipping his arm around her waist. "So, has she turned you into an expert yet?"

"Almost. Under Sophie's coaching, I can't go wrong."

"I'll second that." Duncan kissed his wife's cheek. "Taught me everything I know. Someday I'll tell you the story about how she seduced me. Now she's got me carrying around her boxes, sweeping the floor, kissing her feet."

"I wish!" Sophie's genuine laughter filled the room. Her eyes glistened as she watched her husband.

John had never touched her with such easy intimacy. Even early in their marriage. But the way Leo's gaze had scoured her at the doorway earlier had made her toes curl and insides get all steamy. Steamier than she ever recalled feeling around her husband.

Rose shook off the distraction, mad at herself for losing focus around Leo so often. "How long have you lovebirds been married?"

"About a year and a half."

"Nice."

Those who wrote in to Rose's column had problems, making her sad life seem like less of an anomaly. Watching these two gave Rose hope to someday meet someone special.

She cut a glance between them. "Is it hard to work together and live together?"

"Not as long as Duncan does what I ask," Sophie said matter-of-factly, but her lips twitched.

"She jokes, but always with an ounce of truth." He kissed Sophie's cheek. "On that note, I'm off to help Trent."

As he left the room, Rose asked Sophie. "Do you two have kids?"

"We do. From both our former lives."

"It's not easy blending families."

"You're right. Most days, it's okay." Sophie shrugged. "The kids, they can cause stress for us."

A statement Rose had heard from many clients in the past.

"Do you have any children?" Sophie corked the merlot.

"No. We never did." She wondered if John would've tried to frame her for those donations if they had a family, but it was a question she'd never have answered.

The back room door swung open and a giggling Meg entered with Charlie on her heels.

"Oh, Charlie, you're so funny."

"What are you two up to?" Sophie smiled.

"Miss Meg here is sharing her infinite wisdom with me." Charlie stared at her with adoration so genuine it had to be real. "She has such a positive way of viewing the world."

"Well, I hated seeing you down in the slumps."

Charlie and Sophie glanced at each other, then Sophie said, "You mean down in the dumps, hon?"

"Dumps. Slumps." Meg waved her hand in a dismissive gesture. "Nobody wants to be in them."

Charlie's hazel eyes sparkled. "Couldn't agree more."

The aura of romance surrounded Rose. New love. Married love. These couples both carried ease that hadn't existed in her past relationships. Being raised in the public eye, she always wore a shield to hide a piece of herself. Her parents had encouraged it. But had she kept it up even with the people close to her later in life? If so, had it stolen her chances at truly loving another person?

Seeing these couples made her want to live it, breathe it, understand what the concept meant. It could help her complete the work assignment her editor had given her. Or at least find a way to write something worthwhile on the topic of love. Because at the moment, she really had nothing good to say about it.

Chapter 8

"No. I'm not positive he took the money, Jo, but where else could it be?" Rose pressed the phone to her shoulder and chopped a clove of garlic, inhaling the pungent aroma rising off the cutting board.

"And you checked everywhere else?" Joanne asked for the second time.

"Everywhere except the spot it's been hidden."

"Okay, okay. Calm down. I just can't imagine someone like him doing such a thing."

"Are you speaking as a fellow writer or a judge of human behavior?"

"Both. As an author, he earns big bucks and doesn't need your money. And yes, he sounds anxious to have you gone, but stealing?"

"Why couldn't Leo's fears about not getting his book done drive him to steal? Desperation can make people do crazy things." Rose scraped the garlic into a pan of hot oil and dropped a few handfuls of kale in, too. More quietly, she added, "Look at me, running from North Carolina."

"With a good reason."

"Exactly. Oh, I stopped at the drugstore in town and found one of Leo's books. I can't remember the name."

"The Wolfe Wars? It's being made into a movie."

"No." Rose thought for a second. "The Gospel According to…oh, some guy."

"Stan. That's the one I told you the critics panned, but I noticed the book still made the NY Times Bestseller list. I wouldn't be upset if I were him."

"No?"

"Maybe a little."

"Well, he's clearly bothered about his writing, considering he'd steal—"

"Allegedly steal."

"—my money." Rose sliced a chicken breast on an angle then took a small end piece and tossed it on the floor for Bella, who gobbled it up. "At least I have the place to myself. He's gone tonight."

"Where'd he go?"

"I don't know." She laughed. "I'm not privy to his private business."

"I've gotta tell you, I'm not sure I'd want to be in that big house by myself."

"Thanks for planting the seed. I wasn't afraid, but now that you mention it…"

"Sorry."

Rose shut off the burner and spooned the kale onto her dinner plate. "On the plus side, right now I'm in the kitchen, wearing a T-shirt without a bra. Freedom only a woman understands."

"Amen, sister."

Rose chuckled. "Oh, and once he left, it also gave me a chance to scour the main floor to see if he hid my money anywhere. Nothing turned up. Which leaves the upstairs left to check. He was quite specific about not going up there. Do you think going up there crosses a line?"

"The question is, do you?"

She searched deep, balancing the act of penetrating his privacy against his possible act of theft. "Yes, it *does* cross a line. Only in this instance I'm making an exception. If I find my money, maybe I can go back to my original plan to hunker down in this house and stay out of the public eye."

"Then you've justified your actions…although I still think you're barking up the wrong tree."

"Maybe. I won't know unless I check. Let's hope he doesn't have cameras up there to spy on me while he's gone."

"Next time I need plot help, I'm coming to you. Your imagination is showing real promise."

They both laughed; then Joanne got serious. "Think John suspects anything yet?"

"Probably not. It's been just five days since I left. We've gone weeks without speaking. The private investigator is watching him in DC, and I will hopefully hear from him any day now."

"You may need a good lawyer pretty soon."

"I know. One step at a time. My dinner is done. How about I call you after my first day on the job? Maybe I'll become an expert in wines."

"Glad to see you taking a step onto the sunny side of life."

"Don't go overboard." Rose said goodbye.

As she hung up, the home's silence seemed to shout. A creak from upstairs. An odd noise in the basement. A shiver rushed up Rose's spine before she rationalized it was only the hot water heater. She grabbed her phone off the counter and sent Joanne a short text.

Thanks again. Now I'm hearing noises.

Her gaze landed on a boxy General Electric transistor radio on the counter, plugged into the wall. Rose went over and twisted the round dials until she found a rock station. After putting Bella's dinner bowl on the floor, she got Leo's book from her room and returned to her meal.

She ate slowly and read the first few chapters, surprised by how the story read so beautifully. Pushing her plate aside, she sat for another hour reading. Pain jumped off the paper in some scenes, wrapping Emma up into the world of a man so deeply wounded and tangled in his own needs that he couldn't live.

She finally closed the book and washed out her pans. The story had been labeled as fiction, yet she couldn't separate the angst she'd sometimes see in Leo's eyes during his less pleasant moments. How much of Leo was in this story?

Once finished, she used a dishtowel to dry her hands and considered checking upstairs for the missing money. Nerves danced inside her belly. Snooping. So morally wrong. Only if he *had* taken her cash, that was wrong, too. Sure, two wrongs don't make a right, but in this case, the dishonest move might make things right for her.

Rose coaxed Bella into the apartment, shut her inside, and headed for the staircase to the second level. She flipped on the stairwell light and took slow steps up, her heartbeat pulsing faster as she neared the top. At the landing, she paused as Leo's request echoed inside her mind. An image of her missing envelope silenced his "rules" and propelled her forward.

Most of the doors in the hallway were shut, but as she passed the only open one, she glanced inside. The hallway light cast a bright beam into the large bedroom, the same one she'd looked inside the other day when she came up here. On the nightstand was a glass of water, bottle of Tylenol, and small stack of hardcover books. She entered and turned on a light. The mahogany dresser with heavy brass hardware held some toiletries, not that he'd be stupid enough to leave her money in plain sight.

She quickly canvassed the dresser drawers. At the bed, she lifted the thick mattress and slipped her hand along the box spring. Nothing.

Rose turned to the nightstand. An unframed, close up photograph of a very pretty woman with golden hair and eager eyes rested on top. She lifted it, studied it for a second then turned it over. *"I have nothing to give you but my heart."*

She quickly put it down, ignoring the shame worming through her and lifting another picture in an antique silver frame. Leo wore a dark suit, a red rose tucked in the lapel, and every hair combed into place. Next to him was the blond beauty from the other photo, her arm looped through his. She wore a flowing, fitted white dress and carried a bouquet of red roses. Leo stared at her, his face beaming with such an intense outpouring of affection that it made Rose's heart flutter. Blue Moon Lake glistened in the background, like stardust stirred by their obvious love. Rose couldn't remember when anybody had ever looked at her with such devotion.

She left the room, more curious about Leo than before. His exterior didn't quite match something she sensed was hidden inside.

For a few long seconds, she stood in the hallway thinking through the next steps. Just as she turned, committed to finishing her task, a groan sounded from above. A creak followed. Fear brushed the back of her neck.

The last tenant's departure came to mind, along with the haunting story from Meg about a murder taking place here decades earlier. A gruesome murder.

Not that she believed in this stuff, but she rushed downstairs. Daylight would be a better time to venture up into the attic.

* * * *

"Yes, it was good to meet you, too, um…Theresa." Leo's face hurt. Forcing himself to smile again at the attractive friend of his sister's was the way this game was played. A game he had little interest in, although his sister's persistence at matchmaking was admirable.

"I look forward to reading your books." Theresa headed for her car, turning once to flash him her brilliant smile. She did have a pretty smile.

Mallory's voice dropped to a whisper. "You almost forgot her name, didn't you?"

"What? Of course not." He put his arm around his sister's shoulders and glanced down at her. "Shorty."

"Don't change the subject. How could you forget her name?" Mallory shook her head and the flipped edges of her ash-blond hair jiggled. "We just sat at dinner together for more than two hours."

He lowered his arm and tucked a hand in his sports jacket pocket. "I didn't forget. It was a dramatic pause. To show her I'm the kind of writer who uses those techniques in real life, not only my fiction. I think it may have worked. She said she'd buy one of my books."

Mallory rolled her eyes.

Stan chuckled. "Aw, let him off the hook, Mal." He hit the unlock button on their new car, another Mercedes Sedan. "So, what do you think of the new wheels, Leo?"

Leo's brother-in-law's passion for cars always transformed him from a prematurely gray investment banker to sounding like a sixteen-year-old who worked in a garage.

"Impressive. Sleeker than the last one. How's the mileage on this thing?"

"We were talking about your blind date." Mallory held up her hand, a rather militant pose for someone who held a Gucci bag in the other. Both men knew enough to listen and turned her way. "Did you like Theresa?"

"She was pleasant. Pretty smile."

"Pleasant?" Mallory pulled a disgusted face as she walked around the car and opened the front passenger door then slipped inside. "Guess I bombed."

Leo climbed into the backseat as Stan started the car. "You didn't bomb." He shut his door, buckled up, and searched for words to make her feel better. "Attraction can't be forced."

"I hope you don't mind me saying this…" Mallory turned around, her expression serious. "Camille would want you to date." She quickly turned her back on him.

Stan drove out of the parking lot. The fragile edges of Leo's heart wilted, leaving him disappointed in himself by the truth in Mallory's remark. For several minutes, he sat and sulked. He wanted things right with his sister, the one person who always had his honesty.

Finally he replied, "Mal, I have gone out. Just because I don't tell you everything, doesn't mean it's not happening. And I'm trying to move on. Honest to God."

"Okay. As long as you're dong it." More quietly, she asked, "Are you angry with me for trying?"

"I'd never get angry with my favorite sister."

She turned around, already smiling. "You dork. I'm your only sister, but that stupid joke never gets old."

"Good, then you'll hear it again. Now about my only brother…" Leo let it hang. Unfinished. A little like his real relationship with Everett.

"Please stop letting him eat away at you."

"Too late. That house is in my name, too. Jesus, if he'd accepted my offer to buy out his half, we wouldn't have to go through this."

"Dad hoped that by leaving it to both of you, you'd somehow come together. You both loved the place."

Like they had both loved Camille.

Leo let the ache of his loss own him for a moment, suddenly certain his love for his wife stood on solid footing. Not a way to punish his brother over a childhood filled with sibling rivalry abuses.

One summer in particular, in their adolescent years, it had grown worse. Everett and his pranks. All childish and mean spirited. All leaving a mark on Leo. Like the red food dye soaked on Leo's toothbrush and switching the contents of his dresser drawers. Another day he'd poured vinegar in Leo's soda when he'd turned his back. Back then, Leo wondered if the rituals were a strange way to show brotherly love. Deep down, though, they always stung.

Dad! How about a little time for your real son?

Everett's hateful words, uttered during a deep conversation about books between Leo and his dad. The remark made clear the motive behind Everett's hurtful actions that summer.

"Does that sound right, Leo?"

He tuned into his sister's voice and let his childhood pain wash away. "I'm sorry. What?"

"That Everett hasn't been to the house since we buried dad at the cemetery in town."

"Sounds about right. When he has come back, he usually heads for his place on Montauk. This renting out bullshit, it's a way to get back at me."

Mallory glanced back. The headlights from the car behind them caught her worried expression. "Maybe I'll call him."

"Please don't. We're grown men who should be able to handle this ourselves. I'm just venting. You've always been my sounding board. Besides, I emailed and called again. Ball's in his court."

Leo stared out the car window. The final straw drawn in his battle with his brother had been at Camille's funeral when Everett uttered four hateful words.

You didn't deserve her.

Despite everything, though, Leo let go of his anger. He closed his eyes, taking a moment to feel thankful for the chances and the love he'd been given. The desperation to feel grounded in the love of a family he could truly call his own slipped through his fingers the day Camille died. And he didn't want to lose what family he had left.

Chapter 9

Low murmurings roused Rose. She tossed. Turned. Fought with a force keeping her legs bound. All as she slipped between consciousness and dreamland. Where soft voices breathed unnatural whisperings, the sounds making her heart beat faster. And faster. And faster.

She woke and bolted upright, blinking into the dark room. Goosebumps tingled along her spine and her heart raced. A nearly full moon outside cast a shine into the room, enough for her to see the top sheet tangled around her leg. As she worked it free, she glanced at the alarm clock. One thirty. She lay back down and breathed slowly, trying to stay calm and forget the strange dream. Squeezing her eyes tight, she concentrated on better things. Drifting, drifting, drifting...

A hiss. A faint laugh. A gentle moan. She stirred again and a breathy whisper whooshed by her. She wanted to rush, escape from the terrifying sounds but hard as she kicked, she couldn't escape from the confines of the bed. Opening her mouth, she tried to scream, only her vocal cords had frozen. The terror she was truly alone and unheard stole her ability to move....

Her eyes flashed open as her own voice reverberated inside her mind as she moaned, unheard by anybody. Darkness greeted her. Her skin was cool and clammy, and the racing beat of her heart pounded in her ears.

This time she sat up and flipped on the light. Rubbing her bare arms, she realized her sheet had fallen to the floor this time. She glanced to the clock. Two o'clock. Bella lifted her head off the dog bed and her ears perked. Had she heard the sounds, too?

Rose got up, threw on her bathrobe, and opened the apartment door. Flipping on lights along the way, she checked the back door leading outside to the kitchen, the front door near the staircase, and peeked around the lower level. When she returned to the kitchen, she stood in one place, listening to the silent house. Nothing but the loud thud of her heart echoed in her ears.

She hurried back to the apartment. Wide awake now, she went to the table near the sofa to grab a book she'd been reading to help her get back to sleep. As she reached for it, she noticed the photograph of the Drake's again face down.

A chill crawled up the back of her neck. This table might have a leveling issue. She wobbled it, but it held steady. Rather than dwell on the finding, she took the photo and tossed it into the drawer of the end table.

After going to the bathroom, she went back to bed. Bella stood and came to Rose's bedside, this time her expression registering concern... well, for a dog. Rose patted the top of her comforter. "Come on. I could use some company."

Bella hopped up and snuggled at Rose's side. She hugged Bella, and it made her feel a little better. As she read, though, she strained her ears to hear each creak and groan oozing from the walls of the old house.

* * * *

For the first time since arriving at the Drake estate, Rose longed for Leo.

Not because of the eerie sounds giving her a horrible night's rest, but the idea she might not be able to have a morning cup o' Joe. She yawned while trying to make sense of the disassembled percolator in the drying rack near the sink. This one appeared to have gone through WWII. How on earth did that man produce a decent cup of coffee using *this* contraption each morning?

She lifted the dented, scratched steel base and considered the other components. After trying different configurations, she found that, like a puzzle, the pieces only fit properly one way. Measurements lines on the metal had faded long ago, probably around the time Richard Nixon resigned from office.

She reached for the blue coffee can on the counter. Even though Leo wasn't around, she'd make a full pot to get her through the day. After filling the basket, she tossed in one extra spoonful for good measure, added enough water to reach the top of the carafe, and flipped on the gas burner. Leo wasn't the only one who could make coffee. She'd take a quick shower and let it brew.

She turned to go to her apartment. A glimpse toward the staircase at the end of the center hallway reminded her how she'd raced from the attic like a scared little puppy last night. On this sunny morning, the task didn't seem so daunting.

"Come on, Bella. We've got a job to finish."

The dog followed her up the stairs, bravely passing her at the top and running straight for the attic door. She'd swear this dog could read her mind.

Rose took one step and stopped. What if Leo had come home earlier, like in the middle of the night? That might explain the noises she heard when trying to sleep.

She tiptoed toward his bedroom, holding her breath. At the sight of his empty bed, she exhaled her relief and hurried past.

At the door to his office, she hesitated and knocked. "Leo? Are you there?"

Bella woofed.

No answer. She slowly opened the door, but Bella impatiently wedged between Rose's legs and ambled up the stairs. Rose followed.

At the top, the attic opened to a semi-finished room with sparse furnishings. A pine desk near the window had a few nicks in the legs but was otherwise functional. A table pushed to one of the walls held a bunch of messy papers, a legal pad, and several pens. On one side of the table stood a tall file cabinet and the other a trashcan filled with crumpled pieces of paper. An oversized fabric chair faced the room's one window, stationed to see outside.

Bella ran from corner to corner, sniffing like an airport drug canine on the scent of the bust of the century. Rose walked to his desk and chuckled at the ironclad typewriter, undoubtedly over fifty years old. Using her finger, she pressed the rounded button for the letter K and the metal key raised slowly then struck the cylinder-shaped black bar where paper belonged. *Wait'll Joanne learns that Leo uses one of these contraptions.*

Next to it sat a stack of papers. A cover sheet said *Street Views*. To look any further seemed a violation, so she kept moving.

Rose turned a full three hundred sixty degrees, trying to figure out where he might hide money. A twin bed covered by a white-and-brown, psychedelic-swirled bedspread was positioned against the wall, beneath the slanted ceiling. While she slipped her hands between the mattress and box spring, she examined a creepy wall poster from Stephen King's *The Shining* and was glad she hadn't come up here last night.

She walked over to the metal filing cabinet. First she tugged on the top drawer but it didn't open. The lock button was pushed in. Damn. Moving to the desk, she opened the drawer but only found some business cards and some paperclips.

At the messy table, her gaze landed on a legal pad. The top sheet was scribbled with dates and names, plus several descriptive words sounding like personality traits. The word *theme* was written multiple times and underlined.

Next to the table was a floor to ceiling bookshelf. She browsed each row, the books stacked orderly and tight. Certainly with no wiggle room for something as thick as her envelope.

On the bottom shelf was a stack of magazines. Leo's image stared up at her from a *Writer's Digest* cover. She lifted it. Dressed in a plain black T-shirt, he crossed his arms near his chest showcasing the same biceps she'd admired her first morning here. In the photo he wore the thin, wire-rimmed glasses that she'd seen him wearing whenever he read. The eyewear gave him a scholarly appeal, perfect for the publication. Rose flipped to his interview.

WD: Tell us about winning the Pulitzer Prize. Did it come as a shock to you?

Drake: Sure, I was surprised. Writers tell the story inside of them. Not once in the process do I stop and worry about awards or how the public will receive my work. Yes, I hope the finished product is well received, but it's secondary to the message of my novel.

WD: In The Gospel According to Stan *there are two brothers. At times, the lines between the good brother and bad becomes blurred. Was this intentional?*

Drake: Very much so. Even in a case where it may seem obvious who the bad people are in life, we really never fully understand what goes on in someone's private world. Inside their heads. Good and evil could be only illusions. Labels we designate to make things fit into a perfect world.

Rose speculated over how much of this fictionalized work rested in his relationship with Everett. According to Leo, Everett was to blame for her showing up at the house. Were they both to blame for some obvious strain in their relationship?

She carefully closed the magazine and sifted through the rest of the stack. A *Time* magazine with him on the cover caught her eye. He looked the same. Wispy, layered bangs brushed his dark brow, but this time his hair hung a little longer, over his ears.

A day-old layer of whiskers shaded the cheeks of his long face and chiseled chin. His soft expression carried none of the tenseness she observed in real life. The first few buttons of a white dress shirt lay open, showing off his thick neck and a smattering of chest hair. He stared face-on at the camera, those soft, serious dark eyes stirring her interest.

She tore her gaze from the mesmerizing image to the words next to the photo. *Pulitzer Prize and Sex Appeal...Meet Leo Drake.* Under different circumstances, meeting a man like Leo would have been nice. A relationship with someone like a writer, who wanted to live in a quiet town far from the public eye, could offer the simple life she'd always wanted.

She flipped open the magazine and found the article about him. One photo showed him with the beautiful woman from the picture in his bedroom. The caption read, "Drake and wife, the late actress Camille Caron."

An actress? Interesting—

Rose sniffed. Coffee. Oh good.... She sniffed again. Burning coffee! She threw the magazine back into the bookcase. "Come on, Bella!"

She hurried down the stairs and into the kitchen. Water and wet grounds covered the stove and dripped along the oven door, stopping at a pile on the floor. The stench of burnt coffee filled the air.

Rose cleaned up, annoyed at herself for being so careless. After wiping the last sopping grounds, she tossed out the paper towel, opened the refrigerator, and pulled out a Coke. At this point, caffeine was caffeine.

* * * *

Leo bumped open the back door with his hip and entered the kitchen. Muted rock music played behind the closed door of Emma's apartment. He sniffed. Burnt food? Before she'd arrived, whenever he left, he'd return to the same quiet house. Now he was never sure what he'd walk into.

He hurried upstairs and tossed his overnight bag onto his bed, anxious to get to work. His fingers itched to get on the keyboard. Talking about his current project on *Good Morning Boston* got the creative juices flowing; the interest expressed by the show's host a good sign.

As he neared the attic, the partially opened door sent a prickle up the back of his neck.

He climbed the steps fast and entered the warm room, glancing everywhere for signs someone had been snooping around. Nothing caught his eye, and he went over and opened a window. Not only was Emma's presence a surprise a minute, but distracting enough to make him do dumb things, like leave his office door open.

He yawned on his way over to his worktable for a legal pad. A quick outline of the next few chapters would be a good way to start work. A *Time* magazine lying on the floor caught his eye. He picked it up, noting it was an old issue previously stored in the pile on his shelf. The partially opened door raised more suspicions about his tenant.

He pictured her snooping around his house for her missing money, going places he'd specifically asked her to keep away from. If she did, much as it annoyed him, he'd give her credit for persistence. He might do the same in her shoes.

She could be gone soon anyway—at least if the recording he'd left on had gone off at the right time and had the desired effect. He returned the magazine to the stack.

Another yawn escaped. At this rate, he'd fall asleep before he could type one paragraph.

He left the attic and went to the kitchen. The burnt scent lingered. Flipping the window over the sink open, he glanced into the drying rack where the percolator lay sideways and assembled, not in the pieces he'd left yesterday after washing it out. Dried crumbs of coffee stuck to the edges. He took the stem to the trashcan and wiped off the mess. Coffee-stained paper towels filled the pail. He should've shown Emma how to use this. People were so spoiled by today's easy devices.

Once he got the coffee heating on the stove, he took down two mugs. His stomach growled, so he grabbed some chips and sat down with his notepad.

The apartment door down the hall opened. Bella entered the kitchen, spotted Leo, and trotted over with a happy gait.

"Hey baby." He rubbed her chest, cooing softly, "Did you miss me?"

"Not really." Emma entered, her bare feet shuffling on the floor.

Leo smiled, the obvious disdain for him strangely stimulating. For some reason most women tended to his whims, leaving him feeling as needy as he did as a child. But not this one. Not one bit of fuss.

Emma squinted through her lopsided black glasses at the percolating pot. "At last. Coffee."

Her disheveled red waves were pinned back on each side with little brown barrettes. She glanced at her dog and raised a brow, but Leo didn't want to offend Bella by taking away his attention, and Bella didn't seem to want to leave. He took in Emma's fitted tank top and flannel bottoms, the fabric's pattern a collage of cartoon dogs. "Nice pants."

She shrugged. "One of the perks of working at home. This hairdo is the other."

He ignored what he'd heard from eavesdropping and figured it wouldn't kill him to be nice to her. The way he used to behave around a pretty woman. "And what kind of work do you do?"

"Travel agent. It's computerized, like everything these days. An easy job to do from a remote location." She glanced at the stove; then her gaze drifted to the counter then to him. "Why do you do that? Take down a mug for me each day."

"Habit." Heat crept up his neck from her intense stare. "My family had a rule...first one up made the coffee and got down mugs for everyone."

He pretended to read his notes, but instead could only think about the day Camille had told him how much she loved when he took the time to remember her with a ready mug and hot coffee. He looked up. Emma watched him, her stare intense, like she'd caught wind of his thoughts.

Leo embraced the ache in his chest and said, "It scored big points with my wife after we married. The little things...they mean everything."

She nodded, watching him in the most knowing kind of way. "Yes. I suppose they do."

Sadness resonating in her eyes sliced right through a place he reserved for those close to him. He wanted to ask her more, learn what details rested in her answer, but he discarded the notion fast as it entered his head. "Any problems while I was gone?"

"Problems? Like wha—oh yes, there was a big problem."

Leo tried not to smile. How could he get lucky enough to have this fake haunting work twice?

Emma pushed her large glasses against the bridge of her nose. "I think something is wrong with your coffee maker."

"It's worked fine for decades."

"Exactly. Its days are numbered." She went to the cabinet near the sink and took down a glass. "Why don't you donate that thing to the Smithsonian? They can put it next to Archie Bunker's chair. Gosh, I'll even spring for new drip-maker."

Leo laughed. How did she relax him so easily, leave him calmer than he'd felt all day? The same calm that swept over him around Bella. And he rarely opened up to strangers about life with Camille, yet he'd just handed her a piece of himself on a platter.

Guilt over trying to scare her with the dumb recording ambushed him out of nowhere. A foolish stunt, and one she thankfully hadn't noticed last night.

"A drip-maker is a generous offer, but we don't need one. Based on evidence in the garbage pail, I'm going to guess you used too much water or grounds."

Her ivory skin reddened and she glanced to the garbage pail as if it had betrayed her. She filled the glass with water. "Is the coffee ready yet?"

"Almost." He leaned back and stretched his legs, taking note of how oddly cute her derriere looked with puppies prancing around on the curves. "The percolator has been in my family since I was a kid. People want things instantly. No one appreciates the value of time spent crafting a good cup of coffee. A symphony of actions, exact measurements."

"I suppose. I never thought about it much before." She drank her water and watched him over the rim. When she finished, she put the glass in the sink. "Well, thank you for making me coffee. I do appreciate it."

"Any time." An idea hit him and, without overthinking it, he rose and moved to her side. "This coffee is about done. You want a few tips on using this, in case you try again yourself?"

"Are you kidding? I'm going on Amazon right now and ordering something manufactured in the past decade."

"Very funny." He tried to keep up the act of being annoyed, but a smile crept to his lips as he shut off the burner. He waggled a finger at her to move closer to the stove. "Come on. Percolator Coffee 101 is about to start."

She laughed and stepped to his side. "Guess my grade in this class can't get any worse."

"You didn't do too badly. I'd give you a C for your first attempt. Your assembly was about ninety percent correct."

"C? I'm an A student."

He grinned and their gazes met, lighting a spark inside him. "I'll bet you are. Pay attention. First, you don't want to overcook the coffee. Boil for no more than three minutes. How long was it on yesterday?"

She blushed. "Let's say more than three minutes."

He suspected way longer, but kept it to himself and lifted the pot to fill their mugs. Normally, he wouldn't take time to explain his beloved old coffee maker to someone, but he wanted to show it to her, for reasons he couldn't quite define.

She reached out to take a mug and he rested his hand over hers. Her soft skin reminded him how he missed touching a woman. "Hold your horses. This lesson isn't over."

She rolled her eyes but didn't move away. "Fine. My horses are held."

He removed his hand, but the touch left an invisible imprint on his skin. "Based on the assembled pot I found this morning, you were almost there, but the basket lid probably wasn't on."

"A basket lid?"

He removed the top from the pot he just brewed and pointed at a flat cylinder piece. "Look familiar?"

"No. So this is what keeps the grounds down, huh?" She studied the part with serious consideration, like she expected a quiz on the topic. "It explains my mess."

Her long lashes flickered behind the eyeglass frames. He inhaled a mixture of coffee and the floral scent of her hair. Their nearness, and the need for his help, cued him into a certain vulnerability she possessed, like she wasn't as tough as she seemed. Unexpected need for her stirred inside his chest, leaving him strangely desiring this woman who didn't seem to fit properly in the skin she'd arrived in.

"Got it. Basket lid. Three minutes." She smiled. "Thank you for the lesson, Mr. Coffee."

She laughed and stepped away, going to the cabinet. Her nearness had made a piece of him melt.

He returned to his seat and struggled to erase the warmth smothering his chest, almost afraid to feel so good. Emma busied herself removing a bag of salad and making her lunch. Leo tried to get back into his outline, but couldn't. Instead, he noted the movement of her slender arm and roundness of her buttocks beneath the flannel. He dragged his gaze along the curve of her waist and to the generous curves of her chest outlined in the ribbed tank top. Despite her offbeat wardrobe, she glowed with a womanly aura.

Emma glanced sideways and caught him staring. He looked at his pad and quickly scribbled, writing an earlier thought with an unsteady hand. Taking a seat on the opposite side of the table, she quietly ate and occasionally talked to Bella.

Feeling back in control of himself, he cleared his throat.

She lifted her gaze from her plate.

"Any other problems while I was gone?"

"No. Why do you ask?"

"My office door was open."

Her cheeks went pink. "Did you forget to shut it?"

"I usually don't." He returned to his notes, but added, "With your missing money, I'd wondered if you decided to search upstairs."

"I thought you didn't take my money."

He looked up to answer, and this time wished she'd believe him. "I didn't."

She lifted a brow that in as much pointed the finger of guilt at him, stood confidently, and brought her bowl to the sink. When she turned around her lovely, crystal-blue eyes pegged him in place. "Could've been your ghosts."

"Hmmm. You could be right." He worked on a neutral expression, because right now he couldn't get a handle on what he wanted from her.

She stared at him for a moment then shook her head. "Come on, Bella."

He watched her walk down the hallway until she disappeared, and all he could think about was how comforting and sexy he found those flannel bottoms.

Chapter 10

"This one is 'Delilah's Dream.'" Rose poured a sample tasting into each of the foursome's glasses, more confident in her tasks than she'd been at the start of her shift. "The goat on this label happens to live right on this property." The group loved the tidbit. Rose continued, talking about the wine attributes. She waited while they tasted and removed the next bottle. "Next we'll move on to this propriety blend of cabernet and cabernet franc, aged on French oak."

As she poured, the tasting room door opened. She glanced up and held in a gasp as Leo strode across the room with a man and woman she'd never seen before.

The coffee pot assembly earlier had been an unexpected and strangely tantalizing moment of tenderness between them. His attention had turned her inside out. His touch made her core warm. She couldn't remember when she'd last flirted with a man or why Leo's instruction would warrant such behavior.

Hell, they'd been making coffee. It had been about making coffee…right?

No…it was more. His physical nearness had evoked a need. She missed being with a man. Being held by strong arms. The way they'd touch her skin, at times carefully like she was made of porcelain, other times more demanding, pushed by their own needs.

She returned to her customers, reciting the wine descriptions off the cards Sophie had given her. Every so often, her gaze would drift across the room to where Leo sat talking to his friends. Sudden affection for him swarmed her. Leo's gesture earlier had opened a door. It welcomed her into his world of old gadgets and rituals. An unusual place, filled with family history and offering the kind of comforting roots she'd craved her entire life.

She gave herself a mental swat, along with a stern reminder to keep her guard up around him. He was still the number one suspect with her missing cash. Plus, up until today, all his actions suggested he wanted her gone.

The group ordered half a case of Delilah's Dream. She was about to go in back for a box when Jay came up to her side. His long, graying hair was tied back in a ponytail today. "You're doing great."

"Thanks. I'm getting more comfortable."

"Good." He motioned across the room. "I'll ring up this up. Why don't you go help your landlord and his friends? Have I mentioned I think Leo is a great guy?"

"I didn't know you knew him."

"Yup. I just met him this year. He helped us name some bottles recently. See if they want a glass of wine or are here for a tasting."

"Sure." Rose's voice squeaked a little too high as she tried to sound like she didn't mind. Only it was inevitable Leo would see her, so she might as well deal with it. She grabbed a few wine lists and headed over.

Leo sat next to an attractive woman with delicate features and short brown hair. Their chairs were close enough that their legs brushed beneath the table. He scowled and carried on quite passionately to the man across the table from him, who listened and nodded every so often.

As Rose approached, the other man glanced up. His fair blond hair was styled with intended messiness and his classic handsome face could've made him a Hollywood star. Besides a gray casual shirt with the fitted look of something from Banana Republic, his well-pressed jeans were a perfect shade of indigo blue. His gaze skimmed Rose and he grinned, showcasing Crest-bright teeth.

Leo glanced up and his eyes widened. "What are you doing here?"

Before she could reply, Hollywood interrupted. "Wow, Leo. No wonder you're striking out with the ladies these days."

The woman laughed, but it sounded forced.

"I'm working," Rose replied. "Welcome to Litchfield Hills Vineyard." She focused on his companions with a bright smile. "Would you like to see our wine-by-the-glass listing or are you here for a tasting?"

Hollywood leaned back in his seat, crossed his arms, and swept her with his gaze. "We're just having drinks, sweetheart."

"Wine by the glass, it is." She bit back an urge to lecture him on his demeaning treatment. "Here's a list of what we have, including both a red and white flight if you'd like to sample a few different kinds."

Leo leaned toward her and lowered his voice. "Since when have you been working here?"

He sounded annoyed and she regretted falling for his suave moves back at the house earlier.

"Since someone stole my money." She gave him a hard stare and refused to back down. "Could be someone right under our own roof. Like someone who wants me to leave."

Leo narrowed his eyes. "I told you—"

Hollywood chuckled. "You two know each other?"

Leo sighed. "This is my new tenant. Emma, this is my agent, Seth. He'll be staying with us tonight. And Susan."

"Nice to meet you both. Have you been to the vineyard before?"

"No, but I'm glad we came." Seth motioned to the woman. "Susan and I were passing through for a work retreat. Since my favorite client is hiding out here, I figured visiting wasn't a bad idea."

"I'm not hiding out," Leo mumbled. "I'm working."

The woman patted Leo's hand but didn't remove it when through. "Ignore him. He's trying to get you worked up."

Seth laughed easily, clearly a man who didn't take life as seriously as Leo. "I'm teasing you, buddy. Anyway, nice to meet you, Emma. I think I'll try the flight of reds."

"I'll take the white flight." Susan studied Rose through dark, pretty eyes. Was this Leo's girlfriend?

"Good choice." Rose admired the woman's soft linen dress. It flowed to her feet and delicate sandals peeked out near the bottom hem.

She looked at Leo. "And you?"

Aggravation flickered behind his crisp, fawn eyes. "A glass of the cabernet franc."

She nodded. "Be right back." As Rose walked off, she could feel the burn of their gazes on her.

The dark glasses slipped a notch down her nose, practically taunting her with a reminder she wasn't herself. It took everything in her not to yanked them off her face and toss them against the wall. Rose wanted to return to her old wardrobe and her old self. In these new clothes she didn't feel pretty or normal. And for some reason, right now, her appearance mattered.

* * * *

Leo told the story of Emma's arrival, all the while struggling to keep from staring at her as she beamed politely at another customer. A smile so endearing he wished he'd been more polite when she'd come to their table. Surprises were never his thing.

"She's cute." Seth openly gawked at her. "I don't know what you're complaining about."

"Because it's hard to get work done with someone running around the house."

Leo's temples throbbed. He wanted to grab Seth's chin and jerk his eyes back toward their small group. His agent tended to have a one-track mind when it came to the opposite sex, but doing this with Emma—well, it crossed a line.

Let's face it. He'd walked in here annoyed with Seth.

"Something's missing," Seth had said about Leo's manuscript, spoken in Seth's usual confident way. His agent could spot a mediocre novel from a bestseller in an instant. Leo expected those words, but hearing it face-to-face made him stew. He couldn't deny how Seth had said the same thing about the novel the critics panned. During the review phases of that particular manuscript, Leo had argued so passionately with Seth about any changes that Seth caved.

This time, Leo needed to listen to his agent. Only he still had no idea how to get this book on the right path.

"Well?" Seth stared at him with a frown.

"What'd you say?"

"I asked what you meant about her running around the house. She doesn't strike me as the noisy type." Seth shook his head. "God, you are so particular sometimes."

"You wouldn't understand," Leo said firmly. "It's a distraction. And now I find a place in town where I like to stop in for a drink, and she's here, too."

"You could've been nicer," Susan said quietly, shooting him a reprimanding glance. "I'm pretty sure she thinks you stole her money."

"Why would I...she lost it!"

"And then trying to throw her out." Seth made a "tsk-tsk" sound. "You know, if you'd told Everett you were going to live at the house in the first—"

"I did tell Everett. He ignored me, remember?"

"Oh, right." Seth's gaze drifted to the bar and Leo followed it. Emma had leaned over and lifted a wine bottle out of a box, the position exposing the backside he'd admired a few times himself lately.

"She's off limits," Leo growled at Seth. "Don't complicate this renter arrangement thing for me."

"Aw, come on. She's like a schoolmarm in those glasses, but with that crazy red hair, I'd bet some kinky stuff lurks beneath the surface." Seth squinted in her direction. "She looks familiar."

"Did you hear a thing I said?"

"Knock it off, Seth." Susan elbowed his arm. "This is supposed to be a fun night out."

"All right, all right. I don't know why you're so tense, Leo. You've got a decent start to the book. It needs a little something, that's all. What, though, I can't figure out."

"My exact problem," Leo mumbled. Annoyance hammered at him, although the bulk of it pounded at his chest, a bit like...no. Jealousy?

Seth continued to stare in Emma's direction.

"Seth!"

The agent slowly turned to Leo. "What?"

"Read my lips....Stay away from her. There's more to her than meets the eye."

Emma neared with their drinks so he shut up and waited until she was far enough away. He leaned into the table. "There's something strange going on with her. She's telling people in Northbridge one story about her life, but her friend came by the other day and I heard a different version. The stories don't match. Sounds to me like she's running away from something."

"Like what?" Seth picked up one of the small sample-sized wine glasses and swirled the contents.

"She told the real estate agent her ex-husband won't leave her alone, so that's the reason she's in Northbridge. Yet, when a friend came by, she talked about her dyed hair and, possibly, even using a different name."

Susan snorted. "Lots of women color their hair."

"But why carry all that cash, change your name, buy a new wardrobe? And, if she came here from Boston, why shop at a store in Virginia?"

"How do you know that? Did you go into her apartment?" Seth said, a little too loudly.

"Shhh. Keep it down." He glanced over Susan's shoulder, relieved to see Emma talking to Jay near the bar. "Not intentionally. The dog got out. I brought her to the apartment and..." Leo wasn't about to tell them how he'd worried Bella had choked to death. "I noticed the receipt and clothing when I returned the dog."

Seth laughed. "You know what I love?"

"What?" Leo raised his glass, took a long drink, the red wine soothing his angst.

"That you're curious. Always a good sign. And I'm thinking about your story so far and pretty sure I know what's missing." He glanced Emma's way for a second, a smirk on his face. "You need a character like her. Imagine how she'd play off your protagonist?"

The idea hit like a thunderbolt, the missing link now so obvious. A whirlwind of excitement owning Leo whenever ideas for a new novel fell into place lifted his spirits. Emma's profile and mystery was a perfect fit for the third main character in his story. "Holy shit." He looked at Seth. "I think you're right."

Susan eyed him skeptically. "Are you seriously considering it?"

"You bet." Leo patted Seth on the shoulder as relief and excitement coursed through him.

How had he missed everything her presence stirred inside him? So focused on the goal, he forgot how to play the game. "I knew a talk with my agent would go a long way. But now I'm even more serious about what I said before…" He worked hard to muster up an angry grimace at Seth. "Please stop gawking at my muse."

* * * *

"Good morning, sunshine."

Seth's velvety smooth voice surprised Rose. She dropped the photograph of Leo she'd found pushed far back in a drawer while searching for a potholder and turned around.

Seth leaned against the doorway, hair damp, nicely pressed jeans, a button-down shirt. A more pulled together look than her cropped yoga pants and clearance rack T-shirt imprinted with a Jedi on a clover that read, "Who needs luck when you're a Jedi?"

"Good morning." She casually shoved the photo back near a canister set so he didn't catch her snooping. The Halloween picture of Leo wearing a dress and his wife in a man's pinstriped suit was hilarious and an unexpected find. Maybe he *did* have a lighter side.

"Did you sleep well?" Seth walked toward her.

"I did. And you?"

"So-so. It's quiet around here. Takes some getting used to." He glanced at Bella, whose nose was buried inside her dish. "Leo didn't tell me about a dog."

"Meet Bella."

On cue, she lifted her head and eyed Seth with some suspicion before returning to her bowl.

He inhaled and stopped a few feet away from Rose. "There's nothing quite like the smell of fresh coffee."

"I can't make any promises on the taste. This is my second try using this contraption. I miss my Keurig."

"That's Leo. You can take the boy from the past, but can't take the past out of the boy." Seth grinned. "He still drives his parents' old '63 Mercedes sedan when he comes here and I'm pretty sure he's waiting for the Beatles to appear on the Ed Sullivan show."

She laughed, but it hit her all these artifacts seemed to fit into one harmonious and homey feel, despite how they hadn't at first. "I guess there's something to be said for embracing the old ways."

He didn't respond. Instead, he quietly studied her, the over-analysis as disruptive as a buzzing fly. She lifted her hand to adjust the glasses, a habit she'd gotten into lately, but her fingertips grazed her bare temple.

Panicked, she swung around to the countertop, where she'd left the eyewear. "I think coffee's almost ready." She retrieved the glasses and slipped them on casually, as if her heart wasn't about to burst from her chest. "Want me to pour you a cup?"

"Sure. I'll get the cream and sugar."

She got down four mugs, remembering what Leo had shared yesterday about his family.

Seth found everything else without asking for directions. She filled two mugs, and as Seth came to the counter, she handed him his cup. He poured half-and-half and offered it to her. "So where's your Keurig?"

"My Keurig?" Her own words came back to bite her in the ass. It was sitting on her counter in North Carolina. She mixed her coffee and avoided his eyes. "Oh, I let my ex-husband keep it. Some things aren't worth fighting over."

"And where is he?"

"Near Boston, where we lived because of his work." Rose sat at the table and he followed.

"What does he—"

"How about you? You work in Manhattan, but are you originally from the city?"

"No. Maryland." He tilted his head, his gaze canvassing her face.

"Hungry?" Rose jumped up and went to the cabinet. She removed a package of muffins and put them in the center of the table. "Help yourself. You know, I've never met a literary agent. How does one fall into that field?"

"My career started in print journalism, working in DC. I wrote a book—nonfiction—and pitched it to a college buddy who ran a literary agency. He signed me on, and two years later, asked if I wanted to become an agent. Leo was my tenth client, and my ticket to success." He reached for a muffin. "And what do you do?"

"Travel agent. And of course my new job at the vineyard."

"So, you think Leo took your money?"

She shrugged, but wondered what Leo had told them about her. "It's the only explanation I have."

Seth chuckled. "You really ruffled his feathers."

"I've searched everywhere. Last I remember I carried it inside when I moved in. He's the only other person who's been in the house."

"That you know of."

"Well, yes." She sipped the hot coffee and considered that her accusation was a possible knee-jerk reaction because of her larger problems. "Who else could've been in here?"

"I can't say, but I can attest to the fact Leo's not the kind of guy to steal."

"Even if he wants me to leave?"

Seth thought about it. "Yeah, even then. His edges are a little rough since losing his wife, but he's been through a lot. At his core, he'd do anything for those close to him. His work means everything and wanting you out of here is all about his book. Not personal."

She considered the endorsement and the morsels of his past she'd seen around the house. "What happened to his wife?"

Seth frowned. "Died of cancer. Only a few months after she was diagnosed. The same year his book got the Pulitzer Prize."

"How awful." Rose's eyes watered, surprising because she hadn't shed a single tear for herself lately. Staying strong was all she'd had. But a losing a loved one hurt. A hurt she understood.

Seth pressed her hand in his large ones. "Sorry. I didn't mean to upset you."

"Good morning." Leo entered, his gaze focused on their hands, his jaw muscle flexed tight. "Looks like someone mastered the coffee pot."

Rose pulled her hands away from Seth and her cheeks burned. Guilty of nothing, and yet Leo's reaction made her feel plenty uncomfortable. "Yes. Much better than my first attempt."

Leo nodded and the tenseness around his eyes slowly disappeared.

"It's delicious." Seth winked at Rose. "I think Emma handles that old percolator better than you do."

"Of course you do." Leo glanced to the counter, his gaze drifting from the coffee maker to the mugs she'd left out. He walked over, picked one of them up, and gave her a gentle smile.

Susan padded in wearing a kimono-like bathrobe, hemmed to just above the kneecap of her long, lovely legs. "Morning all."

If she'd slept, it must've been motionless, because her hair still looked perfect as last night.

Leo filled both mugs and handed one to Susan, their eyes meeting for a brief second with an affectionate message Rose couldn't miss.

"I forgot how early you get up." Susan spoke softly, casting a heat to the message.

So much more resided in the weight of the remark, leaving Rose curious about his relationship with this woman. Yesterday during the coffee-making lesson, his sexy quietness carried a powerful undercurrent she'd seen him turn off and on at will. One capable of softening the most skeptical person, like her.

Leo stepped away and the smile vanished from Susan's face as she watched him. He went toward the sink, but paused near the partially opened drawer Rose had been inside earlier. "Why's that photo on the counter?"

Rose shot up from her seat, brushed by him, and swiped it up. "Sorry. I needed an oven mitt and found this in the drawer instead.

"Wonder how it got in there." He frowned and held out his opened palm. "I should take it. Wouldn't want it to get in the wrong hands."

"What is it?" Seth asked.

Leo lowered his arm. "A picture from the Halloween party Ben Steinberg threw in the Hamptons. You were there. I went dressed as a woman and Camille went as a man." He chuckled softly. "How she ever convinced me to do that is beyond me. It was fun, though."

"Fantastic party," Seth agreed. "Everyone thought you showed cover girl potential, buddy."

"Those heels were killing me." Leo cracked a grin and again held out his hand to Emma. "Not my proudest moment, though. I'll take that now."

"I wouldn't give that over so quickly, Emma." Seth leaned back in his chair and slipped his hands behind his head. "I'll bet the tabloids would find a little gem like that front-page worthy."

She clutched it to her chest and grinned at Leo. "You may be right, Seth. I could extend my stay in this house years. Indefinitely, even."

Leo looked between them, shaking his head and scowling. "Ha-ha. Neither of you is funny."

Seth chuckled. "You never could take a joke."

"Not true. The picture is proof." He turned to Emma with a deadpan expression and, again, put out his hand. "Okay. You've had your fun."

Rose kept the photo pressed to her chest, enjoying a brief moment of power. "Fun? This is about more than fun. You'd better watch out, Leo… blackmail is sweet."

Leo hooded his lids, not angry but heated in a whole other way. A sly grin crossed his lips and his voice grew deep with huskiness. "Indeed, dear Emma. But revenge is sweeter."

Her belly tingled as his frisky gaze pinned her in place. Heat brushed her cheeks. Playful Leo was…well, sexy. He raised a brow and reached out with an opened palm, still watching her in a way that left her feeling exposed and vulnerable to his charm. She held out the picture. As he took it, their hands brushed.

Her pulse raced as she returned to her seat. After taking a muffin, she removed the paper wrapping and tried to get a handle on the pendulum-like emotions for her landlord.

Chapter 11

Leo lost all track of time, pounding at the keys of his typewriter after Susan and Seth left. Images of these past days with Emma guided every single stroke.

…Her arrival on the cold, damp night.

…The determination in her eyes when he'd asked her to leave.

…Each delicious, well-hidden curve often visible beneath her odd clothing choices.

…Joyful frolicking with Bella.

The details served as a missing link to his story. Seth, in all his genius, knew what made a solid plot tick. Leo typed furiously. So in the zone that a knock at his office door hit his ears like an exploding bomb.

"What?" he yelled, as he continued with the stream of consciousness ramblings he'd edit later into shape. His fingers moved fast, the click from the striking keys on paper a symphony of sounds like true music to his ears.

"I wondered—"

"One sec." He finished typing his thought then turned to face her.

There she stood, the woman he couldn't stop thinking about. Who, unbeknownst to her, had become fictionalized material.

The same woman in his thoughts when Susan had pressed her lips to his for a goodnight kiss last night, a little too generously, and made a big-hearted offer they sleep together. She'd assured him she was fine with the friends with benefits thing. If his read was correct, though, she didn't seem fine with it. He'd made an excuse about an early day and given her a warm hug. He'd quickly retired to his room, ignoring his erection. Especially because he hadn't been sure his urges were meant for Susan.

"What's up?"

Emma wore well-fitted jeans, hanging low on her hips, with a tucked-in camisole and button-down beige vineyard shirt. His gaze skirted along her flat torso to her slender thighs. Why on earth did she often wear clothing that kept her lovely figure hidden?

"So you actually write your books on that thing?" Her sloped nose crinkled as she stared at his typewriter.

"I only write my first drafts on it."

"Uh-huh. And you know about this new invention the rest of us use called the computer?" She raised her light brows, a detail he'd not taken notice of before, but it confirmed her hair color wasn't natural.

Her ease at speaking her mind around him was refreshing. He couldn't recall when a woman had last teased him since he'd become a writing success. "Yes, I own one. I type the next draft into the computer, when starting my edits."

"One day we're taking a road trip to Best Buy. Besides computers, they even sell coffee makers that use electricity. A little invention of Ben Franklin's."

He laughed and made a mental note to add sarcasm to his character. "Did you come up here to tell me about the modern day advances of mankind or something else?"

"Nah, on the mankind thing, I merely seized the opening." She grinned. "Oh, your agent is nice. Interesting."

"Yeah, he's a good guy." This morning's jealous reaction when he saw Seth holding Emma's hand still bothered him. "I hope he didn't come on too strong."

She shrugged, but behind her eyes he noticed some discomfort. "There are times in a woman's life when even someone like Seth can boost your morale."

He pocketed the remark, curious over her reaction and why a beautiful woman like her would need any kind of morale boost.

"The reason I'm here is because I need a favor."

"A favor? From the man who stole your money?"

She drew in her full lower lip, somehow making the small gesture quite sexy. "Listen, I'm just frustrated because it's gone."

"Understood. So what's the favor?"

"My shift at the vineyard is a long one today, from three this afternoon until around ten. Bella will probably be okay, but...uh....well, the hours cross into her dinner time, and she might need to go out, too."

Emma obviously didn't know about his rendezvous with the dog each time she left, and he considered telling her.

"Aaaand…" She drew in a breath. "Since you're here, I was wondering if you wouldn't mind feeding her around six, and maybe take her out after she finishes eating."

She watched him in such a way he knew if he didn't help her, she'd figure out something else. A chance he didn't want to take. For years, nobody needed him for anything. He hadn't cared. Now, though, the idea appealed to him.

"Sure. Leave me some written instructions."

Her brows lifted. "Oh. Okay good."

He turned around and aligned his fingers on the smooth, round typewriter keys. "Put the leash where I can find it, too." He struck a few keys, anxious to pick up where he'd left off, although a part of him enjoyed this short distraction. More than he wanted to admit.

"Thank you," she said softly.

"Any time."

She didn't move for a second and Leo couldn't bring himself to look at her. Instead, he moved his fingers on the keyboard, faster and faster until the attic door clicked shut. He exhaled. If he'd seen any gratitude in her expression, she'd sink even more deeply under his skin, a place he still wasn't sure he could handle.

He got up and went to his notebook to add his latest observations about his Emma-like character to his notes. The newly fictionalized Amanda had a small frame, seductive red hair, and oversized black-framed glasses. He'd made her Emma, even down to her peculiar outfits and entering his protagonist's life due to a betrayal, forcing her to run from the world she knows.

So many questions about her were left unanswered, like about Emma's real life betrayal from a man named John. And what was she like before disguising herself to live in Northbridge? How had she been raised, and why did he sense neediness in her, yet inherently understand she could stand on her own two feet?

He wanted answers but couldn't blurt out his demands. The only solution was to fictionalize what he didn't know. Another part of his desire to know came from a more personal place. Who was the real Emma? If he raised the questions, she'd know he eavesdropped. She might also suspect the truth: something about her being in this house had become personal to him.

He returned to his typewriter. Five minutes later, a car started outside. He went to the window. Emma backed out her small car and disappeared down the driveway.

Perhaps his character needed a dog? He headed downstairs, happy for the excuse to bring Bella up to his office without it being a secret this time.

* * * *

"Our work day is done, Bella." Leo stood and stretched his arms over his head. A glance at the clock radio on his desk showed three hours had passed since returning to work. He couldn't recall when he'd last lost track of time while working. "Let's go eat."

Bella flew off the bed, knocking off a crumpled ball of paper she'd been chewing to the floor. Leo tossed it in the trashcan and headed down the stairs behind her.

For the first time in the months, he'd accomplished something worthwhile. On top of his productivity, he'd enjoyed having the quiet, low-commitment company of Bella with him while he worked. The second Emma left, he'd visit the local shelter.

They neared the kitchen. Bella ran ahead and stopped to stare up at her empty bowl on the counter. Leo read the instructions Emma left there and measured the kibble.

"You deserve a treat." He went to the refrigerator and removed a leftover piece of steak. Bella's droopy eyes went wide with anticipation.

He cut the meat into small pieces and mixed it with the other food. Spoiling her brought him a whole new kind of delight.

Tonight he planned to tackle a meatloaf recipe his mom used to make. Emma's cooking affected him. Each time she made dinner, she left behind a trail of scents reminiscent of home, family, and dinners with loved ones. Junk food and takeout paled by comparison.

He reached into the cabinet and removed the ancient white-checkered Better Homes and Gardens recipe collection, taking care not to let any of the tattered loose-leaf pages fall out. As the book slid off the shelf, a thin paperback hidden beneath it dropped onto the counter. He put down the cookbook and took the other. The ecru cover showed a simple sketch of an old Victorian house and the words "Connecticut Ghost Sightings" above the drawing. He chuckled. So unlike the way books were marketed nowadays.

When they were kids they'd read this, finding one tale scarier than the next. Leo flipped through the pages, stopping on the story about the Drake's house. His parents had always said it wasn't true, but the kids never believed them. In all his time here, though, nothing paranormal ever happened in this place. At least not that he'd seen.

His cell phone vibrated against the kitchen table. He stuck the haunting book between the flour and sugar canister.

Mallory's name flashed on the phone's display and he answered.

"Hey, you left a book on the guest room nightstand. Need it mailed back?"

"No. I finished it. Read it or pass it along."

"Will do. Listen, the real reason I'm calling is to let you know Everett called me from Switzerland."

"Oh? What did he want?"

"I think he was fishing, trying to see if he tripped you up by getting another tenant. Honestly, he makes me ashamed sometimes."

"Yes, well, the dislike he feels for me runs deep. Then again, I guess I didn't help matters with Camille." He shut his eyes and owned the heavy weight pressing to his chest. "It's history now."

"Yes, it is. I gave him an earful about how he abuses his role as executor of dad's estate. There's no reason why he can't sell you the house."

"I appreciate your concern. But if you try to convince him, he'll only get angry with you, too."

"I don't care. This is stupid. He's changed so much over the years, worse than ever. Dad wouldn't stand for this, and I told him so."

Leo's heart swelled with gratitude and love for his sister. "Did he show any signs of breaking his silence with me?"

"The dad remark bothered him. I could tell. But Everett won't budge unless he thinks it's his choice. Maybe he'll come around."

Bella lifted her nose from the bowl and glanced at Leo. He crouched down to pet her. "Thank you for trying. I'd better run. I've got a few things to do. Did I tell you the tenant has a dog?"

"No. What kind?"

"A basset. I'm thinking of getting one after she leaves."

"The tenant is a woman? You didn't mention that."

"You didn't ask."

"I just assumed it was a man."

"Assuming. Your first mistake."

She laughed. "You're impossible."

"I know. Want to get together in a few weeks?"

They talked briefly about possible weekends; then he hung up. Bella came to his side. He stroked the thick fur around her neck as a happy commotion bubbled inside him.

He'd had so many good feelings lately. Lightness to his step. Eagerness to get out of bed each morning. The house carried a certain life, almost like the days of his childhood. An unexpected awareness passed over him, like the lifting of a dense fog.

All this goodness happened with the arrival of a stranger and her dog.

As of this moment, he'd been writing better than he had all year. A month or two and he could get this manuscript whipped into perfect shape and delivered to Seth on schedule. Perhaps the book could release on the date they planned.

Leo stood. "Let's take a walk."

He leashed Bella as a new problem occurred to him. Emma had become his material. His muse. If she left, could he continue this story without her around?

* * * *

"Emma?"

Rose paused her conversation with Sophie, her fake name still foreign sounding at times. Veronica approached them at the bar, the pretty brunette looking classy in a simple black knit top, dark jeans, and a strand of pearls.

Rose smiled. "Hey, that last duet you and Trent sang was beautiful. You guys really draw a nice crowd."

"Oh. Thanks. We love doing it. I wanted to ask you something, but before I forget…" Turning to Sophie, she asked, "Did you talk to Emma about joining us Thursday night?"

"Oops." Sophie shrugged. "We've been so busy it slipped my mind. Emma, want to join us for our monthly gals get together?"

Jay groaned from where he stood at the end of bar, restocking one of the serving stations. "Better be careful how you answer. They do some crazy shit."

Sophie cast an annoyed glare her brother's way. "We do themes, Jay. It's not crazy. It's fun."

Jay grinned and winked at Rose. It wasn't the first time she'd witnessed him get his sister riled up over nothing.

Trent came up alongside Veronica and put an arm around her shoulder. "I agree with Jay. It's like a cult."

Gentle and humorous bickering ensued. Rose listened and laughed along. This group was so easy and made her feel right at home. The happiness in her chest faded as quickly as it had appeared. One drawback to living under a false identity was getting close to people. Getting too friendly would make her lies seem even worse if they ever learned the truth about why she'd appeared in Northbridge.

Their loud laughter drew Rose back to the group. Sophie handed over two water bottles to Trent and Veronica.

Trent twisted the top off his and quietly asked Veronica, "Pearls, did you ask about Leo?"

"I was about to." She looked at Rose. "I run the public library. Since you've got an inside connection to Leo Drake, any chance you could see if he'd be interested in speaking for us?"

"I could try." Rose debated, not sure if it pushed a boundary with Leo or not.

"That's great. People love to hear about authors, their process, what it takes to complete a book, get published in today's market."

Rose chuckled. "It actually is interesting. I learned that Leo writes his first pass on a typewriter, not a computer."

Veronica raised a perfectly plucked brow. "Really? See. This is the kind of stuff people like to know. You mean an electric one?"

"Are you kidding? It's an ironclad relic from another era."

Sophie laughed. "At least it's not a feather pen."

"Now, now ladies." Jay frowned. "That's my buddy you're making jokes about."

The phone on the wall rang. Jay stepped over to answer, shaking his head at them.

"I'll ask him, Veronica," Rose glanced between the two women. "And I'll definitely join you guys this week. Got a theme yet?"

Before Sophie could answer, Jay hung up and said loudly, "Hope you guys enjoyed the short break. A tour bus is on the way."

Rose grabbed a sponge to wipe up the counter and get ready for the next wave of guests. A new kind of happiness churned inside of her. Being here brought the kind of contentment she'd been seeking her entire life. In spite of pretending to be someone else, she was actually just being herself. She couldn't remember the last time she wore those shoes.

Chapter 12

As Rose stepped from the shower into the steamy bathroom, Dan Montgomery's early morning call weighed heavy on her mind. His investigative staff was only human. He couldn't help it if the guy assigned to her case got a mild bout of the flu, and his already swamped staff couldn't work on her case. Still, disappointment stole the hope that got her through each day.

She rubbed the soft cotton towel against her wet skin. This wasn't the end of the world. Dan hoped the staffer might be out of bed in three to five days. Besides, it wasn't as if the FBI or Department of Justice were knocking at the door a second time, demanding she explain those deposits. Not today anyway.

Rose wrapped the towel around her body and tucked the corner between her breasts. Over a week ago she'd arrived in Northbridge. In some ways, she already felt settled. A job. New friends. Scenic setting, in a lovely New England small town.

Scratch. Scratch.

She stuck her head out of the bathroom door and the scratch sounded again.

Bella's persistence was both admirable and annoying. Rose picked her underwear up off the tiled floor and tossed them into a tall plastic garbage bag on the bedroom floor—her makeshift hamper. Today she'd search in town for a real one. This visit here might not be ending any time soon.

Bella whined.

"Jeesh, being a half-hour off schedule for a lousy bowl of morning kibbles doesn't warrant this much drama."

The dog scratched again.

Rose still had to dry her hair and get dressed. As of last night, though, Leo had left her a note with a lifted house rule; Bella could have the run of the place. Less need for doggy supervision gave Rose more options.

She went to the apartment door. Bella flipped her head around and grunted.

"Yeah, yeah. I heard you. You know, the vet said you were a teeny bit heavy, which I overlooked. But if you can't wait a half hour for food, well, then, I worry for you, my friend."

Bella lifted her paw, a threat she was fully prepared to scratch again if needed. "Okay, okay. Let's go before you wear down a hole in the door."

They entered the hallway. Rose paused, taking a minute to stand outside her door and listen to the home's silence. Leo must still be sleeping. She double-checked to make sure the towel knot was secure and hurried to the kitchen.

After taking the dish off the floor, she stretched up to the cabinet, removed the container of kibbles, and filled the dish.

"Eat up, pups." She bent at the knees, taking care not to lean over in the towel.

She started to put away the kibbles away. The container bumped a canister set as she lifted it, knocking out a thin paperback wedged between them. She shelved the dog food and picked up the book. *Connecticut Hauntings*. She opened the cover. The table of contents showed about twenty stories, but one in particular stopped her cold.

In the Quiet of the Night—A Tale of Northbridge.

Meg had said a man once shot his wife in this house, a story too much like the past Rose gladly kept hidden. She swallowed old fears, not about ghosts, but about how humans were capable of some horrible actions.

Yet curiosity drew her to the story about this house in particular. She skimmed the parts talking about how Reginald Cotswald met Anna Worthington, the early years of their marriage and building this house in an area known as the Upper East Side of the lake back in 1923. She reluctantly turned to the last page of the story, fear of what she'd find as daunting as the night she'd walked into her parents' bedroom decades ago.

In the quiet of winter, the Cotswalds visited the lake house for the very last time. Neighbors heard gunfire late one night. When authorities checked, they found Mrs. Cotswald in the couple's bed, a bullet through her head. Mr. Cotswald later told police his wife had been having an affair with one of her husband's competitors.

Since that day, people harbor suspicions Mrs. Cotswald's ghost haunts the property.

Rose closed the book and shut her eyes. Her hands trembled and a hard lump settled in her gut.

Crimes of passion. A phrase most fourteen-year-olds wouldn't know. A scene no fourteen-year-old should have to face. Yet she had. Even though it happened close to twenty-five years ago, Rose could still hear the gunshot waking her on that humid July night, a sound she'd first believed was a July fourth firecracker.

She had sat up in her bed, the home's quiet almost more terrifying than the angry tones of her parents' earlier argument. An affair. A divorce. Megan Allen's name, repeated over and over. The celebrity was starring in a film with her father at the time and tabloids screamed about their involvement.

A second bang sounded, this one definitely from inside the house. She'd slowly lifted the sheet, got out of her bed, and left her room.

She'd tapped on the outside of their bedroom door. "Mom? Dad?"

Silence.

Rose had slowly opened her parents' bedroom door, just a crack. A splattered bloodstain on the ivory bedspread made her still. Terror wrapped her in a tight hold, cutting off her breath. She'd pushed the door further. Her father lay on his back, legs out. A dark red stain saturated the front of his shirt.

A chill rushed Rose's body. Another body could be seen from the corner of her eye across the room. She'd dared to look. Her mother lay still, dropped like a heap on her side. A halo of blood formed above her scalp, a single bullet shot to her temple. A pistol rested on the floor, not far from her mother's hand. Terror seized her muscles and a chill left her skin icy cold. She'd run from their bedroom, unable to feel her feet all the way to the first level, inhaling gulps of air, trying to breathe so she could speak to the 9-1-1 operator.

After that day, the press hounded her every single time she went out in public. Headlines screamed "Orphaned Emmaline Won't Talk" or "Emmaline's Horror;" then they'd write whatever they could scrape up from neighbors and friends of her parents about what had happened—both before and after they died.

A tear rolling down Rose's cheek ended the horrible memory. She forced her eyes open, thankful to be in this dated kitchen and no longer that desperate child. It had taken leaving California for her to escape the notoriety.

Goose bumps prickled her skin, reminding her she stood in only a towel. She returned the book where she found it just as footsteps stomped near the front door and someone put a key in the lock. She hurried back to her apartment.

* * * *

Leo sat in front of his typewriter unable to work, still stunned by what had just happened.

If he hadn't gone to Sunny Side Up for coffee and an egg sandwich, he'd never have been on his back step and reaching for the door as Emma hurried toward the kitchen counter, wrapped in only a short towel.

If he'd only just walked away, he'd be happily working right now. Instead, he'd paused, debating what to do. All while he'd watched her for all of a few seconds, a small amount of time that threatened to railroad his entire day.

The terrycloth had covered just the essentials. The fabric edge brushed snuggly to the crescent curves of her bottom and exposed toned thighs. Sunlight streaking through the kitchen window landed between her shoulder blades, making her skin sparkle like it had been sprinkled with glitter. She rose on tiptoes to reach something in the cabinet. The motion had lifted the back of the towel enough for the moon curves of her cheeks to sneak out and give him a delectable peek. Slow heat had spread through his groin. The very sign he'd needed to remind him to stop. He quickly snuck away, waited a few minutes, and then entered through the front door, making a huge racket so she could disappear in case she was still in the kitchen.

He pushed himself away from the desk and moved to the attic window. Leo's mind wandered from the shimmering lake view to the way the water sparkled on Emma's backside. He imagined removing her towel, drying her damp skin, taking in the rest of those curves—

The loud slam of the downstairs door woke him from the fantasy. Emma came into view in the back yard with Bella. Gone was the sex kitten in the towel. Instead, she wore a short-sleeved shirt with denim bib overalls. All she needed was a cowboy hat and a piece of straw stuck between her lips and they'd hire her at the dairy farm down the road.

Leo turned to reach for his coffee, only to find the cup empty. He walked down the attic stairs and opened the door. About to step out, he paused at something on the floor.

What the hell? He leaned closer. Another pair of silk bikini panties? These weren't here when he'd come up to his office twenty minutes ago. Navy, with lace trim. He lifted them. Were they Susan's from her brief visit? He suddenly remembered the white pair left on the stairs a few days ago, still in his cabinet. Panties he'd assumed were Emma's. So if these were hers…

The thought dangled on its own with a new and uncomfortable notion settling in. One time he and Seth had gone to LA for Leo's appearance on *Conan*. After the taping, they'd been hanging out at their hotel bar. Seth had made friends with a lovely brunette flight attendant and Leo sat nearby, nursing a drink. A pretty woman Leo had noticed alone at a nearby table wandered over to him and after some brief, enjoyable flirting, she disappeared to the ladies' room. When she'd returned, she reached into her purse and pulled out a thong. Running a hand along his leg, she dropped the garment on his lap. "Maybe you'd like to join me upstairs."

His body had said yes, but he'd said no, worried he'd end up as the feature story on her blog or read about it in some trashy tabloid. Could Emma purposely be leaving these here as a suggestion she's interested in him? She hardly seemed the type, although women were so hard to read. But what if she was?

He considered her behavior. Emma had shown very little interest in his celebrity status. Not once had she gushed over his work. In fact, other than a mocking remark about his typewriter and trying to analyze why he had writer's block, she hadn't said much about him being an author.

But maybe she *had been* impressed. His ego inflated a little.

He touched the smooth panty fabric with the pads of his finger, pictured the navy color against the pale crescents of her bottom. A brief fantasy ensued, one where he removed the skimpy towel she wore earlier and found these silky delights underneath. God, he'd yank off those clunky glasses, stare into her gorgeous blue eyes, slip his hands…He stopped himself too late as needs for her took over and his unmet desires were stiff, wanting more.

God, he'd never get any writing done today. Hell, if he did, the book would be shelved under "erotica."

An awareness of everything he'd avoided since losing Camille hit him, startling as a blast of frigid air on a hot day. His feelings for Emma went beyond this hard-on. She made him entertain emotions he'd been trying to avoid. A joyful swelling bloomed inside his chest. Happiness. Like waking each day for something besides work really did matter.

He balled the panties into a wad, the find suddenly more daunting than a minute ago. Returning them would be awkward, or worse, tempting. Leaving them near her door would prove he'd seen them and said nothing. An insult like that might make her pack up and leave. No. He wasn't sure that was what he wanted. Not now. She served as his muse, but that wasn't all. She also brought him a new kind of distraction. One he couldn't decide what he should do about.

He walked up the attic stairs and tossed the panties into the filing cabinet near the first pair. Parts of his life had turned into fodder for fiction, only he wasn't sure that was such a good thing.

* * * *

Bella walked through the shriveled yellow blooms of a forsythia bush that separated Leo's property from the neighbors. Left off leash, she sniffed close to the edge of leggy branches, now filling in with leaves.

Incessant chirping nearby drew Rose's attention to a tree where two nervous robins fluttered around a nest. She moved closer and the adult birds took off. Before she could peek inside, Bella seized the lack of supervision and disappeared into the neighbor's yard.

Rose squeezed between the branches, shoulder first. "Bella! Here!"

As she emerged, an older man kneeling near a garden bed glanced their way. Bella hurled toward him.

The neighbor smiled and waved to Rose. "I'll hold her," he yelled.

Rose caught up and snapped on the dog's leash. "Thanks." Rose inhaled to catch her breath. "She usually stays by me. I'm Emma Morris. I'm renting next door."

"Nice to meet you, Emma. Leo told me a renter had moved in. I'm Harry Gallagher." Harry tipped the visor of a wool Gatsby cap. He had a crooked nose and sparkling gray-blue eyes. "And this must be Bella." He leaned over and scratched the dog's head then glanced up and squinted in the sun. "Leo told me about her, too. Have you had her long?" Harry straightened upright and pressed his hand to his lower back.

"No. I got her from a shelter a few years ago."

"Around here?"

"No. In Massachusetts, where I just moved from. Are you originally from Northbridge?"

"No. This was our summer house for many years, like the Drakes. But I retired, oh, about twenty years ago and decided to spend the non-snowy seasons here. My grandparents built the house, so we've had the place in the family for a long, long time."

"It's beautiful." Rose studied the exterior: white clapboard like most of New England, a flat roof, multiple brick chimneys, and a cupola in the roof's center. "Different than the Drakes'."

"New England Greek revival, or so I'm told."

Bella bumped Harry's knees with her nose, so he leaned over and patted her chest.

"You must have known the entire Drake family."

"I did." He stopped petting the dog. "Wonderful family. Shame the mother died at such a young age."

"Oh?"

"Oh yes. Mrs. Drake died when the kids were almost done with high school. Heart problems. Then, a few years ago, Philip Drake died from a stroke. Sixty-eight. Had just retired, too." He shook his head, squinted into the sun. "Damn shame. A good man. Very good man."

"So you've known Leo since he was a boy?"

"I remember the first year the family came with him." He dropped his voice. "Leo's adopted, but was a foster child for brief spell at first. Such a scared, quiet little boy. Sweet kid. Tough time at first." Sadness spread across his face, yet he chose not to share. "The Drake kids played with mine in the summers when we all visited."

Leo's background filled in. She tried to imagine him as a scared little boy, because nothing other than his undone manuscript seemed to scare him now.

The dog tugged at the leash, but Rose drew her closer and told her to sit. "Everett actually rented the place to me. Nobody was expecting Leo to be at the house when I arrived."

"Funny. He just kind of showed up the day the old tenant left." Harry chuckled. "The tenant said the house was haunted. I've heard lots of rumors. Up until this last renter, nobody has ever gone running."

Leo had appeared as soon as the tenant left? What a coincidence.

The shrill ring of the phone sounded from inside the house, traveling through the screened-in patio.

"Expecting a call from my daughter. Let's talk again soon." Harry hurried inside.

Rose returned to Leo's back yard. Her picture of Leo and his life had filled in from the brief talk. Harry's remarks had also shed some light on the last tenant's leaving, and she wondered if Leo played a role.

Surely a Pulitzer Prize–winning author wasn't capable of such antics. Or was he?

Chapter 13

Dear Dr. Rose, I recently signed up for online dating and struck up a conversation with a man who had no photograph on his profile. No biggie, I thought. Only a shallow person would care about appearance.

Rose lowered the letter and tapped her foot to the English pop singer Dusty Springfield, playing off the vinyl record on an old turntable in the corner of the room. Attraction. A perfect topic for this month's column, and one many readers would relate to. She sure did.

Take Leo. Physically very attractive. Intelligent, almost to the point of overconfident, although he seemed to know when to reel it in. And those gorgeous cocoa eyes, a deadly combination of serious and alluring.

Rose got lost for a minute in Dusty's lyrics about her pounding heart over a man. Yes, she felt it. Lately moments around Leo caused that same reaction. She missed a man's touch. The last time she'd made love was too long ago.

She shook off the weight of self-pity, finished the reader's letter, and started a response. Digging through the pile, she located two letters to go with the theme. As she considered her answers, the burden of her larger assignment for the magazine weighed on her mind. Yesterday, she'd left her editor a message that they needed to talk about it. Rose had come up with an idea and wanted reassurance it was a good one.

Up until now, she didn't have the guts to tell her editor the task about love felt out of her grasp. Nobody knew she was a fraud. When she and John formally announced to the public they were divorced, she'd be labeled the biggest hypocrite on the planet. Her boss couldn't know the truth yet—after all, she'd signed an agreement not to tell anyone—but she could give her fair warning that her advice columnist might someday drop a bomb to the public.

Rose grabbed her cell phone.

On the fourth ring, the Editor-in-Chief of *Sophisticate* magazine answered. "Mia Durbin-Brown here."

"Guess who? I'll give you a hint. I'm your favorite columnist."

Mia laughed easy and gentle, in true uptown girl fashion. "Hi, Rose. Sorry I didn't call back. Yesterday was a nightmare. How's the weather down there?"

It took her a quick second to remember Mia believed she was in her happy home with the junior senator from North Carolina "Oh, typical May weather. Warmer than where you are, I'll bet."

"It's lovely right now. I thought that dreary winter would never end"

Rose loved working with Mia, who'd taken over the Manhattan-based magazine ten years ago as it teetered on the edge of failure. Now the publication thrived with the timeless elegance of English Ivy. She pictured the fashion-forward editor in her twenty-fifth story office overlooking Manhattan, long legs crossed as she tipped back in her chair.

"I wanted to talk about the special feature piece you gave me."

"Okay. Have you come up with an angle? Maybe how you fell in love with your husband? Readers would love that."

"That's what I wanted to discuss. I haven't mentioned this, but things on the home front aren't going so well these days."

"I'm sorry. You always seem so problem free."

"No marriage is problem free." She noted the defensiveness in her tone so switched to a softer one. "Unfortunately we're beyond repair. It's possible our marital status will change after the elections, when we have time to really talk about our problems. To be honest, I'm worried. The magazine's readers are wonderful, but people can be so unforgiving when someone like me has real-life problems."

"Listen, we'll find a way to deal with it when the time comes. I'm pretty sure if it's handled correctly, readers will identify with you by the time we finish."

"Thanks for the support. You've always been a great boss and friend. So I'd like to talk about this love study."

"Do you want to put it off?"

"No. Oddly enough it has me thinking about my own life. Like when I first met John and what drew me to him. In fact, working on this special piece has been pretty eye-opening."

"As long as you are okay doing the story…"

"I am. But I wanted to brainstorm with someone. You're it."

"Then tell me what you're thinking."

"I'd like to expand on the study premise a bit. Besides why we fall in love, what makes couples stay in love. I just met an adorable couple on the brink of real dating." Meg and Charlie seemed to be trying but couldn't quite get there. "And there's a few other couples in varying stages of their relationships with some real everyday issues married pairs face. I find myself curious what they might learn by doing this."

"That's a great angle. My last marriage might not have fallen apart if I'd tried this. So run with it. Call if you want to talk more, but I know you'll get there. You always do."

Rose hung up, glad about her boss's reaction, but an unexplained sadness took hold. Love. Mysterious and elusive. Had she ever known *true* love? The kind people lived for. The kind that inspired poetry. The kind that lasted forever.

John's appeal had been something else, more about having a rooted family. Not a sensation stirring inside her heart. Romance had always fallen into the category of made-up Hollywood things. Watching her parents' phony attempts to appear happily married painted a sad picture of where love and trust could lead two people.

Her throat grew thick. So many wrongs, forcing her to put faith in nobody but herself. The admission squeezed at her chest until a wall she'd built around it to keep pain away cracked in places.

All her life, she'd felt alone. Until this moment, it had never seemed to matter that much because she accepted it as part of how she survived. Overdue emotion stole a bit of the resistance coating her heart, and Rose surrendered to a real good cry.

* * * *

Leo tossed the tartan plaid dog bed into the car's backseat, next to a bag from Breckenridge Dairy Farm. In all his trips to Southbridge, he'd never once noticed the pet store in the brick strip mall. Yet today, on his way home from town to buy some pastries for tomorrow's breakfast, a sign near the store reading "Sale - Dog Beds" made him slow and turn in.

He buckled up and pulled out of the parking lot. The new bed for Bella was an impulse purchase, justified by his plans to get a dog after Emma left. Until that time, he'd leave the bed near the dining room sliders, where Bella often slept in a stream of sunlight.

Leo followed the country road, blasting Tom Petty on the radio, who crooned about the great wide open. Leo loved the song following a man's rise to music success and the fickle nature of entertainment stardom. A sentiment Leo fully understood. Lately the stings of their critiques seemed to have lost some of the power it once had over him. Especially today. The combined warm spring air rushing his skin and bright sun spilling through trees lifted his spirits.

Ten minutes later, he pulled down his tree-lined driveway and parked next to Emma's car. He bundled his purchases in his arms. Once in the kitchen, he put down the bags, tore the tag off the dog bed, and headed down the hallway. He didn't want Emma to know he'd spent money on the dog to avoid giving her the wrong impression.

At Emma's shut door, he paused and listened. Music. The familiar scratchy sound of vinyl. Rainy summer afternoons growing up, he and the other kids who vacationed here would hang out in the apartment and play board games while listening to records.

He knocked a few times.

The music lowered and she came to the door. She smiled at him, but it seemed forced and didn't mask the sadness in her eyes. "Hi. What's up?"

"Sorry to interrupt."

"You're not. I'm just working."

Bella pushed past her legs and went to Leo's side. He pet her and glanced up at Emma. "You found the record player."

"I hope you don't mind."

"Not at all." He waited for one of her sarcastic remarks, the type that made him laugh. "What? No suggestions that I update to an eight-track player? Or get myself a Walkman?"

She shrugged. "Guess you caught me on a slow day."

"I was just teasing."

"Yes, I know." She smiled feebly, but his good humor nose-dived.

An awkward moment of silence passed. Their gazes locked. Vulnerability in her eyes made him want to pull her into a hug. The dog bed slipped from his fingers. "Are you okay?"

"I'll be fine. But thanks."

Fine, but not happy.

"What's that?" She motioned to the bed, where Bella sniffed at the edges.

"Oh, a friend of mine bought this, but their dog didn't like it. He was about to toss it out, but I said I'd take it. Bella seems to like a spot in the dining room. I figured she might like a bed over there, especially now that she can wander the house." His cheeks warmed at hearing himself babble. He drew in a breath and vowed to shut up.

"Are you sure her wandering around the house is okay? She won't bother you?"

"Not at all. It's not the big deal I made when you arrived."

Bella climbed onto the bed and turned in a circle, then plunked down.

"You like that Bella-bug?" Emma asked quietly.

Bella lifted her head, and he'd have sworn she grinned.

Emma met Leo's gaze, happiness shining in her eyes. "I think that's a yes."

"Good. I'll put it in the dining room." He called the dog off, lifted the bed, and turned to leave.

"Leo?"

He stopped and looked back.

"Thank you for thinking of Bella." She smiled so generous and genuine it warmed his heart.

He smiled back. "It was my pleasure. She's a special dog."

Her expression got serious, and she stared into his eyes with a curious gaze. Softly, she said, "I'll be going out tonight for a little while. If it turns out she's too much of a pain or taking over the whole house, please go ahead and shut her inside the apartment."

"It'll be okay. She keeps me company, too." He hung onto the image of her expression, relaxed and filled with interest. An expression he wished he saw more often.

Chapter 14

Rose had been quietly noting details in Sophie and Duncan's spacious kitchen, their craftsman-styled house a spectacular display of architecture. At least she was, until Meg had marched into the room a minute ago and demanded their attention, her endearing cheery disposition nowhere in sight.

Meg's forehead creased and she scanned the ladies standing around the kitchen island. "When Sophie suggested we do a Scottish *Outlander* theme, I took it quite seriously. Like I always do. Remember on RomCom night…" Meg paused and donned a stern expression as she focused on Bernadette Felton, who'd started to chuckle. "Do you think this is funny?"

Rose had met Bernadette for the first time tonight and learned she was married to the local pastor at the Methodist Church, was a lawyer, and also a local activist.

Bernadette nodded, her brown layers brushing her shoulder. "Aye, lassie," she quipped using a halfway decent brogue. "It's hilarious." Her voice returned to normal as she removed a plastic wrap from a casserole dish and glanced up at Meg. "Don't get your panties all twisted. I was joking when I said to bring haggis. You know, sarcasm?"

"Well I didn't know. Good God, those pictures online were gross." Meg's nose crinkled. "And nobody around here sells sheep's pluck either. The butcher at Bellantoni's laughed for five minutes after I asked for some. He told me I should hop a plane to Edinburgh."

More laughter ensued and Meg's frown deepened.

"Good for you for trying, though." Rose felt badly for poor Meg and didn't join the others. "What exactly is sheep's pluck?"

Meg twisted her nose into a disgusted face. "Sheep's heart, liver, and lung."

Bernadette put her dish with the others, came to Meg's side, and rested a hand on her shoulder. "I'm sorry you went through all that."

Veronica, so pretty and proper in her own way, sat with her back straight, making her long neck seem even longer. "So if you didn't make haggis, what did you bring?"

Meg frowned. "Hamburgers and hot dogs."

"A perfect substitute," Bernadette said right away, and the others agreed.

Rose found herself a little envious. They'd all been friends since elementary school. When Rose high-tailed it out of California, she'd forfeited her childhood friendships.

"They'll go perfect with my tatties." Bernadette took a seat across from Rose.

Sophie snorted a laugh. "Your what?"

"Tatties is a Scottish national side dish, usually served with haggis. Burgers and hot dogs are close enough. God only knows what they make those hot dogs from." She smiled nicely at Meg then quickly glanced Sophie's way. "I still can't believe you didn't tell Duncan my idea."

Sophie rolled her eyes. "To come visit us tonight in a kilt? No, I didn't tell him! He'd have been embarrassed."

"But imagine if he did." Meg's eyes grew wide and her cheeks turned pink.

Bernadette raised her eyebrows. "See? I'm not the only one. Ronnie?"

Veronica shook her head. "No thank you. I don't want to see my brother-in-law wearing a kilt. Theme or no theme."

"All right, ladies." Sophie slapped her palms on the table. "We haven't even started drinking the scotch and are already headed down a bad path." She turned to Rose. "There's no backing out of this gathering now."

"Are you kidding? I wouldn't miss this for anything."

Rose had accepted the invitation somewhat reluctantly but was so glad she came. Not only were these women fun, but they'd be perfect candidates to answer the question for her *Sophisticate* piece. All she needed to do was ease into the topic without scaring them off.

* * * *

"Now where'd your owner go, Bella?" Leo lowered his plate from the kitchen table to the floor so Bella could lick off the remains of his dinner.

Emma left a half hour earlier, dressed in fitted black jeans and a silky shirt, which was cinched at the waist and flowing along her torso. She'd even done something different with that flyaway haircut instead of pinning it back in barrettes, overall looking cute and more grown up than usual.

He lifted a page from the chapter he'd typed this afternoon, slowly rereading the passage giving him so much trouble. Intimacy. In real life, he'd been with plenty of women, so why was writing it now from his male character's perspective so hard?

He sat quietly as happier moments with his wife played out. Shared secrets. Passion in unexpected places. The joy of her laugh, a contagious little giggle that always made all their problems disappear. The edges of each memory blurred and he couldn't get focus. Emotions denied since her death were stuck behind a door with a rusted bolt.

He lowered the papers and closed his eyes, tying to visualize the power of the scene. His character was a man with two women circling his orbit. One, an exact replica of his ex-wife, brought him the comfort found in old, damaged state of being. The other offered a new adventure. Around her, he found himself jerked from his comfort zone in a way that was exhilarating and frightening at the same time. His character found himself drawn to it like an addiction.

Leo opened his eyes, struck by a new awareness of his character. He was a man who possessed all the desire, but none of the ability to dive into a new life.

Like Leo.

He owned the idea, letting it sink inside of him. Emma both exhilarated and terrified Leo, too. Walking around with her secrets. Wearing that little towel. Enticing him with her silk undergarments.

What exactly did she want from him? She seemed so straightforward, not someone who'd drop hints, like leaving her panties at his door. Had he imagined a sign of closeness earlier when he'd delivered the dog bed? She'd studied him, as if for the first time she saw past the horrible man he'd become. Or was something inside him softening and allowing her in?

At that moment, another reason for her leaving the underwear unexpectedly hit him from behind. He'd been too stupid, so blinded by his lust he'd almost missed it. Perhaps those little drop offs were an intentional effort to make him uncomfortable having her around. So uncomfortable he'd return her money. The money he hadn't taken. She'd been surprisingly quiet about it for days.

Yes. That made more sense. Idiot. Good thing he hadn't pranced to her apartment door with a proposition.

He patted Bella. "Your owner confuses me."

Bella lifted her bloodshot eyes, a sure sign of agreement.

A raw pain swelled in his heart, kick-started by some blend of old feelings for his wife and uncertain feelings for Emma. He'd vowed after losing Camille to never again allow himself to care that much about someone. Yet here he stood three years later, behind a wall losing its bricks. Proving a point he didn't want to prove; Emma's presence showed he *did* need love.

The enormity pressed to his chest and he allowed it to own him. He wished Emma were here right now. Instead, he put down his manuscript and went down the hallway to the laundry room to see if his clothes were dry.

As he passed her doorway, he spotted a business card lying on the floor just outside the opened apartment door. He picked it up and read "Dan Montgomery, Private Investigator, Specializing in Computer Crimes." The phone number exchange was one he didn't recognize. A private investigator? Emma had some big problems, but if she needed a PI, they must be mighty large ones. The jumbled thoughts in his head about what she hid became an even bigger mess.

Bella trotted over to Leo. He scratched the dog's chest, considering the latest bizarre find. His somber mood improved as his mind whirled with excitement over the idea of using this angle in his story. He wished he could talk to Emma openly and find out why she needed a PI's help. He slipped his phone out of the back pocket of his jeans and noted the card's information so he could do some research later. Then he left the card where he'd found it.

"Come on, Bella. The Dairy Inn just reopened for the season and we could both use a treat."

He grabbed his keys off the counter and whistled a tune as they walked out to his car. Surely Emma wouldn't mind if he treated Bella to a small cup of vanilla. While they enjoyed their ice cream, he'd use his phone Internet to learn more about Dan Montgomery.

* * * *

Rose's eyes burned. She pushed aside the scotch after trying for an hour to drink it. "I'm sorry. This is gross. If a sexy Scotsman in a kilt were to spoon feed this to me and promise to spend the night, I still couldn't finish it."

Sophie and Bernadette laughed. They were both sipping theirs on the rocks and with ease Rose couldn't grasp.

"You were brave for trying." Meg patted her hand. "I'll get you a glass of the wine I'm drinking."

Sophie speared another hot dog with her fork. "Back to our bitch session."

Rose had been listening quietly. What started as some honest remarks about their husbands had turned into a major upheaval of small problems mounting to bigger complaints.

"I'm just tipsy enough that later I might tell Duncan what I think about the boost in his daughter's school allowance that he handed over without even a bit of discussion. She's got him wrapped around her finger, that one does."

Bernadette's cheeks flared brighter crimson as she nursed her second glass. "I can top that. Dave was too tired to help me look over a problem with one of our bills when he got home the other night, but the second the church organist called, telling him she needed a ride somewhere, he got up and drove her."

"Well, Bern." Meg shrugged. "He is the pastor."

"Yes. He's not a taxi service, though. He'd just put in a long day and didn't have time for me, but he did for a parishioner?" She raised a hand. "Before you all tell me I'm mean, hear me out. Dave gives one hundred and fifty percent to the church, which makes me proud of him. I ask for very little. That night I needed help and he said no." Bernadette frowned. "Why does he have time for everyone else, but not me?"

Meg patted Bernadette's hand. "Honey, Dave adores you. He's a good man. It's sometimes easier to say no to the people we love."

Veronica nodded. "Good point."

Bernadette's tense expression softened. "I know you're right. Sometimes, complaining feels good." She glanced at Veronica. "Please don't tell me Trent's still perfect?"

The long-necked beauty laughed. "Okay. I won't tell you. I also suggest that you *not* pour another glass of that lethal stuff."

Rose laughed with the others. Over the course of the night, she'd grown a little closer to these women. They loved their men but weren't without issues. Meg's closeness to Charlie had made her eyes sparkle with the mere mention of his name. Sophie's second chance at love with Duncan showed how fate could draw two people together who'd always been meant for each other. Bernadette and Dave were the most unlikely match anybody might have thought of: a lawyer/political activist and her Methodist pastor husband. Yet before she'd started complaining, everything she said about him spoke to the kind of love that evolved over the passage of time. And Veronica shined like a beacon of brightness around Trent. Their romantic ballads sung at the vineyard showed such strong emotion Rose could feel their tenderness in her own heart.

Yet it was real life, not all glamorous and problem-free. Because love wasn't always easy. So what might they see if they tried out the experiment about love?

Rose cleared her throat and they all looked her way. "I'm wondering if you ladies can help me. I'm taking an online psychology class."

She hated having to lie to these lovely women. If she used anything from their discoveries, Rose promised herself she'd tell them the truth about it being for the magazine. By then, she'd be done with this identity ordeal and hopefully have returned to her old self.

"I never got to finish my degree. The divorce seems like a good time to work on finishing. I have to write about a study. A scientist claimed his experiment could make two people fall in love in a lab."

Veronica chuckled. "I never liked science, but would've found that an interesting experiment."

The others nodded their agreement.

"I'm thinking of taking this in another direction, expanding and seeing what happens when someone already in a relationship tries the questions. Like you all…well, you seem to have a variety of stories."

Sophie chuckled. "Variety is right. I met Duncan when he tried to buy the land that I wanted. And Ronnie"—she motioned to Veronica—"she got stuck in an elevator with Trent."

"Yeah, I'm the most conventional story here." Bernadette snorted. "After a stint in the Peace Corps, I came home and Sophie dragged me to church. There I meet the new pastor. Never, in a million years, would I have guessed I'd find something so irresistible about Dave Felton that I'd marry him." She frowned. "Now I feel bad for complaining earlier."

"No marriage is complaint-free." Rose shrugged. "It's normal. Living together is hard work. The trick is to communicate. Like you, Bernadette. You were just hurt because Dave didn't have time for you, but did for someone else."

"You're right." Bernadette slapped her palm on the table. "That's really all it was."

"Sharing makes us vulnerable. Which is why we don't always talk about our feelings. But this study makes me wonder: When we hand our vulnerability to our partner—and they do the same—do you suppose that's what leads to love?"

The formerly rambunctious group stared at her, each holding deep, serious expressions.

"I'm sorry. Heavy stuff?"

"No, thought provoking," said Sophie. "And pretty accurate."

"Except for me." Meg twisted the ends of a napkin in her fingers. "Roy left me. I like Charlie but have no idea how to get him to see it."

"Would everyone be willing to set aside some time, about an hour, and try out these questions with your spouses?" She turned to Meg. "And can you see if Charlie would want to give this a try with you?"

"What kind of questions?" Bernadette arched a brow, suspicion obvious.

"As an example, an easy one might be, 'Would you want to be famous and in what way?'"

"Versus a harder example?" Bernadette eyed Rose skeptically.

"These are a little more revealing, like talking about a terrible memory, for example. Or sharing an embarrassing moment."

"I'm game." Sophie shrugged and lifted her scotch. "Why not? It can only bring us closer to the men in our lives."

Veronica turned to Rose. "Emma, what about you? Have you tried this?"

"No takers at the moment. But if one shows up, I'm willing to give it a whirl." She slipped on a cheerful face, but questions roiled inside her head. Would she put herself out on the precarious limb of love again if given the chance?

Chapter 15

Rose waved goodbye to Veronica, who'd insisted on driving her home from Sophie's house. Everyone had agreed: unfamiliar dark roads and a little too much wine was a bad mix. She flipped on the kitchen lights and squinted. The multiple glasses of wine still swam inside her head, making her steps light and her balance tipsy.

A soft beat pulsed through the ceiling. Leo must be upstairs.

Tonight, while with the ladies, Leo's visit to show her the dog bed would pop into her mind and leave a warm impression inside her chest. His over-anxiousness about the delivery showed it meant something to him. And when he'd realized she'd been upset before he arrived, his concern came across as sincere. Almost sweet.

Lately, she'd been enjoying their banter, catching herself waiting for his smile when she'd tease him about how he loved old things. As she'd handed out the study questions to her new friends before leaving tonight, she'd pondered the idea of trying them with Leo. An idea she dismissed as quickly as it had formed.

She started to walk by the kitchen table and paused. Several pages were lying there, the old typewriter print distinct. She lifted the small stack of papers.

Chapter Eighteen.

Was this the infamous book Leo needed to finish? Just last night, she'd reached the end of *The World According to Stan.* She'd found it well written, deep in very subtle ways, and a work she'd happily recommend to others. With nothing else to compare it to, she couldn't imagine what the critics disliked. If anything, the layers of the story reminded her of layers she believed Leo possessed. Complex layers, the top raw and frustrated, but beneath them a man who clearly wanted more.

She skimmed over the first page then paused. What if writers didn't like their unpublished work read by just anybody? Curiosity owned her, though, and she started at the first line.

One page in, she dropped to the kitchen chair. By the time she reached the third page, she couldn't deny how Leo's keen observations about life and intimate details had her entranced and engaged. By the fifth page, Rose realized something...the woman in this chapter was a redhead running from a past and living under an assumed name. Like her.

Only he didn't know she was living under an assumed name or running from her past. Did he? She read further, worried she might find a senator husband in this tale or learn the character wrote for a magazine column. No other similarities jumped out, thank God.

On the last page, she caught her breath at a passage where the sexual attraction this fictional man showed for the redhead carried some serious heat. If his writing held any truth in reality, did it mean Leo watched her this way, too?

She read on as the pair on paper engaged in a gentle kiss. One filled with such deep meaning Rose's knees went soft. Flipping back a few pages, she again read the women's physical description. Too close to her own appearance for comfort, but Leo couldn't possibly have been thinking of her when he wrote this. But what if he was?

When he'd given her instructions on his coffee pot, his touch left her craving more than the lesson. This afternoon, part of her wanted to fall into his arms at the doorway, enjoy the support found in someone's arms.

A creak in the house made her glance down the hall. The door to her apartment was open wide and Bella hadn't come out to greet her. She went down the hall and walked inside, nearly stepping on a business card lying in the doorway. She lifted it and realized the PI's card must've fallen out of her jacket pocket. She placed it on the coffee table. By now, Bella would've come out to greet her.

"Bella?" Rose searched each room but couldn't find her.

She hurried back to the kitchen and stood for an agonizing moment thinking of her poor pup, possibly lost in the dark woods or wandering in town. About to go outside, she instead headed upstairs.

The music grew louder and she recognized the raspy voice of an acoustic artist she enjoyed. Guess she and Leo had music tastes in common.

A sliver of light sliced into the dark hallway from the partially opened door of Leo's bedroom. She moved near and peeked inside. Leo lay on the made bed on his back, eyes shut, and chest rising with each breath. An open bottle of wine, used glass, and hardcover book turned upside down rested on his small nightstand.

One arm lifted above his head with his palm tucked beneath tufts of his thick hair, raising the loose tails of his button-down shirt and exposing the hard planes of his abdomen against the waist of his jeans. The other arm draped over Bella's shoulder as she stretched out on her side with her back to Leo. The hound slept as soundly as he did.

Rose's heart cracked wide open. He'd grown close to Bella. She'd noticed other signs. Maybe it wasn't only her dog that had found the good beneath Leo's guarded surface. He was starting to rub off on her, too. The power in his writing proved he didn't show the world his inner self. At that moment, she wished the fictional redhead and the on-paper kiss *were* meant for her.

She shifted and the floorboard creaked. Bella lifted her head and blinked. Her tail wagged then she lengthened her elongated body into a stretch. Leo stirred and his eyes fluttered open. He stared at Rose and rubbed the side of his cheek with his hand. A slow awareness settled over his face and his gaze filled with heat. He studied her, sweeping past her lips, lingering on her breasts, traveling to her hips. Each place he stopped created a warm and tingly sensation in its path.

Rose stilled and lifted her chin, empowered by the craving in his eyes. Or was it from the wine and talk about romance? It didn't matter. Let him look.

He seized her in a hypnotic hold. His lips parted, almost touching her without touching. On reflex, her mouth did the same. His eyes softened with the subtle lift of his mouth into a sleepy, sexy smile.

Bella rolled over and jumped off the bed, snapping Rose from her erotic trance.

Leo lifted onto his elbow and ran a hand through his unkempt hair. "Bella wanted some company. Hope you don't mind."

"Not at all."

He stood, the same rumpled man Rose had seen on her first night here. Only the way she saw him tonight wasn't the same. No longer an angry ogre, but a man who lived behind some pain. Who'd had a rough start but found the love of a family to save him from a different path in life. And a man who'd snuggled with Bella, simply to keep her happy.

He watched her carefully while running his palm over his unshaven face. His gaze dropped to the typed pages. "Oh. You have my manuscript?"

The papers. She'd forgotten all about them. "It was on the kitchen table. I suppose I shouldn't have been so nosey." She handed them to him. "I'm sorry."

"My fault. I left them there by mistake." He took it and sat on the edge of the mattress. "Did you read them?"

She nodded.

He studied the pages for a few seconds. "I was in the kitchen reading it over and over to make sure this scene has the emotional punch it needs. What'd you think?"

"Oh, it had punch." Her cheeks burned thinking about what he'd written. "What's the story behind what I read?"

Leo's expression turned pensive. "Generally, she falls out of his usual choices."

"And that's bad?" The room spun a little. Rose pressed fingers to her temples. "Mind if I sit?"

"Be my guest."

Rose sank to the small space on the bed at the same moment Bella hopped back up, hogging a huge amount of space. She shoved her dog gently over. Bella groaned. Leo scratched her head, laughing softly.

"She isn't a typical choice?" Rose asked.

"To be with her is a risk."

"In what way?"

"Being truthful about his feelings for her is a risk. Giving into his needs is a risk. Change is a risk."

Rose thought about her life, where the truth was rarely discussed and she ignored her real problems.

Leo slowly rubbed his hand on his thigh. "He worries he might fall in love with her. And love…well, love changes things. Especially when it disappears."

The weight of his words made her chest tighten. The love of her own parents was something she'd questioned while growing up. Their self-involvement had formed the foundation for a distance she'd kept from people her entire life. She glanced up and caught Leo watching her. For the briefest second, she wanted to share about herself, but remembered her reason for being at this house in the first place so didn't. "And her? What does she know of love?"

"She's finding her way, too, but is less afraid."

"Or so your character thinks."

"How so?"

It could have been the effects of the wine, or a fast developing warmth for Leo, but she couldn't shake the urge to open up to him to see what might happen if she cracked the door she usually hid behind. "I was just thinking about my own framework for adult love. It stemmed from childhood. My parents were self-involved people, leaving me to wonder about their love for me—they paid lip service to the idea but didn't really act the part." She chose each word carefully, not wanting to give away her real identity. "On the surface, those who know me think I have a firm grasp on love, but given who I learned it from..." Speaking the truth made her chest ache and forced her to stop.

He'd studied her, his gaze hopping around her face. "What do you mean?"

"After what's gone on in my life lately, I'd say your character should question his observations. Because what may come across as confidence could be masking a person's uncertainty."

Rose, the queen of over-confidence. Her practice, specializing in relationship counseling, and her column for the magazine were reduced to nothing more than a ruse.

"I see." He said quietly and furrowed his brows. "I'm not sure if you caught this, but my character's appearance..." He drew in a deep breath then let it go. "Well, I knew I wanted her to be pretty, a woman who would make it hard for him to resist, but I struggled to get a visual on the character." The muscles around his eyes softened. "After we met, you seemed to fit the bill. Did I cross a line?"

Had he said pretty? Rose reached up and pushed her glasses to the bridge of her nose. Her cheeks burned as he stared, waiting for an answer. "No, of course not."

Leo tipped his head, smiled softly. "I keep trying to picture those beautiful blue eyes of yours without the glasses." He reached up with both hands to her frames. "May I?"

She nodded and sucked in a quick breath, but he seemed not to notice as he removed them and skimmed her face, as though he was seeing it for the first time.

"Yes, they're exactly as I'd imagined them," he said softly. "Too pretty to be hidden."

"I-I'm not hiding them. I thought the frames were different."

"They are different." His gaze fell to her lips. "You're different, too, Emma. Different in a way that leaves me so damn curious there are moments you are all I think about."

He cupped her chin with one hand and swept her lower lip with his thumb, awakening warmth between her thighs. The fog of the wine unlatched her usual caution. As his hands fell to her shoulders and he drew her close, she didn't resist. He lowered his mouth over hers, kissing her with gentle strokes.

He pulled back, hunger in his gaze. She pressed her lips to his thick neck, then along his strong jaw, then the corner of his mouth. He took hold of the fabric on her blouse, drawing her against him again. He kissed her, a slow blending of their lips. Soft and tender at first, then deeply, holding her head in his hands. She threw her arms around his neck, clung to him so tightly her heart pounded against his chest. A hard shell she'd formed years ago melted like butter resting in the sun.

Leo cupped her face in his hands. "Emma..." he whispered into her mouth. The soft grain of his shadowed cheeks greedily rubbed against her skin, rousing uncontrollable longing.

They kissed. At times soft and exploring, then intensifying with eager demand for each other. He laid her back against the pillow, moved his hands along the curve of her waist, slipping them beneath her blouse and skating over the flesh of her back, making her entire body heat. He paused his thumbs near her ribcage, caressing the area just beneath her breasts.

The shock of something cold and wet near her arm made her jolt. She pulled back. Leo's hands fell away. The dog wedged her large head close and licked Leo's cheek.

Leo shook his head and sat up. "Bella, you could use some mouthwash."

Rose sat upright, smoothing her blouse back to a normal position. What was she doing? Being at this house and with Leo was a temporary stop in her game to outwit her lying ex-husband. Not a place a place for...for this.

"I'm sorry," she said quickly and stood. "I drank too much wine tonight." His brow rose. "Nothing to be sorry about."

He was right, but Rose's tangled emotions took over. How had she let things with Leo get so out of control? "Anyway, Veronica drove me home. She's the director at the library. She asked if you might want to speak at the library someday."

He nodded and stood. "Sure. I'd be happy to."

"I'll let her know. Thanks for watching Bella tonight. Come on," she called to the dog.

Bella jumped off and followed Rose to the door. As she left, the burn of Leo's eyes on her back followed every step.

"Emma?"

She turned around. "Yes?"

"Thank you for the help with my work. This is a solitary job. I appreciate your insights."

"Any time."

She hurried down the hall with her fingertips pressed to her lips, swollen from the kiss. Leo's gently raw edges, so obvious from the first time they met, weren't really about a man who was nasty or uncaring. Rather he was a man who tried to work his way through life's problems.

Exactly why she needed to guard her emotions more closely. At this point in her life, she had no business involving herself with any man.

Chapter 16

Leo pressed the "on" button to his computer, taking advantage of the few free minutes he had before getting to work. Harry had joined him on last night's visit to the Dairy Inn, and he'd forgotten all about researching the investigator on the card he'd found outside Emma's apartment.

During bouts of restless sleep, he rehashed the image of Emma standing in his doorway late last night. Through the foggy haze, he'd caught her watching him, her gaze tender and sweet. Normally he'd get upset at someone reading his material before it reached the final rounds, only he began to think he'd left it there on purpose. A subconscious need to pull her further into his world.

As they'd talked about his book, her vulnerabilities became more apparent. Although she'd cracked open a door, he sensed she held back and chose her words carefully. The small reveal made him crave her all the more, pushing him to remove her glasses and touch her sweet-scented skin. When she had trembled slightly from his touch, it surprised him that a woman who'd given him unfettered access to her most personal undergarments would react in such a way. If Bella hadn't interrupted, how far would they have gone?

Every ounce of last night's encounter would be used in revisions later today, but his interest in understanding her went beyond work into personal. Their intimacy drove him and made him want to fully understand what brought her to his house.

Leo typed "Dan Montgomery, 8-0-4 area code" into the search engine, the PI's information a good placed to start. Listings showed a Facebook account and a faculty listing at a university. None an exact match. He adjusted the search to include the full phone number.

Hewitt Investigations, specialists in high-tech crimes appeared on the screen. Members of the Private Investigator Association of Virginia, they'd been in business for the past fifteen years and belonged to the American College of Forensic Examiners.

Leo followed the link and found a list of investigators. Sure enough, Dan Montgomery's name appeared amongst them as a director for the company. His credentials seemed good: military training in computer crimes, certified by the state, and he'd even worked on some big cases for the government.

So why would Emma need this guy's phone number or help?

* * * *

Rose spread mayonnaise on her turkey sandwich then cut it in half. She tore off a small corner of the meat and dropped it to Bella, who snatched it up from her station at Rose's side.

"I'll give you credit, Bella. Your hope for never-ending handouts inspires me."

Rose glanced up to the clock over the sink. An hour until her afternoon tea with Harry Gallagher, something she'd looked forward to since this morning's invite when she ran into him while walking Bella. The guy was honest and easy to talk to. If he were about thirty years younger, she could find herself swayed by his crystal grayish-blue eyes.

As she stuck the knife in the dishwasher, footsteps skipped lightly on the staircase. Leo. She'd only come out this morning for breakfast *after* she'd heard the scrape of his chair and creak of his steps returning upstairs. A silly move, almost junior high. But the tender moment between them last night had left her shamefully craving more of his kisses, more of his touch.

Caution seemed smart. Rose had never depended on anybody and didn't plan on starting now.

He hit the bottom step and Bella took off. Rose struggled to appear poised and aloof to convey a message the kiss hadn't left her uneasy or wanting more. Liar. It had railroaded her dreams and every waking move.

Leo's voice dripped sweet with baby talk from outside the kitchen entrance. "Hello there, Bella. You're such a g'girl."

Heat stirred in Rose's belly with the ridiculous notion she wished he'd give her some sweet talk. Seconds later, he walked into the kitchen.

Rose slid her sandwich onto a plate and turned around, smiling away any embarrassment from last night. "Hello."

Dark jeans, a fitted heather pullover with a V-dip, and sockless loafers. He looked handsome and dressier than usual for working alone in an attic. Her Hello Kitty plush bottoms and matching T-shirt—emblazed with the aforementioned kitty wearing glasses like Rose's and the phrase "talk nerdy to me" along the shirt bottom—made her feel frumpy and silly.

"Hello." He studied her on his way to the sink then he arched a brow and, in a rather husky voice, said, "Or should I say 'Hello kitty?'"

The part of her she'd just zipped tight unraveled. Heat crept up her neck. She tucked a few stray hairs behind her ear. "Oh right, my pants." *Idiot. Of course it's the pants.* "Oh, thanks for hanging out with Bella last night."

"It was my pleasure." He paused near her for a moment then continued to the sink with his mug. "I had a productive writing morning. Our talk helped." He cleared his throat.

Was he implying more? She lifted her empty glass from the counter.

"Good." She scooted to the sink and reached for the faucet at the same time he did. Their hands brushed and she jerked back.

He watched her, his gaze penetrating, unwavering. "After you."

Bella howled and ran to the kitchen door. Leo put down his mug, strolled there, too, and peered out the window. "Stay here, Bella." He blocked her with his leg and slipped outside.

Rose went over and watched as Leo approached a little red compact car with New York plates. A woman with short dark hair in her mid-twenties got out and smiled at him. They hugged. Leo was a good head taller than her, just like Rose. The woman motioned to the lake. Together they walked toward the dock. Smiling and chatting. She said something and Leo laughed, even put a hand on her shoulder as he answered.

Another woman in his life? She'd thought he dated Susan, a fact conveniently missing from her thought process while she made out with him last night.

Rose turned away, yet the oddest sensation crowded her chest. Jealousy? The ridiculous notion sunk deeper. She wanted to slap herself across the face. After all, she was here under false pretenses, taking flight from her problems. She had no right.

"Come on, Bells. I've got to return a call and get to work."

She took her lunch and returned to the apartment before Leo entered with his... his what? Once inside, she shut the door tight, like it might keep desires unleashed for him from escaping again.

Putting down her lunch on the coffee table, she lifted the business card found on the floor last night. Before she could dial, voices carried from the kitchen; then an army of footsteps went upstairs. Jeesh, not even offering her lunch before luring her into his den of iniquity?

She dialed Dan, pushing aside her hurt and concentrating on bigger worries. On the fourth ring, he answered.

"Hi, Dan. It's Rose Richardson."

"Hey! We finally connect. Boy, have I got some news for you."

A scratching sound at the door made her glance over. Bella lifted her paw and scratched the door again. "Good news, I hope." Rose went over and opened it partway. Bella stuck her head out into the hallway but didn't go further.

"In the long run, yes. We've made some decent progress. Have you ever heard the term 'straw donor'?"

"Sure." She returned to the sofa. "When someone advances money to another party, who then makes a campaign contribution in their own name. It's illegal because of the limits a single person can *actually* give to a campaign."

"Exactly. It seems your husband has been a very busy man. In short, he's made it appear as if your inheritance went into his campaign using third parties, but his name isn't on anything."

"How did you find the third parties?"

"Every single one was filtered through an email account with the address senatorswife@yahoo.com. Sound familiar?"

"No. Not at all. I only have my work email address and a personal account through our internet provider."

"Well, this Yahoo account is listed as belonging to you. Although, anybody could have used your name and set it up without your knowledge. From this account, we've found emails—supposedly sent by you—asking quite a few people to use *your* money to donate to John's campaign."

"Like who? Can I have some names?"

"Bernard Johnson, Francis Arconti, Susan Stern, Sean McAllister."

"I never heard of any of those people. I wonder if John knows them."

"My thoughts exactly. We're going to see if we can connect any of these people to John, but figured we'd run them by you first. I'm going to send you an email with the full list. It's possible he's set up this account, pretending to be you. The Department of Justice and FBI don't take straw donations lightly."

A pit grew in Rose's gut. "I know."

"I have two goals right now. First, find a connection between John and the people who made donations. Second, we have to prove he was behind the transfers made from your Bank of North Carolina account to the donors. I'm hoping, if we can bring to light what he's done illegally with your money, that'll give us leverage to get his phone records subpoenaed. Whoever he spoke to the night you overheard him is our only hope to prove to the authorities how John planned you harm."

She shuddered, reminded of John's chilling threat. "Will the financial records side of this be hard to prove?"

He hesitated a little too long. "Hard to say. This has been tougher than I'd expected. But give me more time and stay where you are. Oh, one other thing"—Dan paused, making Rose's stomach dip—"one of my sources caught wind that the Department of Justice is getting antsy about making an arrest for the donation. Try to stay low key."

"Trust me. I'm not going anywhere."

* * * *

"As you can see, this now combines your blog and webpage." Pam leaned back in her chair and looked at Leo. "Well, what do you think?"

Leo studied the screen of his laptop, impressed with the new author website his assistant had pulled together. "Great work. Exactly what I pictured when we talked." He glanced at her. "Will you need much content on this blog from me?"

"Maybe a little, but you concentrate on your books. I'll re-run some interviews on here and do some promo."

"Are updates easy?"

"Just a matter of telling the web designer to replace the old with the new."

"Like everything else in life," he grumbled then grinned.

She laughed. "Seth says you're an eighty-year-old man in a forty-year-old body."

"Seth is a sixteen-year-old teenage boy in a forty-year-old body." He snorted a chuckle. "Nothing wrong with appreciating the simpler things in life."

She scribbled on her pad and smiled. "Nope, you're right."

He stood. "I'm going downstairs to get some water before we go through mail. Want something?"

"No thanks."

At the bottom of the attic stairs, Leo swung open the door. He stepped out, his foot landing on a bright red pair of bikini panties on the floor. He quickly swiped them up; a quick buzz of irritation over Emma's games shot through him.

Why would she keep doing this? Especially when she'd apologized for the kiss and acted skittish when their hands bumped at the sink earlier. She sent more mixed messages than the Enigma machine, and her secrets were just as hard to break.

He tucked the panties in the back pocket of his jeans and struggled on how to handle this strangely passive-aggressive communication Emma seemed hell bent on keeping up.

As he neared the kitchen, her voice drifted from the other room. He went toward her door. This time he'd return the damn panties. Later, after Pam left, he'd confront her and demand to know what she really wanted from him.

Leo stood steps away from slipping them over the knob when her voice came closer to the threshold. He scampered back into the kitchen, clutching the panties in his hand and feeling every bit the fool.

No woman had ever left him this baffled. He pulled a bottle of water from the refrigerator. As he passed the hallway, he stopped and reconsidered his plan to get rid of the undergarment. Rose's voice got louder.

"I'm sure it's illegal, Joanne," she said, her tone filled with frustration. "Plenty of people have been convicted by the DOJ for using straw donors. I sure as hell don't plan to be one of them. John is a sick man."

Straw donors? Was she involved in politics?

Bella stuck her head outside the apartment, spotted Leo, and scampered toward him.

Two seconds later, Emma stuck her head out. She raised a brow at Leo. "Did you need me?"

"No." He patted Bella a few times and walked away, the panties tightly balled in his fist. She called the dog and, a second later, closed the door.

Her secrets, now handed to him on a platter. A whole new angle to consider in his relationship with her. Something illegal went on in her world, a possible explanation why she arrived in Northbridge with a changed appearance, a lot of money, and a PI's phone number.

As he passed his bedroom, he tossed the silky undergarment on his bed, unsure what to do about not only the panties, but also his mounting feelings for a woman caught in the midst of something criminal.

* * * *

"And then my daughter Gretchen stood up in the canoe and the boat tipped, landing them all in the icy cold water." Harry laughed over the memory. "Kids. They just don't listen. But they sure had fun together."

Rose imagined the canoe filled with Leo, his siblings, and Harry's two kids tipping into the icy April water. Even today, on this sunny May afternoon, a moderate breeze had them wearing sweatshirts as they sat in lawn chairs near Harry's boathouse. Bella lay nearby on her back, basking in the sun's heat.

Rose sipped her iced tea. "Sounds like this place is filled with memories."

"Oh yes. A lifetime of them." He stared out at the shimmering lake, his thoughts his own.

A chubby bird landed on a tree branch not far away. "There's another one," Rose whispered. "What kind is that?"

"In the flycatcher family, I think." He picked up the binoculars off the table and pointed them at the branch. "Ah, a tyrant flycatcher."

He handed them off to her, and she noticed him jot down the name on a pad he'd brought out with their drinks.

After peeking at the cute bird, she lowered the binoculars. "So you keep track of the birds you spot?"

"It's been a hobby of mine since retirement. So far this year, I've seen at least ten different kinds of warblers. The Northwest hills of the state are home to a number of rarities this time of year."

"So these birds that come through here, do they stay for a while and leave closer to winter?"

"It varies. Some species will be stay in Connecticut and breed. Others will pass through on their way to more northerly territories."

"Mind if I see your list?"

He handed it over. "Not at all. Nobody usually asks."

While she studied it, Harry's words resonated. She'd migrated here, most definitely just passing through. At least the birds had a purpose. For all Rose's movement, she definitely lacked purpose.

She put down the list and studied the lake. Surrounded by gently rolling hills, this place was beautiful and lush. People in Northbridge were nice. Why had she always thought New Englanders weren't friendly? Perhaps a little too much of her life lived in the south. The people she'd met here welcomed her, appreciated her hard work.

Then there was Leo's kiss. What had it meant? She really didn't know him at all, yet that kiss…when had she last been kissed like it mattered? Maybe never.

The jealousy over his upstairs guest returned, definitely an unwarranted reaction. Especially when she was just passing through like the migratory birds.

Someday she'd leave this town. The mere idea opened a gap inside her chest that stung. At what point had she become so…so attached to this place?

"Emma?"

She snapped out of her thoughts and found Harry watching her. "I'm sorry? What?"

"You okay?"

She smiled and it helped ease some of the sadness inside her. "Oh, just thinking about how I'm glad I found a home at Blue Moon Lake. At least for a while."

"You don't really know how long you're staying then?"

"No." Rose slipped her fingers around the edge of Adirondack chair arm, wishing she could enjoy seeing this lake change through all the seasons. "Eventually I'll need to deal with my ex. Escape doesn't make our problems disappear."

"Wise words." A bird chirped in a weeping willow tree near Leo's yard. Harry picked up his binoculars and viewed the tree, but added, "With that attitude, you'll get things worked out."

The irony in his statement wasn't wasted on her. Her "do what I say, not what I do attitude" had reached a new low. Running from her problems had only given them more power.

Two large geese landed on the lawn near the dip into the lake. Bella's head lifted. She writhed in the grass like a worm until finally managing to get up on all fours. As she chased away the birds, they squawked loudly and ascended over the lake.

The second she got good news from the PI, Rose would be running off. The problem: she wasn't sure she wanted to leave.

For once, she had an urge to lead an honest life, where secrets didn't exist and she could simply be herself.

Chapter 17

Leo's heart thrashed wildly in his chest as he ran, and yet…oh God, he grew harder by the minute. The slender model, with flaming red hair, the most perfect lips, and wearing silky lingerie topped off with a cowboy hat, swung a lasso. She nipped his heels. Run! Faster. Faster. The rope slipped around his chest and pulled tight. Using all his strength, he fought to free himself but a force stopped him when he slammed his skull into a hard surface…

Leo's head crashed into the attic eaves above his bed, fully waking him. "Ow! Damn it!"

The piercing pain did little to ease a morning hard-on thanks to the bizarre erotic dream.

Blinking into the morning sun streaming through the window, he considered the signals in his subconscious that kicked off the madness. His gaze drifted to the worktable, where he'd been working until midnight. Yesterday's pair of panties now sat next to his story outline. He fell back onto the pillow and laughed. The cowboy hat must've been about the baggy overalls Emma owned, but the absurdity of everything else that played out somehow eased his pain.

He wished Emma were as easy to figure out as the dream. She certainly hid her problems well. If not for overhearing her conversations, he might know very little about them and think she had it all together. Yet he couldn't let go of the rope pulling him to her. He'd hand over a million bucks to know her endgame with the panty teasers.

Leo rolled out of the twin bed, rubbing the sore spot on his temple. He picked up the latest silk offering and tossed them into the file cabinet with the others. A perfect line up of red, white, and blue. Very patriotic, and a twist considering his recent finding she was involved in politics.

Plenty of people have been convicted for using straw donors.

Answers, all Leo wanted, only led to more questions. Like who she'd spoken to on the phone, and what had John done to make him a "sick man?" A humbling thought struck him…had she ever left panties at this John person's door?

A clank sounded from the lower level. If he caught her at breakfast, maybe he could strike up a conversation, get her to talk about herself and separate fact from fiction. On the second floor, he made a quick stop in the bathroom then went to the kitchen in his wrinkled T-shirt and sweatpants.

"Good morning." A plate of unappetizing scrambled egg whites, plated with slices of apple, sat on the table. Leo noted Rose's Hello Kitty flannels again, but he refrained from teasing this time. "Nice day."

"It is." She poured coffee, meeting his gaze for a brief moment. "Want some?"

"Please. Thanks."

Bella sat looking out into backyard from the sliding door in the dining room. Leo paid his morning respects. When he reentered the kitchen, Emma glanced his way.

"I heard a bang upstairs. Everything okay?"

"Yup." The sensation in his groin when waking briefly returned, but he ignored it and removed a thick bagel from the breadbox. After getting the butter from the refrigerator, he put both on the table.

"Your commitment to poor eating is admirable." She smiled and sat down. After taking a napkin, she placed it on her lap.

He grabbed a knife from the drawer and joined her at the table. "Thank you." He laid down a napkin and sliced the bagel on it, noting she winced when he did. "According to my doctor, my cholesterol is still under two hundred."

She shook her head. "Of course it is. You probably can drop five pounds in a day by just thinking about it, too."

He chuckled and buttered his bagel, selecting work as a good topic to start a discussion. "Since you're a travel agent, mind if I ask you a work-related question?"

"Shoot."

"I'm thinking about taking a trip. What do you recommend this time of year?"

"It really depends on the type of travel you like." She sipped her coffee and waited for an answer with raised brow.

"A trip to Europe sounds nice."

"For someone single, or a romantic destination?"

"Single, I'd say."

"Really?"

He looked up. "Yes. Why?"

"Just because there seems to be an array of women in your life." Her cheeks turned pink as she pushed the eggs with her fork.

"Oh? Care to tell me about them?"

She lowered the fork and met his gaze. "There's Susan. And then whoever stopped by yesterday."

"You mean my assistant?"

She blinked. "Oh."

"You disappeared before I could introduce you."

She blushed again. "But you and Susan, you seemed—"

"We used to date. We're just friends. And my assistant and I worked upstairs instead of in here just in case *you* needed to use the kitchen."

She lifted a slice of apple and nibbled at one corner. Uncertainty showed in her eyes, and he wasn't sure how to read it.

"I see," she finally said.

"Is this about our kiss?" he asked softly, certain it was exactly the reason.

"God no! Definitely not. I just…I was curious because you asked about travel plans."

They ate for a moment in silence. It unquestionably *was* about their kiss, but to probe crossed a line. He debated about where to go next with this poor attempt at conversation. Instead of helping him learn more about her, he'd only confessed the dire status of his romantic life.

Before he could come up with anything, she said, "I was wondering what's up with you and your brother? How is it he didn't know you were at the house when he rented the place to me?"

"We don't talk much."

"If you both own this place, don't you need to talk?"

"Yes, my father thought so, too. Why he left us both ownership. Dad has probably spent a lot of time rolling over in his grave."

"So what's the problem?"

Leo lifted his bagel to take a bite but paused. "How about we discuss the weather or world peace?"

"Sometimes it takes one party reaching out." She tucked a flyaway strand of her brassy red hair behind one ear. "I'm just saying…"

"The reconciling email I sent to my brother has gone unanswered. Any other ideas, Dr. Freud?" He bit into the bagel and chewed hard.

"Just offering some help." She shrugged and finished off the apple slice.

Here he'd hoped to get some information out of her, but she easily pried his most private thoughts from him. Next he'd be confessing how things weren't always horrible with he and Everett, the way they'd escalated in their teenage years, and how his engagement to Camille shut off all communication between the brothers.

His muscles twitched to regain control of this conversation. "Do you have any siblings?"

"Me? No." She shook her head. "An only child."

He pocketed the tidbit, one seeming true, not part of the persona she played.

"Oh, yesterday I had a nice visit with Harry, from next door."

"Since when are you friends with him?" Did she have a whole life here he didn't know about?

"We met a few days ago. Bella's doing, actually. He told me you two met on your first summer here."

"We did. I wouldn't have started a writing journal if it weren't for him. It was actually pretty good therapy for a kid like—well, anyway, he's great with kids."

Her eyes pierced him. "What were you about to say?"

"Harry treated me different than most adults, like he didn't know my story."

"Your story?"

"The early years of my life. My birth mother was a drug addict and died from an overdose."

"I'm sorry. That must've been difficult for you."

Leo shrugged, although it didn't omit the weight of sharing such a personal detail with her. "Harry was great though. Treated me regular, a real novelty those days."

"I'll bet it was. Sometimes well-intentioned adults forget what children are feeling." She studied him for a few seconds. "But it sounded like you kids have some great memories from those days. At least Harry enjoyed sharing them."

"Yeah, we did. The first time we met—I was five at the time—I was drawn over to these enormous sunflowers near his garden. I asked if I could climb them—like Jack climbed the beanstalk. Instead, he showed me the tree-fort built for his kids. Suggested I climb up there. I think it was the start of a beautiful friendship," Leo added, doing his best Bogart imitation with the classic movie line.

She laughed, so sweet and tender his heart thumped a little faster.

"So that was when the Drakes adopted you?"

"Yup. Two summers after my mom died." Leo suddenly felt as if someone had stripped him naked in a crowded room. He remembered his commitment to learn about her. "What about your childhood?"

She looked down at her shirt and made a brushing motion with her hand, but he didn't see anything there. "Oh, you know. Nothing too interesting." She passed a feeble smile and stood, picking up her plate and mug. "I'd better get to work. Lots to get done."

She put her dirty plates in the dishwasher and disappeared down the hallway.

The intimate talk reminded him of moments with Camille, where they'd lie together after making love and talk about the roadmap of their lives. Details bringing them closer. Turning their passion into the intimacy found in love. It made him yearn to be close to a woman again.

More than ever, he didn't simply want to know Emma's story. He *needed* to know it.

* * * *

"Are you behind this mess?" Rose worked hard to sound stern.

Bella lifted her bloodshot eyes in a pitiful display of innocence worthy of an Oscar.

Rose scoured the half-emptied hamper bag on the floor. The clothes she'd put in there were pulled out, left in a mess. She stuffed clothing back into her makeshift hamper, a plastic garbage pail bag. Not quite the laundry chute going straight to the cellar in her bedroom back in North Carolina. And easy access for Bella.

"I'm onto you." Rose narrowed her eyes at the dog, who blinked back with the innocence of a bribe-taking politician.

Rose lifted the bag and headed out the apartment door to the laundry room at the end of the hallway. Bella followed. Halfway down, she nearly stepped on a pair of underpants on the floor. She swiped them up, not certain how they'd fallen out of the bag.

At the alcove area that held a washer and dryer, she dumped in her laundry and added some detergent. Just as she swiped the start button, a snort from Bella drew Rose's attention to the corner near the machine.

Bella lifted her paw and scratched at the wall.

"Stop, Bella."

Bella ignored her and scratched again. This time, a section of the wall fell out.

"Damn it." Rose lowered herself to her hands and knees. She bumped against the dog, gently pushing her aside. A perfectly shaped rectangular piece of sheetrock lay on the linoleum laundry room floor, leaving a big gaping hole in the wall.

"Thanks a lot. Leo will have a fit if he sees this. I'm throwing you under the bus for this one. He's got a soft spot for you, anyway."

Bella pushed past Rose and sniffed at the opening.

Rose lifted the piece, about a one-by-two-foot cut. She held the section up to the wall, hoping she could insert it back in place and Leo would be none the wiser. As she sized up the Sheetrock to refit it into the wall, the overhead light caught a glimmer of something inside the opening. Rose reluctantly stuck her hand inside, felt around, and removed a smooth metal object. A recorder. Black and silver, with a few buttons. She hit the "power" button and a little green light came on.

Record, play, rewind. A timer. Huh? Was Leo's house under surveillance? Or…wait. Was he listening to her? She studied the device more closely. She'd never seen anything quite like this before.

She hit play.

Static-sounding voices—a little like white noise—started to play, going on for a good twenty seconds. She nearly jumped when a creepy, low moan started. A voice. Yet not a voice. Muted, as if someone covered the microphone and made the sound.

She sat on the floor and pondered the facts. Her bedroom, on the other side of this wall, would certainly hear sounds from this area. The night she'd sworn she heard ghostly sounds, they had been similar to what she'd just replayed.

She stuck the device back inside the hole and replaced the fallen Sheetrock. A rather strange puzzle of facts sat before her. It started with Leo's insistence that she understand the prior tenant believed the house was haunted. The second piece was Harry's comment that Leo moved right in immediately after the tenant fled.

Did Leo scare out the first tenant? Had he tried to do the same to her? Their kiss, so tender, so loving, wasn't the touch of a man who wanted her to leave. But desperation made people do bizarre things. But this recorder—and even the moved photographs—all pointed to the possible notion Leo might have tried to pull the same prank on her that he'd played on the last tenant.

She smiled. Leo wasn't the only one who could pull pranks. He needed to put his haunting days behind him for good. Or at least he should learn he couldn't pull those stunts on everyone. The question was what could she do?

* * * *

Rose approached the turn to the vineyard for her Friday night shift. Her cell phone rang. She pulled over. Dan Montgomery's number flashed across the display, so she answered.

"Rose. I'm glad I caught you."

Dan always sounded in control and businesslike, so this semi-panicked tone made her gut tighten with worry.

"Two things. My guy following your husband said he left DC and pulled into the driveway at your house in North Carolina five minutes ago."

Rose closed her eyes and imagined him walking in to find the message she'd left behind.

"Did you write what we discussed on the note?"

"Yes. I told him how I knew what he'd done and if he reported me, I would tell the authorities about his involvement."

"Perfect." Dan exhaled. "I suspect he went home because he knows something is up. Maybe he's tried to reach you."

"It's possible. I left my cell phone right next to the note on the kitchen counter. So he doesn't try."

"Good. There's one more thing you should know. One of my sources heard the Department of Justice and FBI are one step from a full-scale investigation of John's campaign accounts. If the authorities go public with the news, John's face will be all over the TV and internet." Dan paused, and more quietly added, "Possibly yours, too."

Rose rested her forehead on the top of the steering wheel as her body went cold.

"Has anybody recognized you yet?" Dan asked.

"I don't think so," she mumbled, feeling as if she were drowning from her worst fears closing in on her.

"Then just stay put. We're close to finding enough evidence to prove you didn't do this, but we need a few days. Maybe until the end of next week. I'll call you if I learn anything more."

She said goodbye and hung up. Her job at the vineyard waited, a public place she'd enjoyed the other day now carrying the threat of an approaching storm. The FBI inched closer. How much time did that give her? If even one person made the connection, the gig here in Northbridge could be over.

The urge to run owned her. This time, however, it abated quickly. She was tired of running. Besides, she didn't have any money to make another getaway.

Her money. Where the heck could it have gone? She'd searched the whole house and tore apart her own belongings. One place she hadn't checked was Leo's locked file cabinet. After their kiss, and how they seemed to be growing closer, she wanted to believe he hadn't taken it. If someone submitted this question to Dr. Rose, she'd tell them to open the channels, learn to trust. So why couldn't she?

Therapy during her psychologist training had shown Rose how she'd lost all ability to trust people the day her parents died. Their problems and drama overshadowed their love for her. At least, she'd spent a good portion of her life feeling that way.

But when she met John, she *had* handed him her trust. Spilled the one secret about her real identity, a fact she'd told no one since leaving California. And he'd gone and used her trust against her.

Much as she wanted to believe Leo at his word, just handing over such a valuable commodity wouldn't come easily.

She could try the honest approach: ask if he'd open it for her and let her confirm the money wasn't there.

No. If she were in his shoes, she'd be insulted not to be taken at her word. Besides, for her own peace of mind, she had to check that one last place. If she found nothing, she'd take it as a sign to let go of the distrust guiding her all these years. A first step in moving beyond a life of skepticism in others.

There must be a key. Maybe on the key ring he always tossed into the small dish on the kitchen counter.

Rose tried to ignore the internal nagging reminding her that rationalizing wrong moves could be a very bad thing.

Chapter 18

Rose cleaned the bar area, her feet aching and her face sore from smiling while talking up the wines at Litchfield Hills Vineyards. Dan's call left her jumpy, glancing over her shoulder each time the door opened, suspicious of guests she didn't know. She'd never been so glad to have a work shift come to an end.

Sophie exited the storage room and came over to the bar with a box of new wine glasses. "Thanks for starting the cleanup, Emma. You're always right on top of things. Whenever Trent plays, we get large crowds. I'm exhausted."

"I'll sleep well tonight."

Laughter in the corner of the room made her turn. Trent and his wife, Veronica, packed their gear on the other side of the tasting room. They'd performed together earlier. Their affectionate glances at each other suggested they couldn't wait to get home and be alone.

Dave Felton, Bernadette's husband, walked toward the in-love pair. It surprised Rose to see Dave wearing jeans and a button-down shirt when they'd met earlier, although logically she understood clergy didn't walk around all day in their preaching apparel. Talking with him had sparked an idea on how she could get back at Leo for his little haunting stunt.

On his way past her, Dave yelled, "Hey, Trent, I'll give you a hand carrying those out."

The trance between the love-lost couple was broken as they glanced his way, smiling, but their disappointment seemed obvious. Same way Rose had felt when Bella's damp nose interrupted her kiss with Leo the other night. Just how far they'd have gone if it weren't for the canine intervention was a question she wanted answered. Knowing he wasn't dating either of those women gave Rose permission to daydream about Leo in a romantic light.

"Night, Charlie." Meg exited the back room and came over to the bar, stealing Rose's thoughts.

As Sophie filled the shelves with glasses, she glanced up at Meg. "What on earth is going on with you two? A few nights ago, you weren't sure where you stood with Charlie. Tonight I almost dropped a case of wine when I rounded the corner earlier and found you two lip-locked."

Rose laughed. "So did I. You guys jumped like two kids caught at their lockers by a teacher."

Meg waved them both closer while glancing around the nearly empty room. "It was those questions you gave us during *Outlander* night. I decided to invite Charlie for coffee yesterday morning at Sunny Side Up. I figured I'd tell him about the questions, ask him to give them a try."

"And what happened?" Rose got excited, hoping to finally make some progress on her article.

"Well, we started them. The first questions were easy. Kind of fun. I think they relaxed us both. But then they got a little more personal. Very revealing." Her face softened into a smile; then she sighed. "Talking so openly made me like Charlie even more. We didn't answer all the questions because he needed to get back to work. But then we went out last night, and..." She blushed. "Well, let's just say we got to know each other better."

Sophie reached out and squeezed Meg's hand. "Hon, it's everything you deserve. He's a great guy." She turned to Rose. "Since we're on this topic, Duncan and I tried them. I honestly figured it was a silly exercise, but damned if I wasn't wrong."

"Do you mind sharing?"

"Of course not. It's funny...we both think we know so much about each other, but those questions touched on things we never thought to discuss." She lowered her voice. "The truth is we've been stressed about the kids. It's made us forget about our relationship. But in asking the questions, we talked about things we'd never have brought up otherwise. It was darn right intimate and we both shared unexpected things about ourselves." Sophie's dark eyes took on a faraway look and she smiled. "I didn't think I could love Duncan any more than I do. After talking, I felt like I did."

Veronica and Bernadette came to the bar as Trent and Dave left carrying some equipment.

"What's with the whispering?" Bernadette eyed them skeptically. "Let me guess. Duncan's finally agreed to let us see him in a kilt?" She chuckled, but Sophie just shook her head.

"We're talking about the questions Emma gave us," Meg said. "Did you try them with Dave?"

"Believe it or not, we did." Bernadette's expression softened and Rose focused on her response. "You know, after all my complaining how he never has time for me, he made the time for this. When we finished, it was clear to me exactly why I love him so much it sometimes hurts."

Their positive results would surely make for a great angle on the piece. "Did any one try to stare into each others' eyes for four minutes?"

"God no!" Bernadette's eyes widened with exaggerated horror, although Rose deemed that part of the exercise a bit invasive as well. "Dave wanted to, but for some reason I couldn't even get started. Maybe another night."

"Charlie and I couldn't do it either." Meg's full lower lip bowed into a frown. "I told him that windows were the eyes to the soul, but he only smiled and said maybe another time."

A silence hung over the group. Bernadette quietly said, "I think you mean to say *eyes* are the *window* to the soul."

Meg's forehead rumpled as she quietly thought for a few seconds. "What did I say? Oh, never mind, I meant what you said."

"Trent and I did both, the study and the eye gazing exercise." Veronica spoke quietly, glancing back to the door where the men had left through.

"And…" Bernadette said and they all leaned a little, waiting for an answer.

"Typical Trent. He was eager for us to try it." Veronica fiddled with her pearl necklace, one Rose had never seen her without. "After doing half the questions, he suggested we jump straight to looking into each other's eyes." Veronica crinkled her pert nose. "I told him I couldn't, but he dared me. I caved. I love how he challenges me."

Sophie raised her dark brows. "So how long did you do it?"

"The entire four minutes. It was—well, uncomfortable at first. Only the longer it went, the more I really"—she raised her hands and made air quotes with her nicely manicured fingers—"'saw' into Trent's soul. It was quite unexpected, taking me into a place I'd never have imagined." She glanced around the group. "I know, it probably sounds weird. But I almost hated for it to end."

Rose turned around to search for a pad and pen beneath the bar counter. "Do you guys mind if I use some of your observations in a paper I'm writing? No names, of course."

"I don't mind," Veronica said right away.

"Me either," the others chimed.

The door opened and Dave stuck his head inside. "Bern, I'm tired. Are you ready to go?"

"Yup." She headed for the door and the others returned to their cleaning. Rose scribbled some notes about what she'd just heard.

Dave waved. "G'night, ladies. Emma, I'll see you tomorrow?"

She stopped writing and looked up. "Yes, and thank you."

Tomorrow morning Dave had agreed to join her plan to teach Leo a lesson. She could only hope Leo took it with the good humor she intended.

* * * * *

Leo closed the front section of the Saturday *New York Times* and lowered it to the kitchen table. He went to the stove and poured another cup of coffee. A noise sounded from Emma's apartment. This morning, when he'd entered the kitchen, a mug for him had already been set out next to the warm percolator. Nice she'd been thinking of him, however, he liked when she was around at breakfast and wished she were here now.

Yesterday afternoon she'd squirreled away in her apartment then left for work without a word. Talking openly about his childhood with her scratched at a scab he'd left untouched for years, making obvious the absence of having a special someone. A confidant. A close friend.

Outside the window, the thermometer showed seventy degrees. He pushed open the window and inhaled a dose of fresh spring air. Coffee in hand, he returned to his seat and resumed reading the paper, lost in a story about the conflict in the Middle East.

The door to the apartment unexpectedly banged open. Emma hurried out, dressed in flared yoga pants and loose fitted T-shirt splattered with decorative cupcakes. Her Pink flip-flops slapped the floor. A red and white polka-dot scarf was folded and tied into a knot at the top of her vibrant hair.

"Morning." She bit her lower lip, glanced around the room. "Listen, I'm glad you're up. Got a sec?"

"Sure." He put down the paper. "What's up?"

"I haven't told you but there's been some weird things going inside my apartment."

Bella came to Leo and nudged his hand with her damp nose, clearly not as upset as her owner. He rubbed behind the dog's ear. "Weird? Like what?"

"Noises, things moved. Look, I know I acted like it didn't matter the night you told me this place was haunted, but I even heard voices one night. Scary voices."

"I'm sure you were dreaming." Leo did his best to hide the shame worming around inside him over the stunts he'd pulled. "Emma, this house isn't haunted. You'll be fine."

"I didn't believe it either, but I saw, and heard, it for myself."

"You're worrying needlessly."

"Didn't you tell me your last tenant left for the same reason?"

"Well, I did. But—"

"See. It isn't just me. There's no good explanation for what's been going on in my place. Do you hear things upstairs at night?"

"No." He debated if he should admit to what he'd done, but to do so made him feel like an idiot. "Listen, there's no such thing as ghosts. At least not in this house. Don't worry—"

"Oh, I'm not worrying anymore." Emma walked away from him to the kitchen door. "I've found a solution to our problem." She opened it and waved to someone. "Good morning! Thanks for coming over so fast."

A man with a friendly, round face entered wearing a cleric's robe. He seemed familiar, but Leo couldn't place him.

"Leo, have you met Dave Felton, pastor at the Methodist church?" Emma stepped aside and the pastor approached Leo.

Leo reached out and they shook hands. "Nice to meet you, Pastor."

"Please. Call me Dave. Emma tells me you have a spirit problem here."

"Big problem," Emma answered before Leo could utter a peep. "If you can't help us, Pastor, I don't know what we'll do."

"You may have to call one of those haunting shows. That happened to one of my minister friends."

Leo opened his mouth, but he closed it fast. If he confessed, she'd never let him live this down. And this pastor, who would he tell?

"Now, Leo." Dave removed a Bible and bottle of water from a canvas bag and put them on the table. "I heard the last tenant left because the spirits here were pretty lively. Any idea what exactly happened?"

Leo was about to answer, when Emma interrupted again. "Like I told you, Dave, objects in my room have been moved." She paced in front of the sink. "One picture in particular of Leo's family. And of course, someone was murdered in this house, making the whole spirit thing more plausible."

Leo wanted this to end. If he could get the pastor to leave, he would privately tell her what he'd done. "Be sensible, Emma. That's hardly proof of paranormal activity."

She paused in front of him. "No, it's not. But can you explain the sounds I heard? It's *got* to be paranormal. Those voices," she said in a hushed tone and crossed her arms, rubbed her shoulders. The remorse he'd been fighting over the stupid scheme tripled. "God, they were terrifying. Nothing I ever want to wake up to again."

For the briefest moment he worried she might actually move out. Scared by him and his ridiculous need to have quiet. She wasn't really even that much of a disruption! Had he known then she'd turn out to be the muse he'd been searching for—one who kissed beautifully, too—he'd never have done any of this.

She reached out and touched Leo's forearm. "Honestly, I didn't say anything when it happened because it's not like me to overreact to things. But then I met Dave at the vineyard and figured he might be able to help. You know, I'm worried about you being here, too."

The dark-haired pastor nodded. "Nothing like a good old-fashioned cleansing to get rid of a spirit." He held up the bottle. "Holy water should do the trick."

Holy water? "I don't think this is necess—"

"Why don't we start in the kitchen. Then"—Emma pointed down the hall to her apartment—"we can go straight down that way, where I live. I seem to be hearing a lot more than Leo."

"Sounds good to me." Dave started flinging water directly from the bottle into the air. "Spirits in this house," he chanted, his tone deep and serious, "be gone! Go find peace elsewhere!"

"Emma, please." Leo stood and went to her side, taking her arm to stop her from following in this senseless ritual. He leaned close to ear and whispered, "This is silly. You must be hearing things."

She shook her head and held her index finger to her lips.

Dave kept up his chant, walking around the kitchen table. Bella followed him, and so did Emma. Every so often she'd glance at Leo and wave him over to join them.

Leo couldn't move. If he would've looked like a fool moments ago, he'd look like a bigger fool following in this ghost-cleansing parade.

"Come on, Leo!" Emma said, her voice frantic. "You've got to help us. We need as much power as we can make so this spirit leaves."

The pastor's voice rose. "Ashes to ashes, dust to dust. Hear us from the world of the living, o' wandering ghost. Please return to where you belong."

"This is an old house, with all kinds of creaks and sounds," Leo pleaded.

"Oh no. I'm positive I heard the noises. I even recorded them."

"You recorded them?"

"Yup. Oh, I didn't tell you that?"

"No."

"Hold on." Emma hurried down the hallway, her slapping flip-flops fading as she disappeared into her apartment.

Leo glanced at Dave, who'd stopped tossing the holy water and waited, too. "Do you get a lot of requests for ghost banishing rituals in Northbridge?"

Dave shook his head. "This is the first."

Emma returned. As she neared, she plunked the familiar tape recorder he'd hidden in the wall on the kitchen table.

She pushed the start button. Her lips twitched. The eerie sounds he'd purchased over the Internet played.

"Terrifying, huh?" Her eyes twinkled and she lifted her lips into a slow smile that turned quickly into hysterical laughter. "Oh, really, Leo? Do you want me out *that* badly?"

Dave laughed, too.

Leo couldn't let go of humiliation building inside him. Every part of him, for reasons that didn't exist when he'd pulled these stunts, wanted Emma to see him as better than the man capable of this kind of behavior.

"You should've seen your face." Emma crowed as she laughed harder and fell into a chair.

"Yeah, it's not every day I get to do a fake cleansing." Dave placed the holy water on the kitchen table near the Bible and removed his preaching stole. "Well worth a little of my free time."

Leo narrowed his eyes at them both. But the more they laughed, the easier it was to let go of his embarrassment. He finally joined them, finding relief in the admission. "Busted." He held up his hands and smiled at Emma. "So I'll bet you think you're pretty funny."

"Hilarious." She wiggled her brows, her bright smile making him want to draw her in close and kiss her again, only he remembered the pastor nearby.

"So, Dave, how about a cup of coffee since your work here is done?"

"I'd love one."

For the next half hour, the three of them sat around the table, reminiscing over the shock they claimed existed on Leo's face when Dave started throwing the water. Leo couldn't remember when he'd laughed so hard. Most of all, he found himself comforted by a new fondness for Emma. Somehow, she'd softened him. Made the angry forces inside of him settle. She'd accepted what a pain in the ass he could be sometimes. A side many others would have simply walked away from.

Chapter 19

"Thanks, Joanne." Rose hung up her cell phone. All the levity from this morning's prank had disappeared, replaced by the sharp sting of fear.

Ten minutes earlier, John had called her close friend. Luckily, Joanne had spotted his name on caller ID and ignored it, and his message only said to call back. They both agreed she should ignore his call. Yet panic swallowed Rose whole, and the urge to run whispered in her ear.

Where would she run, though? Further north? Or leave the country and go to Canada? She stopped the line of thinking because one thing prevented her from doing anything…money.

She tugged up a pair of cargo shorts that gapped in the waist, slapped on a thick leather belt to keep them up, and tied her lightweight plaid shirt on her at her hips. The latest worry hung overhead like a dark cloud ready to burst.

After snapping the leash on Bella, she headed for the door. On her way out she noticed Leo's keys sitting in the dish where he liked to leave them. She looked closely, noting a few smaller keys that might fit into his file cabinet. All she needed was for him to leave his office. Getting into that office with his attachment to the place was harder than getting into Harvard. Maybe if he showered later, she could grab these and sneak upstairs.

As she walked down the back steps, she noted a side door leading to the garage left wide open. Suddenly the garage door went up. A car she'd never seen before had been backed in. The front hood of the shiny red vehicle held a distinctive BMW logo. She walked toward the car, curious who this belonged to if Leo drove the ragged Mercedes always parked outside of the garage.

As she got close, Leo exited the garage, leading his bike out by the handlebars. Behind dark sunglasses, his gaze burned through her.

"All this time I thought you kept a horse and buggy in here."

Leo face brightened with a smile and reminded her of one reason she didn't want to leave here. "Did you now?"

"Whose car?"

"Mine. When I'm here, I like to drive ol' Heidi." He thumbed toward the rusty Mercedes. "She's old but still in great…"

Rose barely listened. Her insides purred as she admired the biking shorts hugging Leo's long, muscular legs. The same ones she had the pleasure of admiring her first morning here during the "boxer-briefs only" incident. A short-sleeved, snug-fitted jersey hugged his fit chest.

Bella tugged to see him, so Rose dropped the leash. He pushed his sunglasses to the top of his head, kicked out the stand on the bike, and crouched down with opened arms. "Come on, baby!"

Bella rushed him, her thick paws surprisingly graceful and her long ears swinging to the flow of her gait. She dropped to the ground, rolling over and waiting for a tummy rub. Rose might do the same if it weren't for all the other things stopping her from handing Leo her total trust.

"Such a g'girl you are." Leo crouched down and cooed, sweeping his hand along her belly. A hand with strong veins, and thick fingers smudged with grease. The touch of those sturdy fingers slipping beneath her shirt had remained imprinted in her mind from their ever-so-brief make out session.

Rose turned to the bike. The frame was solid and tall, like Leo. She'd never seen such thick tires on a bicycle. "What kind of bike is this?"

He gazed at Bella with adoration in his eyes; her mouth seemed upturned in a smile of doggie delight. "Huh?" He glanced up.

"Type of bike?"

"Oh. A mountain bike. For riding some nearby trails." He finally rolled back on his heels to stand upright, towering over her. "There are some nice ones in the area. You should try it. Good for endurance, balance, strength. I mean, since you seem so concerned with good health."

Leo's commitment to exercise given how he ate came as a surprise. "Only when it comes to what I put inside my body, not how I move it." She lifted the leash. "Here's my exercise."

He chuckled and squinted into the sun over the lake. "It's sure a beautiful day. Enjoy your walk." He reached for the bike. "I'd better get going while I still feel motivated."

"Any chance you could feed Bella later? I'll be at the vineyard until around ten."

Bella still lay on her back, staring up at them, her ears splayed to each side.

"Sure." Leo switched to a playful voice. "Good news, Bella. You can join me for dinner tonight."

The dog wriggled and jumped up on all fours, shaking ground debris off her body.

Rose grabbed the leash. "You'd better hope nobody finds out your Saturday night date was a real dog."

He let out an unexpected hearty laugh, which left her pleased he liked her dumb joke. Leo studied her and his smile slipped away, replaced by something darker and more serious. An expression she'd seen on the night they'd kissed, making her pulse hasten and insides woozy.

He blinked a few times then lowered his sunglasses and got on the bike. "See you in a bit."

Rose started down the driveway, but as Leo disappeared into the thick trees lining the long driveway, she had an idea. The moment she'd been waiting for. A chance to see if any of those keys on his ring worked for the file cabinet in his office.

She felt bad for not trusting him, but a stronger part of her brain ignored the tug of her conscience and demanded her curiosity be satisfied. She hurried into the kitchen—justified by the desperation owning her soul. Once inside, she swiped the keys from the dish, removed Bella's leash, and headed upstairs.

* * * * *

Leo's gaze dropped to the empty mount near his handlebars. Damn it! He'd wanted to try a new route and needed the phone's GPS. Turning around, he peddled fast, the quarter mile not so far to backtrack.

At the house, he dropped the bike on its side and hurried into the kitchen. As he swiped the phone off the counter, the empty key dish caught his eyes. If he lost those keys again...! Bella trotted over, swarming his legs and disrupting his irritation over the missing items.

He gave her a quick pat. "I thought you were going for a walk?"

The missing keys nagged at him. Twice since arriving here he'd lost them, hence the bowl. He'd been diligent, or so he thought. He remembered going to the den after he'd used the set late yesterday afternoon. Damn it! He couldn't ride until he found them. On his way to the other room, his cell phone rang. He answered.

"Hey, bud." Seth sounded excited. "You near a TV?"

"I can be."

"Put on CNN."

"Okay." He entered the den and glanced at the coffee table and end tables, but no keys. "What's going on? Are we under attack or something?"

Seth snorted. "Not even close. I want you to see something."

Leo found the CNN channel quickly. "What am I looking for?"

"Shh. Just watch."

On the television set, a couple smiled to a large crowd. People carried campaign signs screaming "Richardson for the Senate" and waving American flags. A second later, a woman on stage caught his attention. He blinked, just as the scene cut to another.

The capital building served as a background to a pretty reporter wearing serious eyeglasses and talking into a microphone.

"...Scandals like this are not new in Washington. Senator John Richardson from North Carolina has maintained a flawless record up until now." A clip of a rally started to play. "Seen here at a recent campaign speech in his quest to maintain the senate seat he's held for one term, he denies the accusations of illegal contributions made into his campaign. However, an anonymous tip to the FBI was enough for them to start an investigation..."

The words faded. Leo couldn't pry his gaze from the woman standing near the candidate. She wore a pretty suit and silky blouse. Soft dirty-blonde hair fell to her shoulders and she hung on every word the man at the podium spoke. He made promises to the crowd and she looked on like she believed every word.

Change her hair color, toss on a pair of clunky glasses, and raid a teenager's wardrobe and you'd have...no. He squinted. Emma?

"Anybody there look familiar?" Seth's voice and question jarred Leo. "And I do mean your tenant."

Leo's defenses jumped in out of nowhere. He needed time to think. Sort through the complicated pieces before him. "There is a slight resemblance."

Senator *John* Richardson. Was this the mysterious "John" whose name Leo kept hearing Emma speak about?

The weight of an anvil pressed to his chest. He wished now he hadn't shared so much about Emma's secrets with Seth. If she were operating under a different identity, maybe there was a damn good reason.

"I don't know, Seth. The senator's wife is classy, pulled together. Emma's pretty casual. You should see some of the getups she wears. Maybe it's her doppelgänger." He forced a laugh. "Don't they say everyone has one?"

"I guess. Didn't you say you thought Emma dyed her hair?"

The sadness he'd often seen in her eyes. The lost money. Her hidden problems. All played to the sucker inside him who jumped to a vulnerable woman's defense. "Did I? No, I don't think so."

"You must be tired," Seth grumbled. "It's a pretty strong resemblance in my humble opinion."

"You're showing quite a vivid imagination. Maybe you should write fiction and I'll become your agent."

"Okay, wise ass. After what you said about her, I just thought—ah, whatever. I'd better run."

Seth hung up. Leo searched around the sofa cushions for his missing keys. How did what he'd seen on the news explain why Emma was here? If she really was the senator's wife, why run? Why hide?

He headed through the kitchen, committed to get this bike ride done and use the time to think. The key search would continue later.

Thunk!

He tilted his head, certain the sound came from upstairs. Bella let out a little woof, reminding Leo he'd been surprised to find the dog back inside the house a few minutes ago.

He walked down the hallway to the apartment. Bella ran ahead to the partially opened door and pushed it open with a bump of her nose.

Leo peeked inside. "Emma?"

No answer. Another thunk sounded from above. Leo turned around and headed for the staircase.

* * * *

The key ring in Emma's hand held about seven keys of varying sizes, but only three of them were small enough to fit into the metal lock on the cabinet.

The first didn't fit.

The next almost did, and then it got stuck and took a few panicked seconds to remove.

But the third key slid in with ease and the lock popped open.

She pulled open the top drawer and skimmed through folders marked "contracts," "artwork," and "endorsements," pushing them aside to see if anything had been hidden beneath the hanging folders. Her money envelope didn't appear.

More documents filled the second drawer, mostly of a personal nature. What a fool she'd been not to hand him the trust he'd asked for. She'd check this last one since she was here, but obviously Leo's overtures to her were honest. He deserved the same from her. She opened the drawer.

Some additional paperback copies of his books were stored here. As she poked through them, her fingertips hit a piece of soft fabric in the back. Silk. Curious, Rose gave it a gentle tug. Women's blue bikini underpants. Very strange. A little like hers.

She stuck her hand further into the back and slowly pulled out a second pair. Exactly like hers, in fact. The pair found lying in the hallway earlier returned. Would the dog have found them, taken them out? Had Leo found pairs, too? Embarrassment heated her skin, imaging where else the dog might have left—

"What are you doing?"

Leo's voice hit Rose like a tossed bucket of ice water. He stood at the door, brows bent and confusion clear.

Her heart thumped wildly, but she did her best to recover and find her voice. "Why do you have these?" She held up the underwear.

"Excuse me?" His brows shot up like blasting rockets, but he blushed. "You're in my filing cabinet and—"

"Are these mine?"

"You should know. Haven't you been leaving them around?"

"Why on earth would I do that?"

He shrugged, then his lips curled into a paper-thin grin. "I'd wondered that myself."

"Oh God! Did you think I was leaving them on purpose for you or something?"

His lips pursed, but he didn't answer.

"I am *not* the kind of woman to do something like that."

"That's what I figured." He said quickly. "But, when I found them at my office door and—well, what could I think?"

"At your door? When you got the first pair, why didn't you return them?"

"And that wouldn't have been awkward?" He moved closer and stood over her looking down. His voice switched to a mocking tone. "Oh, Emma. Here's your sexy panties."

Her face heated. "Okay, it might have been a bit uncomfortable. But three pairs?"

"What can I say? It seems I'm shy. And don't change the subject. What are you doing up here with my keys and in my filing cabinet?"

She swallowed down her shame. "I've looked everywhere for my money…except in the cabinet."

He lifted a brow. "Were you up here when I went away for the night?"

A hard lump to form in her throat. The walls came tumbling down. Tears spilled. She tried to blink them away before he noticed, but his face blurred beyond her eyes. "Yes. I'm sorry."

She stood and pushed past him for the door.

He reached for her arm and drew her back. "Emma," he said gently. "Don't run. I did not take your money. Can you start to trust me? Maybe I can help you. Whatever it is…"

She looked up. Pity owned Leo's gaze, like he'd figured out her story and wanted answers. Anger she could handle, but pity was for the weak.

"I have some personal problems…and the money…it was like my insurance." Pressure lifted off her shoulders, not the entire weight of her lies but a little.

"What kind of problems?"

"I'm afraid I can't say. Really, Leo, the less you know, the better for you."

Bella's clumsy gait sounded on the attic staircase. Leo opened his mouth, the stress in his eyes a sure sign he hadn't accepted her answer.

But before he could say a word, Rose spotted Bella. "Well I'll be damned."

Bella waddled over, the pink underpants left in the laundry basket now dangling from her mouth.

Rose went over and swiped them away. "I can't believe it, Bella. Care to tell me what you're up to?"

Leo's laughter echoed off the walls. "I hope you're not expecting an answer."

She narrowed her eyes at him. "It's not funny. I saved that dog at a shelter and she embarrasses me this way?" Emma tossed down the handful of panties and slapped Leo's chest gently. "Stop. It's embarrassing."

"I'm sorry." He held up a hand but kept laughing. "Really, I am."

Rose watched Leo, suddenly more relaxed than she'd ever seen him. She let go of the embarrassment and started to laugh, too. In a way she couldn't quite figure out, she somehow felt like they'd moved a step closer.

He drew her close and kissed her, a gentle sweep at first then so deeply she forgot all about her embarrassment. When he leaned back, he stared into her eyes. "Do you know how those little drop-offs were making me crazy for you? Crazier than I already am?"

"You're crazy for me?"

"I'm headed there."

"Then Bella's unveiling of my dignity was a small price for me to pay."

"I wonder how that dog knew those drop-offs would have a Cupid-like effect on me—although she does have above average dog intelligence."

Rose laughed. "I don't think you've met many dogs."

"Just one before Bella. I'm thinking, for all we know she took your money, too."

"Probably did. To make sure I stay."

Leo's good humor vanished. "Why would you leave? What's wrong?"

Words stuck in her mouth. All the truths she wanted to share. *My name is Rose and everything I've told you is a lie because I'm hiding from my husband and the authorities.*

She inhaled deeply. "I've got too much to sort out before I talk. You've got to trust me on this one."

He studied her like he didn't.

Smart man. She wasn't ready to hand him the truth or drag him any further into her messy life. He didn't know she was a runner. Someone he might want to avoid getting close to. At this moment, she didn't have the heart to tell him. Because there was one other person she hadn't ever trusted: herself. Every relationship she'd ever witnessed growing up had been plastered in Hollywood fakeness. Something she understood at an early age, rendering her incapable of relying on her own feelings for others.

"Give me time," she said quietly. "I apologize for being up here. I should have trusted your word."

Leo slipped his arm around her waist and kissed her again. A warm and sweet kiss, gentle as a soothing ointment to the troubles following her for so long.

He leaned back and slipped a finger beneath her chin and stared into her eyes as his thumb stroked her cheek. "You can trust me, Emma. With anything."

More than any other time in her life, she wanted to believe in someone else. In his arms, she found herself closer to offering it than ever before. Yet, the high stakes of what she faced weren't his problem and she simply couldn't let go.

Chapter 20

Leo watched Emma's car disappear down the driveway. He went straight to his laptop computer on the kitchen table. After skimming the hits on his Internet search, he clicked on a link taking him to a *North Carolina Dispatch News* story.

He scanned the article then his gaze dropped to a photo at the bottom. The caption read, "Vice President Warren Thomas administers the Senate oath to Sen. John Richardson, D-North Carolina, left, with wife Rose Richardson, during a ceremonial re-enactment swearing-in ceremony in the Old Senate Chamber of Capitol Hill in Washington."

Rose Richardson. He stared at the woman's face, comparing her to Emma. The same perfect lips he'd kissed were lifted in a simple smile. The same large blue eyes Leo couldn't get enough of were averted to her husband as he was sworn in. She wore a tasteful skirt and jacket. A gold teardrop necklace dangled just above her cleavage and straight golden hair brushed her shoulders.

He moved to another article, more specifically about the FBI allegations. It discussed alleged illegal contributions made by the senator's campaign. A sidebar piece talked about past instances and the stiff fines that came from doing so, including jail time to the parties involved. Senator Richardson went on record saying, "I am unaware of any illegal donations and am cooperating with the FBI."

An irrational anger swelled inside Leo. He had no idea as to the specifics behind why Emma...Rose...had run off from her life and gone into hiding, but eavesdropping provided him with enough information to know John *had* caused her problems. The single fact alone got his ire up.

He typed "Rose Richardson" into the search bar. Up popped several listings for *Sophisticate*. A tap on the computer mouse took him to the women's magazine. He located her column, *Dr. Rose Says*. A photo showed the same person who'd been at the senator's side.

An advice columnist on the run. The irony wasn't wasted on him.

He exited the computer. No matter who this woman was, Leo vowed to patiently wait for her to share the truth. There had to be a damn good reason she'd leave her life and come here. If it had to do with the investigation, then there had to be a valid reason she'd hide from that, too.

The big house suddenly felt lonelier than ever before. He wished she were home, so he could talk to her. Later he'd stop in at the vineyard for a glass of wine. He could at least make sure she was okay.

A horrible thought struck. What if someone else watched the news and connected the same dots he just had?

* * * *

Rose woke slowly, still half-asleep but immediately wandering in memories of Leo's visit to the vineyard last night. She thought he'd come to see Jay. After he'd tossed out a manly handshake, they'd chatted and laughed for a while.

After a group of her customers had disappeared, he came to the bar and pushed forward his credit card. "I'm here for a tasting."

He'd said it seductively, watching her closely through smoldering eyes and a sexy grin. Throughout the tasting, she'd reminded him about the location of the tip jar. They'd laughed a lot. It had felt nice and unguarded.

Only when she'd returned home, a message from Dan had ruined her good mood with news the FBI had gone public with an investigation about John's illegal campaign money that afternoon. A fact she'd been too busy to notice because she'd been rummaging in Leo's drawers and then left for work. While her name did not come up, he told her to use caution and they'd talk today.

She'd replayed the conversation with Leo a hundred times since then, picking it apart and certain he'd been looking at her differently. Her cell phone rang and she swiped it off the nightstand.

"It's Dan. Did I wake you?"

"No. I'm up. I got your message."

"Expect more today. Can you stay inside?"

"Yes. I'll call in sick to my job."

"Good. We're getting closer, Rose. Please don't worry. I'm adding a resource to this. We'll find a way to stick this on John before the FBI traces it to you."

"I hope so. Call me as soon as you get any new information."

"Will do." Dan hung up.

The nightmare stalking her was suddenly tangible and waiting at her door. Using the phone, she searched the Internet for John's name. An article in the *Times* caught her attention. She went to it and cringed at the photo of John rushing toward a limo as the press surrounded him.

She closed her eyes. Fear stole the life from every muscle. Leaving home. Arriving at a new place. Pretending to be someone else. Deceit snaked around Rose like a cobra. Suffocating. Threatening her well-being. She fell back onto her pillow, curled into a fetal position, and let tears take over. Better than the never-ending diatribe going on inside her head.

When Leo learned the truth, he'd realize he harbored a woman wanted for criminal actions. He didn't strike her as the type to take such news lightly, which meant he probably hadn't seen anything out there yet. It was only a matter of time.

She cried harder, her gut trembling as she remembered finding her parents dead and the terror of her new reality: she was alone in this world. Something inside her clicked that day, caused her to adopt an attitude she'd carried for decades...*it's me against the world.*

But who was she kidding? The decades spent convincing herself she was invincible were a sham. Vulnerable people hurt. Being alone hurt. Hell, loving and losing always hurt. Being used did, too. John used her, from their phony marriage to stealing her funds. Pain had made her hide, back then and now.

A boulder-sized weight pressed against her chest, making it hard to breathe. A pain that was hers alone to tolerate. In Leo's arms, though, she'd been offered brief refuge. To feel that way again would bring sweet relief. However, to go there again without telling him the truth would be an epic lie. Worse than any she'd already told.

* * * *

Refreshed from a hot shower, Rose dressed and wandered to the kitchen. Bella waited near the counter, an impatient gleam in her eyes.

"I got the hint, Bells." She removed an empty container, realizing Leo had used all of what was in there last night. "I hate to tell you, but you'll have to wait a few minutes."

Bella didn't look happy, but did she ever?

Rose grabbed her car keys and went outside, the dog following. Later she'd think about sneaking off to a local pet store and seeing if they carried the brand. It would be good to know where she could buy it; that was, if she lasted here long enough to warrant more than one purchase.

A horrible notion hit out of nowhere. If she got arrested, who would take care of Bella? She imagined John gleefully returning poor Bella to the shelter. Sick over the idea, Rose searched for options. Leo fell at the top of a short list. Would he watch her?

She sighed and pushed the worry aside. One problem at a time, and the FBI was a big problem.

After popping open the car trunk with the remote, she leaned into it. The spare bag of food had been shoved to the back and blocked by jumper cables, a roadside emergency kit, and a few items from home she'd never moved into Leo's house.

She pushed the items aside and dragged out the food. As she did, a plaid blanket inched forward. Beneath the blanket—in the corner—a paper edge stuck out. A flash of awareness spread over her. Could that be…? Leaning further into the trunk, she concentrated all her hope on the object she believed to be her missing cash.

She flipped over the blanket. Relief rushed her as she picked up the envelope. She flipped through the wad of bills, full as the day she'd left.

She mentally retraced her steps on the night she'd arrived, trying to figure out how this ended up in the trunk. The moment her purse tipped inside the trunk on that night as she grabbed a few things for overnight returned. In the dark, she couldn't really see to put everything back inside the purse—but she had assumed it was everything. The envelope must've never been put back and got shoved aside in the shuffle.

Relief swept through her, a sign that things were looking up. Her joy quickly vanished. More than once, she'd accused Leo of being a thief. The puzzled expression on his face flashed before her eyes. His adamant denials.

Embarrassment squirmed through her over all the times she'd insulted his integrity. Under normal circumstances, she'd never behave so poorly.

Rose headed back to the house, forming the words for an apology in her mind. She went to the bottom of the stairs, where she heard noise on the upper level. "Leo?"

She waited but got no response.

Inhaling a deep breath, she moved to the top landing. As she passed the closed bathroom door, it swung open. Steam rushed out. Leo stood in the archway with only a white towel wrapped at his waist.

His dark hair was towel dried and tossed about in many directions. The scent of shaving cream drifted her way, drawing her to his clean-shaven cheeks, showcasing every rugged line. A few drops of moisture dripped from his hair.

"I'm sorry." Rose took a step back. "I thought you were working."

"Soon." He tilted his head, frowned. "Is everything okay?"

A droplet of water fell off his damp hair and hit his solid shoulder. She followed it as it flowed along the curve of his bicep. "Yes. Look what I found." She held up the envelope. "My money. It was in my trunk."

"Huh. You don't say." He pursed his lips then almost smiled. "Well, I'm glad you found it."

"Me too." She placed a hand on his forearm. "I'm truly sorry. I hope you'll forgive me."

His gaze skipped over her, pausing at her chest. "How could I hold a grudge against a woman wearing a Bazinga T-shirt?" He softened his eyes. "How about we call it even after the stunt I tried to pull on you?"

Rose found it hard to move, hard to keep her eyes focused on his face. "Sounds fair."

She slowly took a step back, afraid if she stood here one second longer she'd end up in his bedroom. She couldn't. Not unless he knew the truth about her.

"I'm heading to Sunny Side Up in town for some lunch in a couple hours." His gaze searched her face. "Want to join me?"

Of course she did, but she couldn't be seen in public. A desperate part of her wanted Leo to know everything. Right now, while he stood here barely covered. "I can't. I've got some work to do. But I did want to tell…"

A buzz sounded from the bedroom.

He frowned. "Better get that. I'm expecting a call from Seth. Did you want to tell me something?"

"Only thank you for being so understanding." She turned and hurried down the stairs.

* * * *

"Leo! You never come in on a Sunday. Can I get you something to drink?"

Leo glanced up from the plastic menu and smiled at his favorite waitress at Sunny Side Up. She wore the same teased hairstyle he remembered as a kid and still greeted each customer like they were her favorite. "Hi, Peggy. How about a Coke?"

"Pepsi okay?"

"Sure."

"I know it's lunchtime, but the chef's special is chocolate-covered waffles à la mode. Might satisfy that sweet tooth of yours." She raised an eyebrow, the kind drawn on with pencil.

Leo laughed. "Don't tell me I have a reputation around here?"

"Only for sweets." She winked.

He thought for a second about all Emma's eating habits and how they compared to his. His entire life, he'd paid very little attention to what he ate, but he wasn't getting any younger. "How about a turkey club sandwich with fries…no, hold the fries and give me a salad."

She pulled a pencil from her hair and a small pad from the pocket of her apron. "Changing it up a bit, I see. Change is good." She nodded and walked off.

Leo removed from a bag the *Sophisticate* magazine he'd purchased at Walker's Drugs on his way here. Curiosity about the woman living in his house warranted the purchase. Since she'd refused his lunch offer, he figured he'd take the time to learn more about her role as Dr. Rose Richardson.

This morning, even though she was happy over finding the money, something still bothered her. Mostly likely from the news he'd heard about the FBI the day before. He'd hoped if they went to lunch today, she might be comfortable enough sharing her troubles.

Leo had almost kissed her again this morning as they stood in the hallway. What stopped him was a new reality. One that hit him while they'd laughed together at the vineyard last night.

He'd fallen for a married woman.

Nothing on the Internet suggested she wasn't. Her responsiveness when they did kiss meant something, but armed with his new knowledge, physical contact could only lead to disappointment.

He unfolded the magazine and flipped to the column. "Dr. Rose Says… Relationship Advice You Won't Hear From Your Friends."

The same woman he'd seen with the senator and online appeared in a small box to the left of the column. God, she was cute. A plain blouse and blazer suited her. Nothing like the get-ups Emma wore. And without those ill-fitted glasses, the camera exposed her entire face, picking up a ready shine in her pretty eyes. She tilted her head sideways and held a cup of coffee in her hands. Her closed-lip smile suggested someone had just confided a deep dark secret and she was about to dispense some sensible advice.

He'd seen the smile before, and even recognized those slender, well-manicured fingers. The very hands he'd wanted to touch his freshly scrubbed body earlier.

"Yoo-hoo, Leo?"

The melodic voice jarred his delicious thought. He glanced up as the real estate agent…Marge…no, Meg, waved to him. She followed a group of ladies he recognized toward a table on the other side of the diner. Meg appeared to change her mind and detoured his way, grabbing the hand of a tall brunette.

He quickly shut the magazine.

Meg stopped at his booth. "Leo, this is the Northbridge Library Director, Veronica Sussingham-Jamieson. I thought you two should meet. I mean, you write books and Veronica..." Meg paused and thought. "Well, she runs a building filled with them."

Leo smiled at Meg's remark, finding her way with words actually kind of charming. As he shook Veronica's hand, he said, "I heard from my tenant you'd like to have me speak?"

"We'd be honored to have you come talk with our members."

Leo fished out a business card. "Email me here with possible dates and we can set something up."

"Thank you so much, Mr. Drake."

"Leo, please. It was nice to meet you." He nodded at Meg. "Nice to see you again, too."

Veronica walked off, but Meg didn't. "Are you and Emma doing okay?" She dropped her gaze to the magazine. "I'd never figure you for a man who reads *Sophisticate.*"

He flipped it over. "Well, there's a lot you don't know about me."

Meg pursed her lips and considered him, her expression confused. Or was she curious? "Anyway, is everything okay with your renter arrangement?"

"It's been fine." He hoped she hadn't put things together after seeing the news, like he had. "She's a good tenant."

Her ruby lips curled upward, clear delight lighting her face. "Oh wonderful! I was a little worried. After the communication problem. You know?"

He nodded. "I'm curious, how did my brother find this renter?"

"My office ran an ad. Why?"

"No reason. Did he run reference checks?"

Her face twisted. "I thought you said there were no problems."

"No, none. Just wondering how thorough my brother is as a businessperson. That's all."

"Hmmm, well, you shouldn't worry." She glanced to the table with her friends, where Peggy had just arrived with her pen and pad out. "I'd better go. Glad everything is going well."

Leo returned to the magazine. While waiting for his food, he scoured every word of the Dr. Rose column. When he finished, it occurred to him how Emma was a living and breathing contradiction. Queen of good advice, but her own life a fiasco. So bad, she didn't even stay to face her problems. Running away had to be about something more, something not making the papers.

If she wouldn't tell him what was going on, then maybe it was time for him to let her know he'd figured it out. Only what if she ran from him, too?

Chapter 21

Leo made a quick stop at Bellantoni's Market after lunch. As he exited, he noted black clouds gathered along the surrounding hillside and a foreboding breeze whispering through the trees. He packed the car and pushed the speed limit, hoping to make it home before the approaching downpour. Right before the turnoff for his street, steady sheets of rain clouded his view of the winding road.

Pulling into the driveway, he noticed the kitchen light was on.

He shut off the car and sat there, working up the gumption to run through the heavy torrent. Finally, he put one hand on the door handle and was about to take off when an angry rage of thunder rumbled like a sonic boom, followed by the bright glare of a lightning bolt. A crack immediately filled the air then a nearby transformer sizzled. The kitchen went dark.

He grabbed the grocery bags off the passenger's seat, got out, kicked the car door shut with his foot, and ran. Stepping inside the kitchen doorway, Leo slipped off his sopping wet shoes. Water dripped from his saturated clothing onto the linoleum floor.

Emma came out of her apartment, a frown on her face. She eyed him up and down, grabbed a dishtowel off the counter. "Bella and I were enjoying the lake view, and suddenly over the hills it looked like Armageddon was approaching. You're soaked. Did you walk from town?"

"No. From the car." He set down the groceries on the nearby counter edge and took the dishtowel. "It's coming down hard. A transformer blew in the neighborhood, probably a fallen branch landing on it. The power may not be back until the morning. I heard this storm is hitting a large part of the state. We small towns get power restored last, but there's always a chance we'll get lucky."

He wiped his face dry, taking note how she'd changed into a simple white V-neck pullover and a pair of Levis. Probably more how she normally dressed. Her glasses sat nestled in her hair showcasing her entire face.

Beyond any doubt, a reality hit. This *was* the woman on TV. Unexpected emotion for her crept into his heart and the urge to learn even more rode him hard.

"Thanks." Leo hoped he sounded normal. He lifted the groceries and walked toward the refrigerator.

"Should we check on Harry?" Genuine worry filled her eyes.

"You don't need to worry about him. He's probably already got his generator going."

"A generator? So that means he has power, right?"

Leo nodded and quickly stuck the cold six-pack he'd purchased in the fridge.

"Do you have one?"

"A generator? Nah. I like to rough it."

"What a surprise." She grinned, but it slipped as she glanced around the room. "I should try to get some work done while there's a little daylight."

"Change your plans." He tossed the ground beef he'd purchased into the top freezer and put the powdered donuts on the counter. At one of the drawers, he removed a flashlight. "When the power goes out there are better things to do around here than work."

"What? Eat junk food?"

"Even better." He grinned. "Give me a sec to change and I'll show you what I mean."

Upstairs he tossed on clean jeans and a dry cotton oxford. Once back in the kitchen, he heard Emma moving around inside her apartment. He pulled some hot dogs from the refrigerator and searched a drawer filled with assorted kitchen gadgets until he found two long, metal skewers. From an emergency kit stored in the pantry that his mother had set up years ago, he removed some votive and tapered candles and a battery powered transistor radio.

The storm was a true blessing in disguise. A chance to make her more comfortable around him. Then maybe she'd open up.

He lit the candles in various spots in the den and parted the curtains to let in the little bit of outside light. Going out onto the back porch, he gathered a few logs and kindling and dumped them on the den floor near the brick hearth. Temperatures were expected to drop tonight. You could never trust the New England weather in the spring.

He returned to the kitchen and found her standing in the middle of the room holding her flashlight.

"You're in for a treat." He quickly opened the refrigerator and removed a bottle of wine. "Grab some tumbler glasses from the cabinet and a corkscrew. Meet me in the den."

He went to a large chest near the fireplace and removed his favorite childhood game as she entered the room. Ridiculous, right? Stuck in the house with a beautiful woman and here he was, dragging out a board game brought to him by Santa. He didn't care. She seemed to belong in this house, and he wanted to her to enjoy it in the ways he always had.

She leaned on the trim near the den door. "You're kidding, right?"

"Some good old-fashioned entertainment. No batteries needed." He lowered the board game Trouble onto the coffee table. "I don't want you to worry, but I'm pretty skilled at this."

She made her way over. The glow from the flickering candles made her eyes sparkle. "Or maybe you should be worried. Some say I have the best poker face this side of the Mississippi."

"Good. I love a challenge."

Leo uncorked and poured the wine while she opened the game box and poked through the pieces. "What color do you want?"

"Blue. I've never lost a game when I stick with blue. Don't say you haven't been warned."

"Okay. I won't. You know, I took an undergrad class in college where we talked about the psychology of color."

"Oh?" *Of course you did, Dr. Rose.*

"Blue, the color of trust, honesty, and loyalty."

He poured the wine but didn't feel very loyal or honest. If he were, he'd tell her what he'd figured out from the news.

"There you go." She put his pieces near the box.

He handed her a full glass, leaving his on the table to get the fire started. On his way across the room, he saw she picked out red pegs for herself. "So is red your favorite color?"

"Of course. Red is the choice used by kick-ass Trouble players."

She offered a rebellious raise of her brow, making warm sensation glow inside his Leo's chest.

For the next hour, with the game board between them and the rain pounding a blitzkrieg of water on the roof, they played. Each hooted in victory when they'd send the other person's pieces back. Rolling a six and being granted another turn involved some major grandstanding on both their parts. When Queen's "Bohemian Rhapsody" played on the radio, she surprised him by singing, so he joined her.

Over the rim of his glass, he took a long sip and watched her move her piece. He hadn't enjoyed himself this much in a very long time.

She looked up and smiled warmly. "This *is* fun."

Tenderness rushed his chest as he swallowed the wine, causing a secondary stir inside the vacant folds of his heart.

* * * *

"Victory." Leo slipped his last piece in the slot, securing his third win to her two. "So sugary sweet it's making my teeth hurt."

Rose groaned but was secretly amused by how seriously he took the decades-old children's game. "You did have the home field advantage."

"A sore loser. Like my sister. Best out of seven?"

The wine relaxed her. Each passing game gave their relationship a cozier, more natural feel. She no longer wanted to play games with Leo. Not this game anyway.

"I'm no match for you. You've proven the power of the blue peg."

He chuckled, throaty and sexy, then lifted the wine bottle and tipped it in offering. She extended her glass and he filled it, doing the same to his.

"Want another hot dog?"

"One was enough. I can't believe you got me to eat one."

"I didn't hear you complain afterward. In fact, I'm pretty sure you gave your endorsement."

"It was tasty, but let's not get carried away. I never thought about cooking in a fireplace."

"We'd do it when the power went out or on a rainy day, when Mom had run out of ways to keep us occupied. We'd pretend we were camping, only we slept in here on sleeping bags, made hot dogs and popcorn in the fireplace, sang songs." He leaned back and plunked his legs on the coffee table. Resting his arm on the sofa top, he rubbed her shoulder and stared into the fireplace. "Good times."

The warm glow of the fire and Leo's soft touch made her want to get lost in this scene. So perfect and not pretend. His nearness kicked off a desperate need to learn more about him, even if it meant giving up a piece of herself. Rose had figured out a way both could be accomplished; she'd been toying with the idea for the past fifteen minutes.

Finally she said, "I have a game. It's an experiment, actually."

He moaned. "Science was my worst subject."

"Not that kind of experiment. We ask each other questions, to get to know each other better."

He raised his dark brows. "I'd like that. Any questions?"

"No. I have them in my room."

He reached for the flashlight, tucked near his leg on the sofa and handed it to her as he stood. "Go get them. I'll toss on another log."

Bella lifted her eyelid at the activity but didn't budge from her prime space near the warm fire.

Emma walked around the dark corner into the hallway. The rain had slowed. Every so often heavy winds made the house rattle. She quickly found her briefcase and took what she needed.

When she returned, Leo sat on the sofa, gazing at the flames. She studied his Nordic nose, strong jaw, soft wisps of hairs around his ears. He lifted his drink, slowly brought the rim to his lips. Memories of the tender way he'd kissed her teased her fuzzy state of mind.

He turned and his eyes softened. "All set?"

"I am." She sat in the sofa corner and stretched out her legs until they bumped his thighs.

For this to work, she needed to be completely honest. Truth. A foreign substance in her old world. Not on the day-to-day matters, but her past. Tonight, she'd try to step into a new world of honest relationships, with Leo as her guide. Nobody could be more perfect. He understood why someone would run, because he'd run here. He understood living in a blended world of real life versus fiction, the way she had always lived. She wanted to know about his past and was afraid, but willing, to share hers.

"We'll start with simple questions and work our way up to more difficult ones. Would you like to ask me first?"

He held out his hand. "Sure."

She turned over the list, the symbolism in her gesture so much more than he'd ever realize. Tonight was a chance to end a lifetime of making it hard for others to know her, really get inside her head. A lifetime of secrets. The sacrifice? An inability to sincerely share what she had to offer with another person.

He studied the list. The fireplace flames made his eyes sparkle. He rubbed his chin then lifted his gaze and their eyes met, making her inhale sharply at the intensity.

"Ready?"

"As I'll ever be."

"If you could change anything about the way you were raised, what would it be?"

The truth dancing perilously on her lips and she pushed it right off the cliff. "I would like to have been raised in a normal household."

He lowered the paper. "Define normal."

"Anonymous. Where nobody knows your family name, you live in a quiet neighborhood, go to public school."

"So then you didn't have those things?"

"My parents were actors and got a lot of attention as celebrities. We were always on display. I hated it." She exhaled a breath she'd been subconsciously holding, but confessing it wasn't as hard as she'd anticipated.

He raised a brow. "Stage, television, or movie?"

"Television, some movies."

He slowly nodded and watched her intently. "You had no interest in the field?"

"Never. The lifestyle sounds glamorous on the surface. Pressure for perfection is intense when you're in the public eye. My parents were fake versions of their true selves. One way for the camera. Another behind the scenes. They argued. Drank too much." A knot in her belly tightened from the confession but she also found the release empowering. "Drama was everywhere, except when the press or others were around." Moments from her childhood flashed before her, then, more quietly, she added, "I longed for routine, to go out and have nobody recognize me."

A solemn expression took over Leo's face. "Celebrity can get away from people. Who were your parents?"

Silence no longer kept her life safe; it kept her from living. "Warren and Wendy Holloway. I was their daughter."

He frowned. "I remember they…they both died, didn't they?"

She nodded.

"So you were their only child?"

"Yes." She drew in a deep breath. "I found them. My mom shot my dad then took her life. I was fourteen."

"Oh, wow. I'm sorry."

"Please, don't be. It was long ago." Rose's gut trembled with the admission, an aftershock of exposing her living nightmare.

Leo sat on quietly, thinking God only knew what. She didn't dare ask how much Leo remembered from the news back in the day. She didn't want to know.

She held out her hand. "My turn."

He passed over the paper, watching her with a serious and thoughtful gaze.

She read the questions until settling on one. "For what in your life do you feel most grateful?"

"Easy. Being adopted by the Drakes. Left in the foster care system, I may have reached my full potential, but who really knows? I was developmentally behind. Coming here was tough because I was different than the other kids." Gratitude shined in his eyes. "I owe the Drakes everything. Who watched you after your parents died?"

"My aunt."

He nodded. "Okay. I get to ask you the next one, and I already know the question so you can keep the list. What would you consider a perfect day? Besides playing Trouble during a power outage with me, of course."

She laughed. "This afternoon has been pretty damn near perfect." She rubbed his thigh with her foot.

His hand landed on her ankle, keeping it there and slowly caressing her skin.

His touch served to remind her why the truth was necessary. "A perfect day would be one where I've stopped running."

She averted her gaze to the jumping flames of the fireplace. The story of her life painted a weak picture of her. Twice she'd chosen flight, rather than facing reality. But if she answered his question, it could be a new reality.

"Emma?"

She glanced up, awakened by the sound of her fake name passing his lips. Reaching out and taking his hand, she said, "I'm not Emma. My name is Rose. Let me start at the beginning."

Rose shared everything, while Leo listened. She held his one hand tight the entire time while he massaged her shoulder with the other. From leaving California at the age of eighteen until the moment she arrived in his house and why she fled across state lines. No detail was spared. The sympathy in Leo's eyes helped her move forward. She finally inhaled a deep breath and said, "Now it's gotten worse."

"I know," Leo said quietly.

Rose deflated inside. "For how long?"

"Since yesterday, I recognized you on a news clip." He searched her face, his gaze sad and searching, as if trying to understand everything. "Your name hasn't come up there. Maybe the FBI hasn't found the trail John planted to make you look guilty."

"It's a matter of time. They know the money started in my account."

"How could he frame you? It can't be easy."

"The investigator I hired said John engineered a trail of illegal straw donations, but the paper trail all leads to me. To my inheritance."

"Wouldn't he be afraid of getting caught, too? It's his campaign."

She shrugged. "John's always been the type to take a gamble. He stood a chance nobody would have caught the donations at all. Then he'd have all my money." Rage surged through her veins. Anger at John. Anger at herself, for being so naive. "The problem is that I can't go to the authorities about this without being implicated myself. There's no hard evidence against him. Worse, I'm afraid he might hurt me. Don't forget, I heard him talking on the phone to someone with a plan to have me mugged or somehow hurt with a gun." Her gut trembled because she had no idea if John put those wheels in motion yet. "While I've been in Northbridge, I felt out of harm's way. But if I tell the police what I know, who knows what he's capable of doing?"

"Why would he want you arrested or hurt?"

"I don't know. I'm beginning to wonder if he married as a prop to his campaign or to get his hands on my inheritance. Maybe he never loved me."

She swallowed down a lump in her throat. Leo took her other hand, easing the ache in her chest.

Quietly, she added, "My only hope is the PI finds something to connect him to the transactions. It's a long shot, but I'm not giving up without a fight. I don't want to go to jail and end up convicted for something I didn't do. Any jail time as I wait to prove my innocence could tarnish my reputation. I have my own career to think about."

"Ask Dr. Rose?"

She nodded. "I'm sure the magazine will fire me and my readers won't want to hear my advice ever again."

"Has the PI proven your case yet?"

"Almost. He needs a little more time. You know, I never planned to drag anybody else into this mess. Especially you." She squeezed his hand.

"You're not dragging me any place I don't want to go."

"You don't care that I'm a fugitive from the law?" She cringed, the words becoming closer and closer to the truth.

He shook his head. "You're not yet. Besides, with every passing day, I'm certain you ended up at my doorstop for a reason. But I must ask"—Leo shifted and his thigh gently rubbed against hers—"you are divorced, then?"

"Yes. Just not announced yet."

"So us being together, it's okay?"

She inched closer and kissed him tenderly. "Better than okay."

He watched her with such intensity her heart felt his affection. He cupped her cheek while gazing into her eyes for only a second before he drew her close, pushed his fingers through one side of her hair, and brushed his lips against her cheek.

"Rose," he whispered, leaving an imprint from his warm breath. "Such a beautiful name." He kissed her neck. Her chin. The corner of her mouth.

Never before in her life had she wanted to hand over so much of herself. Her body. Her heart. Her soul.

Leo tugged her close and brushed his lips tenderly to hers. "I promise, you're safe here."

Rose got lost in his kiss. The fabricated reality found by running to Connecticut suddenly felt more real than any other moment of her life.

* * * *

An hour had passed since she'd spilled everything. She'd never felt more free and honest. Spooned comfortably against Leo, Rose nestled into the sofa cushions not caring about the passing time and lulled by the warm fire's sizzle. The conversation and questions had continued, openness unlike any she'd shared with a man.

She sighed, the moment of bliss making her question everything she ever knew as happiness. They'd shared so much tonight. About family and friends. The past and present. Loves and losses.

"I noticed you didn't mention the last part of your experiment when you tossed those questions aside," he said quietly, his warm breath near her ear.

"You mean the part where we stare into each other's eyes for four minutes?"

"Yes."

"For good reason."

"Chicken?"

She rolled around and faced him. "Hell, yeah."

"It's only four minutes."

"That's a long time. I could make a boiled egg or sing an entire song or—"

"Or stare into my eyes." He pressed his forehead to hers. "It might help me with a character thing."

"Tell me you just didn't play the guilt card."

"Writing is a dirty business." Leo grinned then turned his face toward the burning fire for several seconds. "I know this is scary, but it's about trust."

She laughed. "Jeesh, hit me where it hurts. Four minutes, huh?"

"Barely a millisecond of a lifetime, if you think about it."

"Well, when you put it that way."

"Let's sit up." He grinned, a satisfied expression, and as they got upright he reached for his cell phone on the end table. "I'll time us. Let's face each other."

They shifted from their spots on the sofa until meeting at the center, their feet firmly planted on the floor and knees touching.

He looked up. "Ready?"

"No. But don't let that stop you."

"Shhh. Let's start." He tapped the phone, put it down, and stared at her. They stared. And stared. *This is silly.* Right away, Rose smiled, although it didn't shadow her discomfort.

He smiled back, tilted his head, and squinted. Such deep concentration. She'd better get serious too.

One-Mississippi, Two-Mississippi, Three-Mississippi. Her mind drifted from the count, intended to keep her focused. Instead the color of Leo's eyes grabbed her attention. *Four-Mississippi.* Dark as toffee. She loved toffee. *Five-Mississippi.* She studied them more closely. They glistened from the flickering candlelight, changing color like a hypnotic kaleidoscope. Shades of browned butter, sweet as warm caramel. God she wanted something sweet to eat now. Warm and welcoming eyes. Calmness rushed her, leaving a relaxed trail in its wake.

He shifted. His bare foot slid on top of hers and massaged the skin beneath her thin socks with his toes. He softened his eyes with such suggestive insinuation that she squirmed in her seat as her desire flared. Damn him.

He grinned, almost devilish. The slow movements of his toes performed a decadent game of footsie, even more daring than his first attempts. She wanted to scream "rule-breaker" but then she'd be doing the same! Concentrate. Concentrate. Concentrate.

She finally pulled her leg away, proud of herself for not once losing her focus. She forced her face into serious submission and his grin slipped away. She again got lost in his gaze, an unexpectedly more comfortable place than when they'd started.

Seconds ticked. The state of staring became more natural. A blanket of silence covered the room. Small sounds magnified. Leo's breath. The crackle of the fire. Raindrops brushing the sides of the house. A masterpiece playing just for them. His soulful gazed etched into hers. So deep. So bottomless. Beautiful eyes. No longer the eyes of a man but holding the innocence of the boy Leo once was, vulnerable and yet so brave.

The quiet way he'd spoken earlier about being raised by an addict elicited a swift brush of sadness inside her chest. Seconds later it disappeared with her study of the strong man he'd become. A sweet man who'd admitted tonight that he'd fallen for her...and her dog. A smile tugged at her lips thinking of how cute the two of them were together.

She studied his face more closely. The scar near his temple. The downward slope of his thick brows. A crease formed between them as his eyes skipped over her face; then he frowned. The whites of his eyes glistened and Adam's apple rolled. Her heart ached to know what made him sad. Unexpected tears stung at the back of her eyes and his face blurred.

Part of her wanted to pull him into a hug. The other part mourned for herself, over the sad state of past relationships and love, never fully given or received.

He blinked and his eyes scoured her face. A stare reaching deep inside her chest and drawing her to a place physically close to him, despite the lack of touching.

The buzzer on his phone sounded. Neither one of them moved at first; then Leo slowly lifted his hand, cupped her cheek, and swept his thumb across her lower lip. She closed her eyes and kissed his palm, her heart full in a way she'd never experienced.

She looked up. "What'd you think?"

"Powerful," Leo said, his voice quiet, husky. He cleared his throat. "I wasn't sure what to expect, but it was more than I'd asked for. What about you?"

"Once I got over the awkwardness of it, the whole thing was actually nice. I've never looked at someone so carefully."

He nodded and shifted his hand to the back of her neck, massaging slowly. "Not only did I see more of you, but I noticed more about myself. Guess I got a little emotional for a minute."

"Want to talk about it?" She took his hand and squeezed.

"It came from too many things. A life of lost control, I think." His forehead furrowed and concentration marked his face. "Only the more I stared into your eyes, the less I hurt. Does that make sense?"

"Yes. The same thing happened to me."

A wounded expression flashed in his eyes. "You should know, I never wanted to fall in love again. The pain that can come with it...it was just too hard. But you—you make me want to love again."

The words filled her heart. "I understand. Me, too."

Bella's collar jingled. Rose glanced over just as she rolled onto her back, legs up in the air, eyes shut tight.

She laughed. "You're sure it's not Bella causing these strong emotions? You two seem pretty close."

He cast a smile at the dog then wrapped his arms around Rose and drew her close. "I'm pretty sure it's ninety-nine percent you."

Leo kissed her on the corner of her mouth, moved to her lower lip then to her throat, his breath leaving a warm imprint on her skin. Their lips entangled, slow at first, then Leo deepened his hold and explored. The soft grain of his unshaven shadow brushed her cheeks, and she inhaled his clean, soapy scent.

Stretching out on the sofa, they coiled around each other getting lost in kisses so deep she forgot everything else around her. He slipped his hands beneath her shirt, his fingertips grazing her sensitive skin, every inch of her so desperate for attention that she instantly dissolved in his arms.

She wanted more of him, as much as he'd give. Easing her onto her back, he lifted himself above her. Each kiss demanded more. She pressed her palms to his chest, traveled his broad shoulders then massaged the hard planes of his back. His hand inched along her torso, then he swept his thumb beneath her breast and groaned into her mouth. Only when her lungs burned did she lean back and draw in a deep breath. Leo studied her with desire that sent a shiver straight to her belly.

He whispered, "You're no longer facing this alone. I'll be at your side."

Isolation she'd always accepted in her life ripped apart at the seams, making her fall completely under his spell.

Chapter 22

Rose squinted as she woke, blinded by the bright morning sun streaming through a crack in the den curtains. Leo snored gently in her ear, his body mingled with hers so they could fit together on the sofa. The refrigerator hummed in the next room, so power had been restored. Most likely after three a.m., the last time they woke and reached for each other. Rose savored every delicious memory, unlike any relationship from her past.

Last night Leo had roused her heart. Rose couldn't even recall when it had fallen asleep, but she wanted to hold onto this wonderful feeling.

Bella stood and stretched. No doubt her hungry stomach was telling her it was past food o'clock. Rose carefully maneuvered off the sofa so she didn't wake Leo, grabbed her clothes off the floor, and got dressed in the hallway near the kitchen. Bella ambled out, casting an "it's about time" glance. The dog followed Rose to the kitchen. After she slipped on a pair of a flip-flops left near the back door, she quietly urged Bella outside.

Wet grass tickled Rose's toes and an unseasonable chill hung in the air from yesterday's storm. Several downed tree branches showed proof of nature's wild ride. Bella sniffed the ground as though she didn't have a care in the world. "Hurry up, Bells. You know what to do. Then we eat."

The dog's ears lifted at the magic word, and her sniffing took on a more serious manner.

Sticking her hands into the warm pockets of her jeans, Rose wished she were still in the warm spot near Leo's side. Even in her dreams last night, they were together. Playing games. Laughing. Getting crazy lost in each other's eyes. Then she'd wake, and find herself wrapped in his arms. This handsome, smart, and complex man. Someone who understood her, and who she hoped to get closer to.

Bella finished and trotted back to Rose, a "what's next" gleam in her eyes.

"Good girl. Do you wanna eat?"

Her ears lifted and she galloped to the back door.

Ten minutes later, Bella ate her kibbles as the coffee pot rattled on the stove and bacon sizzled in an iron skillet.

"Morning." Leo walked in. His eyes were sleepy and both hair and clothes creased.

She flipped the bacon. "Coffee'll be done soon."

He went to the cabinet and removed two mugs then turned on the counter radio, adjusting it to a news station.

He came up behind her, slipped his arms around her waist, and gently pressed his lips to the back of her neck. "Smells good in here."

"It'll be done in a few minutes."

"Great." He patted her bottom as he moved to a cabinet and removed some plates.

The weather report warned of another possible storm today. News at the top of the hour started. Rose flipped the bacon, listening with half an ear to the first story. The next one started and she paused.

The FBI is searching for wife of Senator John Richardson. Evidence uncovered by the bureau shows illegal campaign donations found in the senator's campaign accounts were made by Rose Richardson, the senator's wife.

Fear rippled through Rose. The report continued. She listened, despite her body going numb and her brief happiness suddenly drowning in hopelessness.

Federal investigators have tried to reach Ms. Richardson, also known to many as Dr. Rose from her column in Sophisticate *magazine. At this time, she has not been reachable for comment. In other news, the Treasury Department today reports...*

Rose removed the bacon, only half-aware of her moving body. Her head spun, skin heated.

Leo came to her side, removed the fork from her hand, and pushed away the hot pan. He held her tight, but it didn't stop her from trembling. She buried her face against his shirt and cried. As he rubbed her back and kissed the top of her head, she stopped thinking about her old problems. She had a new one. Involving Leo in this charade was innocent at the start, but now that he knew, staying here was just plain wrong.

Tears spilled harder and faster. Leo didn't say a word. Right now, being in his arms was the only thing keeping her from falling apart.

"Should I find another place to stay?" she managed to say between breaths.

"You'd better not."

She looked up. "I can't drag you into this mess any further. We're probably breaking some laws standing here right now and talking about this. You're harboring a criminal."

He wiped some wetness from her cheek with his index finger. "Please. Let me help you. Am I going to have to steal your money to get you to stay?" He grinned, even though his worry remained obvious.

"No." She sniffed and managed to almost smile. "You won't have to."

Dropping her head against his chest, she sank against his body and wished she could stay just like this forever.

* * * *

Leo pushed aside his plate and for several minutes tried to concentrate on the newspaper. Rose sat next to him reading another section of the *Times*, no longer upset but quiet.

He reached over, took her hand, and gave it a squeeze. "How are you feeling?"

She glanced up from the magazine section. "Better. This was bound to happen. I suppose hearing my biggest concern on the radio just hit harder than I thought it would."

"Your reaction was justified. Want to talk more about it?"

She shook her head, smiled gently. "No. I want to enjoy this lovely quiet Sunday morning...with you." She squeezed his hand back and let go. "Want more coffee?"

"Sure."

She poured them each another cup then returned to her reading.

But Leo still couldn't concentrate. After hearing the FBI was now looking for her, the reality of their situation burned like acid on Leo's heart. The FBI wanted her and *he* knew where they could find her.

The legalities of this single fact made his head throb. How much did they know about her? Would she let him talk to the PI she'd hired? Was it wrong that he didn't care about his silence over her whereabouts?

Last night she'd shown him she was a strong woman. Behind the fearlessness, though, he sensed she still needed something—or maybe just simply someone. A trunk full of problems had been dragged with her to Northbridge. The single fact fueled Leo's drive to make her problems vanish.

If he didn't, he could lose Rose.

She might run. Taking flight when the going got tough had helped her survive. Maybe she'd changed. Her confession suggested so. But what if she hadn't? He inwardly shuddered and tried not to consider the possibility.

Rose's toes tickled near his ankle. He looked up. She kept reading and appeared to be pretending she hadn't noticed him looking. She slid lower into the seat and her foot moved higher up his calf to his knee where she slowly kneaded her toes, her playful touch making him want to fly off the chair and take her right on the table.

"I guess you *are* feeling better." He grabbed her leg and dragged both her and the chair closer.

The newspaper dropped to the floor and she laughed. "Can I help you?"

Massaging her foot, he asked, "You think teasing me is funny?"

"Funny? That wasn't *at all* what I was going for." She wiggled her toes in his hands. "Mmmm. A foot rub. Perfect foreplay for what I had in mind." She arched a brow.

"Oh? I'd like to hear what you have in mind." He secured her foot on his lap, holding it down with one hand and smoothing the bottom with the thumb of his other.

"The big plans are actually for my landlord. He can be a curmudgeonly fellow, but has a very sweet side."

"Curmudgconly?"

"At times. Anyway, there's a problem in my apartment."

"Forget your landlord. I'm filling in today." He slipped his hand along her thigh until he reached the top. His fingertips grazed, going everywhere but where he was certain she wanted him to go. She shut her eyes, shifted in the seat, and inhaled sharply. Leo's desire soared. "What seems to be your problem?"

Her ivory cheeks now flushed with a pink hue. "Let me show you." She quickly pulled her foot away and stood. Moving to his side, she straddled his lap and he cupped her backside. As she shifted against his hardness, she combed her fingers through his hair and watched him with a fiery gaze. It shifted into an unexpected grin. "I hope you brought your tools."

He groaned. "Please tell me you didn't just say that."

Amidst her laughter, he drew her to him, kissed her hard and deep. No, he'd never get enough of her.

Ding-dong. Ding-dong.

Bella howled.

Rose's body tensed in his arms. "You don't think it's the FBI, do you?"

"Relax. It's a Sunday morning. Probably a holy roller." Leo patted her bottom and winked. "Hold that thought."

She got off him and planted a kiss on his lips. "You know I will."

By the time he reached the door, Bella was there, sniffing at the crack and growling. Just as Leo reached for the handle, it jiggled, the lock turned, and the door sprung open.

Everett stood on the other side. Leo froze. He hadn't seen his brother since his wife's funeral.

The dog howled again. Everett now had a few gray hairs near his temples blended with his faded blond coloring. Leo had never seen him in glasses, but he wore a stylish pair: black rims on the top, rimless on the bottom, upping the urbane air Everett usually carried. They only enhanced his classically handsome face, stirring some of the old jealousy Leo had whenever they met women together.

"Surprise," Everett said, in his usual dry-witted, acerbic tone. "Aren't you going to invite me into my own house?"

Finally. The long-awaited confrontation. "A call would've been nice."

The dog swarmed around Everett's legs. He cast an annoyed glance and ignored the animal. "You always did hate surprises." He sniffed the air. "Coffee. Thank God. I knew you'd have some going."

Leo clenched his fist as he shut the door. Everett seized immediate control the second he entered any setting. He paused at the den doorway and looked inside. Leo thought about the blankets, used wine glasses, and plates scattered about the room from last night.

"You have company?" He continued straight to the kitchen, Leo not far behind.

"Well, hello." Everett's tone carried a surprised ring. "Who would've thought Leo would have a visitor plus a dog? He's such a loner."

Leo entered just as Rose stood and extend a hand. "Hello. Emma Morris. The dog's mine."

Everett took her in from head to toe. "Ah, yes. My renter."

She cut a nervous glance to Leo.

He spotted her eyeglasses on the counter. Silly as he thought they were, he walked over and picked them up, nonchalantly passing them to Rose.

She slipped them on and stiffly smiled. "Thanks. I was looking for these. I'd better get my day started." She turned to Everett. "Nice to meet you."

She hurried down the hall calling for Bella, who glanced at Leo but then followed Rose. Leo watched them disappear, taking all the good air away from the room and leaving only the bad.

Everett, a once reasonable kid, was now a bad adult, filled with rage and power he loved to exert over others. The apartment door clicked shut and Leo wished he were on the other side of it, too.

Leo filled a mug with coffee and placed it on the table. "Does Mallory know you're in the States?"

"No." Everett took off his sports jacket. He tossed it over a chair as he looked around the room. "Nobody knows. I plan to call her. *After* we talk." He sat and lifted the mug to his lips. "Thanks. Long flight. Jesus, this place looks even older than I remembered."

"It's the same as we grew up in. A little weathered, but always feels like home to me."

Everett's gaze met Leo's. "How's the tenant? I see you two are"—he paused then flashed a dirty little grin—"getting along."

"Why did you ignore my message that I was staying at the house?"

"Retribution, dear brother. Are you going to deny you were the one who scared the last tenant away?"

"Well…"

"Come on. I haven't forgotten what we used to do to our aunt." Everett chuckled. Not a sinister laugh, but one of amusement that made Leo remember better times. "I can't believe you're still pulling that stunt out of your hat now."

Leo's guard softened, relieved they were at least speaking. "I even had a few new tricks up my sleeve."

"How come you're not trying to scare her?" Everett glanced down the hallway. "Although from the cozy set up in the den, I have my answer."

"The power went out. We kept each other company." Leo couldn't tell his brother the true nature of his feelings for Rose. Everett's world-class manipulations had no boundaries. "I'm glad you're finally talking to me."

Everett shrugged. "Only out of necessity. Some things are unforgiveable." He inhaled sharply. "Differences aside—"

"God damn it!" Leo slapped his palm on the table. "What the hell is wrong with you? Jesus. Life is short."

"Very cliché. I expect more from you." Everett's jaw tightened and eyes narrowed. "You never asked my permission to be with Camille."

"I didn't need your permission to fall in love."

"With her, you did." Everett's voice cracked.

"How many times have I told you, I hardly knew Camille when you two dated, and when I met her two years after you guys broke up, I figured it was over. Our romance wasn't planned, it just happened."

Everett shut his eyes, brought his fingers to the bridge of his nose. "Please, Leo. Stop."

"Why does it matter after all this time? You're happily married. Jacqueline is a wonderful woman."

Everett lowered his hand and opened his eyes. "I only came here to tell you I'm going to sell you the house. I've set up a meeting with the attorney. This way, you have no need to contact me any longer."

Leo bit back rage building inside him. He couldn't believe his brother would go this far. He'd always hoped someday this tension would end. "God damn you, Everett! Be a man. Tell me what's really bugging you."

"Be a man?" Everett pushed back the chair fast and stood, his cheeks blasting bright red. "I was a man! There was more going on between Camille and me than you know."

"And why is that? Your silence perhaps?"

"You didn't deserve any more than that."

"Spoken like a true grudge-holding, stubborn—"

"She was pregnant."

"What?"

"When we were dating, she got pregnant." Everett quieted. "We discussed marriage, but she lost the baby early in the pregnancy."

Camille had *never* told Leo this, leaving him to wonder how well he really knew his wife.

"It—well, the whole episode changed her. I never wanted to end things. It was her call." Everett fell back into his seat. Pain deeper than Leo had ever seen on him filled his eyes. "I loved her."

Leo understood how Camille's mental health issues were tied into her physical well-being. A pregnancy, then losing a baby, could shift her hormones in ways he could only imagine.

"I'm sorry, Everett. I had no idea. Why didn't you tell me?" Leo suddenly felt anger at Camille for never having shared this with him. Her secrecy carried a manipulative quality that hurt.

"Tell you? Admit the woman I loved chose my brother?" Everett snorted. "It wouldn't have mattered. By the time you two came home, it was clearly too late."

Truth rang in his remark, leaving a sour taste in Leo's mouth. "But, if we'd at least talked—" Leo stopped as the guest apartment door opened.

Bella entered the kitchen dragging her attached leash. Rose entered next, still tucking her camouflage T-shirt into the waistband of a pair of baggy jeans that narrowed at her ankles. This time she wore her glasses, and "happy face" barrettes held back coppery loose hairs from her face. Leo noted his brother's silent observation, screaming of judgment that only someone who flew on private jets and stayed at five-star hotels could have.

"Sorry to interrupt." Her curious gaze drifted between the two men; then she turned to Leo. "Back in a bit."

"Enjoy your walk." He smiled, hoping she'd know he was okay. She gave him an uncomfortable, brief smile back. He'd tell her the good news about the house later.

Everett started intently at Rose, his brows furrowed. "So, Emma?"

She lifted a brow.

"Have we met before?"

"No." Her cheeks turned crimson. Leo wanted to rush over and block his brother's view because she looked guilty as all hell of something. "I have one of those faces."

"Possibly. But…" Everett drummed his fingers, squinted at her. "Oh well, maybe not."

She blinked a few times, but Leo sensed her uneasiness was no doubt spurred by Everett's intense scrutiny.

"I'd better walk the dog." She hurried out the back door.

"You know," Everett said the second the door shut, "I forget names, but I never forget a face."

The remark unnerved Leo. Especially with everything on the news about the FBI investigation. "Can we get back to what you said before? I wish you'd reconsider our relationship. Dad loved us both. He left us this place in the hopes we'd reconcile our differences. I hoped we could, too."

Everett stared passively at Leo, like mentioning their father might have softened his hard shell.

Then a steely glow shadowed his eyes. "I've some recent sales figures from town, similar comps to this place." He reached into the pocket of his jacket and removed a sheet of paper. "I think you'll find this figure for the buy-out a fair asking price."

He handed it to Leo then stood and went to the kitchen window.

Leo studied the information. The price was fair and the term of the deal one he couldn't refuse.

"Interesting. She's out there talking to Harry," Everett mumbled. He suddenly turned around and stared at Leo. "Is she from town? Maybe that's why I remember her."

"No. Boston. She's from Boston."

Everett turned back to the view outside the window.

If Everett recognized her as Rose Richardson, who knew how far he'd go. The worst part was, there wasn't a damn thing Leo could do about it.

Chapter 23

After typing the same sentence twice, Leo got out of the chair and walked to the attic window. The sparkling lake waters usually relaxed him. Not today.

Everett had left an hour ago and Rose hadn't returned from her walk. Leo imagined his brother running into Rose along the road, stopping, and grilling her for information. Either about her relationship with Leo or, worse, why she looked familiar.

Bella's howl made him glance toward the end of the driveway. The dog dashed across the backyard toward Harry, who approached Rose, several steps behind her pet. As they neared, he extended a bunch of lilacs to Rose.

She smiled and took them, burying her nose inside the fragrant flower. Then she gave sly old Harry a peck on the cheek. Leo chuckled. In his younger days, Harry was a man that could've made Leo jealous with such a gesture. Aw, hell. He was a teeny bit jealous now.

She stood chatting with the neighbor, her chin held high, laughing sweetly, as if she didn't have a care in the world. Stoic. Rose struck him as a woman who'd survive, no matter what. Last night, she'd admitted to running at the age of eighteen and building herself a new world.

An uneasy thought trampled him out of nowhere. Maybe that's all she'd been doing here.

After Everett had left, the first thing Leo did up here was go to his computer and search for "Warren and Wendy Holloway." Despite how she'd talked openly about them, his curiosity needed to be satisfied.

The shooting happened in nineteen ninety-two. Leo vaguely recalled seeing it on the news back then. One link showed the handsome couple. Wendy Holloway's pretty, heart-shaped face and smallish mouth reminded him of Rose. Her father, tall with rich dark hair and a profile that could give Rock Hudson a run for his money.

Passion. It drove people to do the unthinkable. In her parents' case it was Warren's affair with another actor, leaving Wendy angry enough to kill her husband and then herself.

The article had shown a photograph of the whole family. The Hollywood couple stood on each side of a preteen girl at a formal event. The young girl possessed the maturing features of the same woman he'd made love to last night. The worry she might leave took another stab at his gut, but he knew he had to put faith in what they'd found.

A knock at the attic door jarred his thoughts. "Come in."

After a stampede of footsteps, both Rose and Bella appeared at the top of steps. Bella got to him first.

He scratched Bella's chest as she dragged her tongue against his cheek, sloppy but rewarding. "How's my girl?" he cooed, earning him a faster tail wag.

"I'm good." Rose grinned and sidled near him like a cat in search of attention. "Working?"

"Sort of. I could use a break." Leo stood and put his arms around her waist, drawing her close. "I'm sorry Everett barged in earlier. I didn't know he was in the States."

"I could tell. Do you think he recognized me?"

"He didn't say anything after you left." Leo opted to keep to himself the few things his brother had said so she wouldn't worry even more.

"What's strange is he seemed familiar to me, too. On my walk, I finally figured out why. I think we met at a fundraiser at Charlie Palmer's restaurant in DC. Mostly CEOs and presidents of some huge firms were there. I could swear I was introduced to Everett. There with another guy who worked for some company in Switzerland. They wanted to open an office in Raleigh. Does that sound like something he'd attend?"

"Possibly. He works and lives in Switzerland at the moment. Even if he figures out who you are, I doubt he'd tell anybody. You shouldn't worry."

Leo tried to look sincere. He trusted his brother about as much as he did a cobra launched to strike, but why concern Rose any more than she was?

He kissed the top of her head. "So, beautiful, why the visit to my lair?"

"Harry invited us over for a barbecue tonight."

"You sure he wants me there? I saw him hand you those flowers."

"Wow. You're jealous enough to spy on me?" She lifted her hand off his shoulder and traced his jawline with her fingertip. "I'd say the trust in this relationship went downhill fast."

"Hell, yeah. Harry's a lady killer."

She laughed. "Those sparkling blue eyes of his are persuasive. He invited Bella, too."

"If Bella's going, then I'm in." He dipped his head and sampled her bottom lip, moving to the side of her mouth then kissing her full on the lips. "Harry's a good guy."

"I think so too." Emma stretched on her toes and brushed her lips to his. Before she could pull away, he slipped a hand behind her head and deepened the kiss. His other hand went beneath her shirt, enjoying a path along her spine as she melted into his hold.

She pulled away, tipping back her head to see him. "You're distracting me before I could finish. I thought we should bring something, even though he said we didn't need to."

"Sure. Want to take a ride into town? Crumbs Bakery probably has something left in their cases."

"If not, I'm sure they'd whip something up for you. You're probably their number one customer."

"Not true. But I do go regularly." He nestled his nose into her hair, inhaled a sweet scent, as delectable as the smell of baking cookies at the bakery. Combing his hands through her hair, he kissed her tenderly. Her throaty sigh of contentment made his needs stir and the problems of today tumble away.

She slipped a few fingers inside the waistband of his sweatpants and her gaze drifted over his shoulder. "Why's there a bed up here?"

"When I was fourteen, my parents let me turn this into my bedroom instead of sharing a room with Everett."

"Did you lure pretty young ladies up here back then to show them your etchings?" She kissed his throat then behind his ear, her warm breath washing over him.

"My etchings? Do I strike you as the type to use such understatement to get what I want?"

"Maybe at that age."

"To answer your question, no. I did not lure any girls up here." He carefully guided her backward to the bed, eased her onto her back, and stretched out alongside her. "But, you know, we never finished what we started before."

She allowed him to take over. He removed her camouflage shirt and went for her baggy jeans. "I'm starting to find your weird wardrobe kind of sexy, you know."

"I hope you're not disappointed by what's on beneath these pants."

He snapped the button and shimmied them down her hips. The enticing red bikini panties once left at his door fit snug to her curves. He ran a hand along the slope of her hip. "You, my dear, could never disappoint me."

* * * *

Rose stuck another dinner dish onto the drying rack, feeling easily at home in Harry's large kitchen.

His colonial, nearly as old as Leo's, had updates galore. The kitchen's black granite countertops, whitewashed cabinets, and shiny hardwood floors were more like Rose's home in North Carolina. Walls throughout the house were painted at least in the past decade. Nothing like the wear and tear found in Leo's house. Still, Leo's place carried charm she now found comforting.

"Hey, gorgeous." Leo entered the room carrying his coffee mug. His gaze hungrily flowed over her body. He'd been in Harry's office helping Harry with a computer problem, the irony not wasted on Rose. "Did I tell you yet that you look very pretty tonight?"

"Three times." She hiked up the sleeve of her pink cardigan, tossed on earlier with a heather-gray skirt that rode a few inches above her knees. "Here I'd thought my Hello Kitty pants were your thing."

As she moved toward the sink to start washing the pans, he put down his mug and took her hands, pulling her to his side. "I like those, too. You even tempt me in your Hee Haw outfit."

She laughed. "My overalls?"

"Yup." He put his hands on her hips. "And that camo shirt gives me a whole new perspective on jungle wear."

He leaned in, lips parted and centimeters from hers, when Harry yelled from the other room. "Leo, I think I may see what's wrong."

He gave her a quick peck and quietly said, "The best laid plans…" He let go and went over to the Mr. Coffee to refill his mug and yelled, "Be right there." He looked at her as he poured. "Give me a few more minutes and then I'll come help clean."

"I'm okay. Take your time."

She dipped her hands into the sudsy water and washed a pot, her thoughts wandering to worries that the FBI might consider Leo an accomplice because she'd been staying at his house.

All afternoon, she'd mentally rehashed what could happen to him if they found out. It left her with one conclusion; the only way to fix this might be to return to the place she'd just run away from.

Hard as she tried to ignore the pain in her chest over leaving him, it might be all she could do. It distanced Leo from her problems. It could—and most likely would—lead to her arrest.

Harry's voice traveled from the den as he explained to Leo about his computer woes. Rose washed another dish, but sadness owned her. Leaving here might be the hardest thing she ever had to do.

* * * *

"So you see, Harry, it's easy. Just click on this next time and you should be okay." Leo was proud of his neighbor. Compared to many other senior citizens, he was damn good on the computer.

The older man shook his head. "I never would've dreamed it was something so simple. Thanks."

Harry shut off the computer, glancing at Leo as he did. "I'm glad you came over with Emma. She's visited me a few times for tea."

"I heard. You two are getting to be fast friends. Like the two of us when I first arrived at the lake years ago."

Harry chuckled. "I'll never forget how you wandered over here, giving your mom a heart attack. She thought you'd drowned."

"I wasn't used to having a parent who paid any attention to my whereabouts."

"Well, you learned fast enough." Harry shut down the computer. "So it's not so bad, having a houseguest? I thought you were happy to finally get the place back to yourself."

"I was. But I'm actually getting more work done with her around."

Harry reached out to pat Leo's hand. "You've got a glimmer in your eye when you look her way. You'd better pay attention to how you feel about her, because I think she's a special one." His expression became more serious. "Did you ever wonder why Emma showed up here?"

"What do you mean?"

Harry frowned then got up and picked up a newspaper from a chair. He pointed to a photograph. "A few cosmetic changes and they'd be twins."

Leo held his breath. Rose's worry that media attention might backfire on her now became his worry. "I guess they do look similar."

"Emma's story about why she's here, it's always sounded vague to me. Do you think there's a chance the woman the FBI are after is her?"

Leo debated, unsure if he should put faith in Harry as he'd done his whole life. Finally he said, "What if it was?"

Harry's brows lifted. "Well, I like Emma. I'd want to understand her side, because all I'm hearing is what the media knows."

Leo drew in a breath and lowered his voice. "Please, Harry. Whatever your suspicions, can you just let them be?"

A noise at the door made them both turn. Bella trampled toward the two men, happy-go-lucky as always. But Rose stood at the door, her arms crossed and expression wary. "What are you two talking about?"

* * * *

"But if you two figured it out, so will the rest of Northbridge." Rose waited behind Leo as he unlocked the back door of his house. "Probably half the town has figured it out by now."

They walked inside and Leo flipped the light switch. The overhead light brightened the kitchen.

He faced her, already frowning. "I told you, it's only because I overheard you talking to your friend Janine."

"Joanne."

"Right. But, that's how I knew you had changed your appearance. Not simply by seeing you with John on the television."

"On that note, I still can't believe you eavesdropped."

He sighed and shut the door behind them. "I'm ashamed and I'm sorry. It just sort of happened." He took her hand and pulled her into a hug. "Let's take this a day at a time. Didn't you say the PI was close to proving you weren't involved?"

"I did."

"Then, a day at a time. Okay?" He slipped his hand along her nape and spread his fingers underneath her hair. "Do you still want to watch the Cary Grant movie?" He grinned. "Nothing like *Mr. Blandings Builds his Dream House* to take away your troubles."

Since he'd suggested it right before they went out, she'd looked forward to cozying up with him on the sofa after dinner at Harry's. Staring into his hopeful eyes, she tried to adopt his less worried attitude and smiled. Rose slipped her arms around his neck. "Sure."

He hugged her, tucking her head beneath his chin. She seemed to fit just right. As he rubbed her back, she somehow felt better.

"Let me go change. Then we can watch the movie."

Once in her room, she shed her clothes and tossed on a pair of stretchy leggings with an oversized T-shirt she'd found at a rest area in Pennsylvania reading, "Does the name Pavlov ring a bell?" It had begged to be purchased.

She hung the skirt and top. On her way out, she took her phone from the purse and found two missed calls from Dan and one message.

Nerves flared, the impact like a sucker punch to her stomach. She'd spent the better part of the day ignoring the news, but a call from Dan demanded her attention. She didn't bother with the message and hit dial. Each ring felt like an hour. By the fifth one, she was about to hang up when a winded voice answered, "Hello."

"Dan?"

"Yeah, Rose. Thank God you got my message."

"I didn't listen to it. What's wrong?"

"Good news. Well, mostly. My guy finished. We've compiled enough evidence to prove you didn't make those straw donations, but I recommend you contact a lawyer."

"Okay. But if you found enough evidence and I get a lawyer, this should be good, right?"

Dan took a deep breath. "My guess is that the FBI will try to get to your husband by going for you. With the latest news, it's time you found an attorney. I can give you the name of one I've worked with before who handles these types of cases."

"Where's the justice in this world? I did nothing. I'm a victim."

"The reason we're doing this the right way. Got a pen?"

"Hold on." Questions twirled in her mind like the start of a cyclone, mounting in urgency with each passing second. She fished through her purse until she found something to write with and swallowed down a hard lump before she spoke. "Ready."

Her hand trembled as she wrote down the name of a lawyer in DC.

"Oh, and stay where you are unless the lawyer says otherwise. I'll be available for conference calls if you need me to go over the evidence we've uncovered. If we do this smartly, you might not serve any jail time."

Might not? Rose wanted to heave. "They would send me? Even if there's proof I'm innocent?"

"They'd need to analyze what we've given them. Look, let's take it one step at a time." Dan's voice attempted to calm, but the damage was done. "Contact the attorney tonight. He's a friend and expecting your call. I told him we needed to get this ball rolling."

"I will."

She called the lawyer, but only got a voice mail. After leaving a message, she went into the bathroom. While brushing her teeth, she stared into the mirror's reflection. A woman Rose *used* to know looked back. Not a grown-up who had a PhD and wrote a respected magazine column. Instead Emmaline Rose stared back. A scared kid, plagued by a need for privacy, routine, and love. Her parents had encouraged the creation of a fantasy world where outsiders would never know their real problems. She hated them for doing that, but hadn't she done the very same in her adulthood?

Reality struck with the force of a speeding truck. Running wasn't the answer. It had never been the answer. It was an illusion, a temporary stop in living a full and honest life.

Her own existence wasn't even clear to her any more. Including this one with Leo. If they were to build on what they'd found in each other, she first needed to fix what she'd left behind.

"I've got the movie ready to go," he yelled from the other room.

"Be right there."

Tomorrow. A new day. A chance to think about what she wanted to make her new reality. She'd be forced to face the demons that followed her. But for tonight, she'd enjoy the peace and love she'd found in Leo's arms.

Chapter 24

Rose sat on the edge of Leo's bed, her cell phone pressed to her ear. "Yes. I understand."

As her lawyer delivered the cold hard facts about her situation, her fingers twirled a loose string on the hem of Leo's T-shirt that she'd slipped on when it got a little chilly during the night. She wished Leo were here now, wrapping her in his hold to take away the sting of the lawyer's words.

Bob Kirkpatrick, Esquire, was evidently an early riser. Said to be the best criminal defense attorney in DC, he offered sensible advice and an outline on what he'd advise she do. Practical as it was, though, her insides ached. The advice conflicted with her heart's desire.

Leo walked in and sat on the bed, making it shake. She didn't turn around, suddenly afraid he'd spot all the agony ripping her apart inside.

Bob finally wrapped up and asked if she had any questions. "Not right now. I'll call if I do."

As soon as she placed the phone on the nightstand, Leo's hands circled her waist. "Lie down with me."

She did and he slipped his leg over hers. "Everything okay?" He draped a hand over the dip in her waist.

"I think so. It was the lawyer. He seems to know what he's doing."

"Good. Don't forget that I'm here to help you every step of the way."

Rose smoothed her hand along the grain of his cheek. "I know you are. And I'm grateful, but I don't want this to be your problem."

He frowned. "I can't help someone I care about?"

"It's not that."

"Then what?"

The night of the blackout, Leo had revealed a lifetime of trying to help the women in his world. His mother. His wife. Even women he'd dated. The pain in his eyes while he'd talked showed his regret over not being able to save them, what he considered his own personal failures. Rose didn't want to be another of the same.

"It's time for me to face everything in my life. For once."

"And I'm saying you don't need to do it alone. That's all."

"That's not all. I *need* to do it alone."

"What's that mean?"

"Look, the past has defined us both. Marrying John was a Band-Aid to fix my need for a quiet family life. Me latching onto you in a crisis is no better."

"You're not latching onto me. It's what we do for the people we care about."

"To a certain extent." Rose took his hands in hers. "Leo, you shared with me the pain of trying to help people you couldn't fix. Your wife, your mother."

"This is different."

"Is it?"

"I think so."

"Well, I don't."

He stared at her and seemed to process the statement. "Fair enough. Have it your way."

He kissed the tip of her chin, nipped at the corner of her lips, then captured her mouth into a tender kiss. Rose surrendered to the heat between them, but her mind wandered. He'd agreed too easily. Leo possessed a quiet persistence, another type of fight she wasn't sure she could handle right now.

Leo pulled away, happiness shining in his eyes. "Hungry?"

Rose didn't want to ruin it by telling him he wasn't listening to her concerns. "Starving."

"How about I get breakfast started? I'll feed Bella, too."

"Sure."

He gave her a quick kiss, rolled out of the bed, and tossed on jeans with a clean T-shirt. Bella followed him to the door. He paused and glanced back at Rose. "Everything will be okay."

"I know." She smiled, because she could tell he wanted to make it good for her. "I'll be right down."

Rose rested her head back on the pillow, staring up at the ceiling and trying to think of how to deal with Leo's need to help her. Bella howled when the doorbell rang. Seconds later, Leo answered. The muffled sounds of a man's voice carried upstairs.

Rose went to the bedroom window. An unfamiliar black sedan parked in the driveway. The plates were not the blue to white ombré found on cars from Connecticut, but more goldenrod, like New York State.

Her mouth went dry. This couldn't be good news. She took light steps to the bedroom door, stuck her head out into the hallway, and held her breath to listen.

"Nope. Can't say I've seen the woman in the picture," Leo said. "Why would you be checking here?"

A stiff, tenor voice replied, "A tip sent us this way."

"Well, surely if she was in my house, I'd know it." Leo chuckled, but a tremor in his laughter belied his humor.

"And the car in the back of the driveway, is it yours?" This man's voice sounded more pleasant, but she didn't like his question.

"The one with the Massachusetts plates?"

"Yes, sir."

"Belongs to a renter living here who works at the local vineyard."

Rose's chest tightened. Leo had lied for her.

"No. She went out with a friend a little while ago," Leo said, sounding pretty convincing. "You know, whoever sent you here could've confused Northbridge with one of the other towns adjoining the lake. Happens all the time."

Rose couldn't tell if they bought it or not. Finally the front door clicked shut. She returned to the window, watching from behind the curtains as two men in dark suits got into the car. One of them was the same agent who'd visited her the first time. A minute later, they disappeared between the thick trees on either side of the driveway. This visit forced her hand, leaving her only one choice.

Footsteps carried down the hallway then Leo entered the room and came up behind her. "Did you hear?"

She nodded. "FBI?"

"Yes." He put his arms around her waist and rested his chin on her shoulder. "I have a bad feeling Everett tipped them off."

"Why?"

"When it came to you, he found a way to hurt me." Leo shook his head. "I'd hoped some of my comments sank in, but I guess not."

She kissed his cheek. "Go ahead and finish breakfast. I'll get dressed and be right down."

He squeezed her and held tight for a minute, then let go. Once he left, she got dressed.

Leo seemed aware of the ways his past played into his choices, perhaps had even grown from his mistakes. But could he let her handle this alone? She considered how he'd just handled the FBI agent and had her answer.

Lifting her cell phone, Rose dialed her lawyer's number and tried to stop struggling tears. In order for her to do the right thing to repair her situation, she'd have to hurt Leo.

"Hi, Bob, it's Rose Richardson again. The FBI was just here."

* * * *

The end.

Leo leaned back in his chair and stretched his arms over his head, sinking into the wonderful feeling of completing this manuscript first draft. Most of the pieces for this book were in place before he met Rose. Her arrival provided the missing link. A few edit rounds and he'd have this turned in not too far off from his deadline.

Leo stood, went to his worktable, and got seated in front of his laptop. Time to start the transfer into a computer file. Rose would surely have something to say about it, like how it was his leap into a new millennium.

He smiled thinking about her as he opened a new file. His mind drifted to the goodbye kiss she'd given him before running off to the grocery store. All she'd cared about was his work progress, so she told him she'd walked Bella and locked her in the apartment so he'd have no disruptions. Now, though, the image he recalled highlighted the sadness in her expression.

Damn FBI! Damn her husband.

Hopefully the attorney's advice would help her through this.

Leo worked for another hour, content in the knowledge he'd soon be having dinner with the woman who'd changed the way he saw his life. Screeching brakes of a diesel truck sounded in the driveway and seconds later the doorbell chimed. Leo got up and went downstairs. The UPS driver handed over a package.

While he opened the box in the kitchen, the house phone rang. He grabbed the cordless phone, seeing his sister's name on the display.

"Hey, Mallory." He removed two books he'd ordered.

"Thanks for the warning shot about Everett's return."

"My pleasure. How was your talk with him?"

"Typical Everett. Short and to the point. He did ask some weird questions about your renter, though."

A pit formed in Leo's gut. "Oh?"

"Yeah. He asked if you two were…well, for lack of a better word, involved."

"What'd you say?"

"I told him not as far as I know. Which is true because you'd have told me. Right?"

"I would have, but, well—it's a very recent thing."

"Is it serious?"

"It's new. Please don't start calling wedding planners."

"Very funny. But really, are you happy?"

"Yes. Very much so."

"Then I'll let it go that you didn't share. But if it comes to wedding plans…"

"You'll be the first person I call."

"Good. Oh, Everett said something else. Pretty out there, if you ask me."

Leo braced himself. "What?"

"He claims she looks like the missing senator's wife who's been on the news lately."

Further proof Everett might have been the reason behind the FBI's visit. Leo wanted to hate his brother, only the pain in Everett's eyes when he revealed the truth about his relationship with Camille left Leo sad and filled with regret. Not that he'd have changed one thing about falling in love with her, but maybe he'd have handled matters more appropriately.

Bella whimpered from inside the apartment. Leo walked down the hallway and opened the door. The dog hurried out, anxious for some reason. Leo's gaze drifted into the main living area and a slow chill spread to his bones.

"Is he right? Does she look…"

His sister's voice faded as he took in Rose's apartment. A bad feeling settled over him. Little signs of her existence always left around, like a pair of kicked-off shoes or her open briefcase, were gone. He entered.

"Can I call you back? Something just came up."

"Sure."

He hung up and squatted down, taking a minute to rub Bella's silky ears. "Hey girl. It's okay."

The spotless living room made his heart sink further. All that remained of her having been there was a filled bowl of water and kibbles.

He went to the bathroom, his head in a haze. All the toiletries were gone. With deepening dread, he stepped into the bedroom. No suitcase. No clothes in the closet. A cleared dresser.

Pain gushed through his chest, like an explosion of his heart. How could she simply leave without a goodbye or taking the dog?

A paper lay in the center of the bed. He went over and picked it up, the hurt cutting through his chest like an axe, making it hard to breath.

Dear Leo,

If you're reading this, you've realized I'm gone. The decision to leave this way didn't come lightly, only trying to say goodbye would have been hard for both of us.

My life is a mess, Leo. For so long I've been running. Yes, it must feel like I'm running from you.

Only I'm not.

I've left, but for a good reason. One I hope means a future for us. Where someday we can have a relationship without the constraints of lies.

Lies about my identity.

Lies about hiding from the FBI.

I can't ask you to be a party to the deceits I've let rule my life, and I can't be with you fully until I make my past and present right. Maybe I should have discussed this with you first, but I didn't want you to try to change my mind.

My lawyer advised me to turn myself in and deal with the aftermath. He will do everything to prove my innocence, but it could be pretty unpleasant at the beginning. I don't want to drag you down that path. With any luck, I'll come out the other end of this a fully vindicated woman and John will land behind bars, where he deserves to be sent.

By now you've noticed I've left my most beloved possession behind. Bella.

As I considered my plans to turn myself in, I worried about her. John never wanted her and I worried she'd end up back at the local dog pound. In fact, there's only one person who I could count on when it came to her. One person who loves Bella as much as me.

I hope you don't object to keeping her until I can get my life in a good place. If you can't, then I will find another place. I promise we will talk soon, but I need to at least get through the next few days or a week.

I'm sorry if my leaving like this hurts you. Sometimes doing the right thing can hurt people we care about. Yet I've left with the full confidence I will face all the demons in my life, both past and present.

When the day comes I return to you, I'll understand if you no longer want me. And if you still have Bella, all I ask is that you return to me the one piece of myself I've left behind.

Rose

Xxoo

Leo fell onto the edge of the bed, the letter dropping from his hands to the floor. Bella wandered over, poked his knee with her nose. He scratched her head but was numb to all other sensations. He processed Rose's note, even though part of him wanted to race after her and track her down.

Only he couldn't. Everything she wrote made sense.

It didn't stop the hurt. Tears stung Leo's eyes and an urge to chase Rose so he could avoid another loss tempted him. But he paused. This time what he'd found with a woman *was* different. She'd left, but she given him something she treasured. A sign of her love and trust.

He stared at the dog, at this moment watching him carefully. Leo patted the bed. "Come on up."

She jumped onto the mattress, plunked down, and leaned against him like she needed his support too. And she did, all while Rose fixed her life.

The obsession to hold up others who weren't strong had followed Leo his entire life. To what end? He'd gained nothing…absolutely nothing. Even if he tried to find Rose, it wasn't what *she* wanted.

Maybe the control he'd craved for so long to make things perfect was nothing he could ever really obtain. This moment, this thing going on with Rose, it was a chance to let the hand of fate determine his future.

He rubbed the dog's back. As he did, the weight of Rose's decision to leave Bella struck a deeper chord. Giving Rose space would prove how much he cared for her and respected her wishes. He respected her bravery, because she'd found the courage to walk into the lion's den on her own.

Courage. Leo dug deep inside himself to grasp the concept, empowered by the fearlessness of a woman he believed he loved. Fear of loss had owned him most of his life. It found him. It followed him. All because he allowed it.

Her leaving could own him, too. Or he could make a decision to change.

It would mean staying afloat and facing another loss, but this time with hope for his future. Live each day with optimism for her return. If she didn't…What if she didn't?

He pushed aside the negative thought. For once, he wouldn't take someone's leaving personally. Who knew where it would end, but if it ended well, life just might be sweeter.

Chapter 25

Rose exited the town car and stared up at the J. Edger Hoover Building. How she'd managed to put one foot in front of the other this morning remained a mystery.

The boxy concrete structure served as a perfect symbol of Washington secrecy and bureaucracy. Bob Kirkpatrick exited behind her. Bob was a tall man and ducked to get out, nearly bumping his head of full, gray hair on the door opening.

A group of reporters waiting near the entrance spotted them and rushed the car. Rose was glad Bob had suggested they come together.

He buttoned his suit jacket, his overall appearance pulled together and confident. "Remember, don't say a word to the press. Let's wait for Dan."

She nodded. Hoisting her purse over the shoulder of her suit jacket, she jutted out her chin in outward confidence. The stampede of her heart told the real story.

"Dr. Richardson, what can you tell us about the allegations made by the FBI?"

"Dr. Rose? Did you do it? Do you have a statement for your readers?"

Reporters yelled. Flashbulbs blinked. Rose glanced over her shoulder in time to see Dan Montgomery climb out of the car. He rushed to her side and used his briefcase to block a reporter shoving a microphone in Rose's face and hollering a question.

He took her elbow. "Head down and move forward." The ex-military PI shot her a comforting grin. He wasn't at all what she'd expected: a bulky man with long hair tied back in a ponytail and a tattoo on the side of his neck. He wore a nice dark suit, white shirt, and striped tie like the lawyer had suggested.

Walking between them should've felt safe, but Rose had never felt more exposed. Since leaving Northbridge the days were one big blur. Meeting with her lawyer. Turning herself in. One day spent in jail, where the lawyer hoped he could get her released on her own recognizance. Then, out of nowhere, someone had posted the $50,000 bail.

Upon release, she'd gone with Bob to his office to discuss today's FBI meeting. Once there, he'd handed her an envelope and a wrapped box.

"This is from the person who posted bail. They'd heard about your arrest on the news."

He'd excused himself to grab coffee. Rose opened it privately, curious who'd offered financial help. Inside the envelope had been a note card with a picture of downtown Northbridge and the lake, where peaceful rolling hills protected the town like a fortress. A penetrable fortress.

Bella and I will wait for you. Remember, a return here holds all the promise of a full moon.

Leo. The bail money was one thing she couldn't get and she'd welcomed his support. Her eyes had watered as she opened the black velvet jeweler box. Inside was a silver crescent moon charm. Dotted with little round diamonds, it dangled from a matching silver chain. She would have to ask him about the quote, one she vaguely remembered found on a postcard in the pantry. She'd put the necklace on, her heart filled with gratitude and affection for the man she couldn't wait to see again.

Dan tugged at her elbow, guiding her from more pleasant memories and into the daunting FBI building. The throng of reporters followed. She reached up and fingered the necklace. The charm held all the power of a talisman, representing every reason why she'd come forward, and every hope for her future.

The receptionist swept them off to a conference room. Inside, two men dressed in dark suits and a woman dressed nearly the same sat waiting at a long table made of oak. All three stood. One of the men stepped forward. His perfectly parted hair and don't-mess-with-me expression made Rose's stomach jittery.

"I'm Deputy Director Lewindowsky." His deep voice meant business. He swept his hand toward the other two people, adding, "Special Agents Susan Moore and Ed Turner."

After introductions, they got seated. Rose folded her clammy hands on the table, so at least she wouldn't appear as nervous as she felt.

Despite what Dan had uncovered, proving her innocence wasn't a shoo-in. But if they got lucky, the evidence uncovered by the PI would turn the tables and refocus the investigation on the real culprit—John.

Director Lewindowsky lifted his smoky gray eyes over the paper in his hands and went straight to her. "Mrs. Richardson, your attorney assures me of your innocence. But the fact remains, you left town. Didn't even tell your husband. You'd better have a good reason why."

She swallowed, but her mouth remained as dry as dust. Fear of someone discovering her past had controlled for too long. If there was ever a time for honesty, it was now.

"Yes. To me it seemed like a very good reason."

"I suggest you tell us, because right now your actions don't make a great case for you."

"Well, Director, after a visit from the FBI, I realized my husband had stolen my inheritance funds. My ex-husband, actually. John and I are divorced, but it's not known by the public yet."

She explained about the confrontation and his threat to tell about her past.

"Fear of the media isn't a good reason to run," the director snapped.

She held up a hand. "You're right. Not for most people, but for me it took on a different light. Before I turned eighteen, my life was anything but normal." All eyes rested on her and her pulse raced, but she kept going. "Back then, I went by another name. Emmaline Rose Holloway." Her chest pulled tight and she drew in a deep breath and shared the story of her past, her voice at times shaky but always moving forward. While she spoke, their silence and stares left her feeling like she'd walked into a room nude, exposing not only bare skin but a part of her soul.

"If that was all, I'd never have run. But later that night, I overheard John on the phone talking to someone about me. I listened. I still don't know who he spoke to, but he wanted them to hurt me, have me mugged—shot—so I'd have more problems than my missing money."

A few raised eyebrows appeared around the room, but she ignored them and continued. "I ran away because I couldn't cope with the idea of being jailed for something I didn't do, coupled with fear I'd be physically harmed by a man who would've used the mugging for political gain. He…" Rose paused, still finding what she'd heard surreal. "He planned to use my being shot to help his campaign on gun reform, a boost for the upcoming elections."

Director Lewindowsky passed a glance to the special agent.

He then looked at Rose. "Do you remember the date you overheard your husband on the phone? We can subpoena the phone records to get the number."

After, she gave him the date, the man with thinning hair leaned forward. She suddenly recognized him as one of the men she'd seen at Leo's front door. "Where have you been this past month, Mrs. Richardson?"

She tensed and thought carefully about her words. "I found a place in Connecticut and ended up renting an apartment in a house near the lake."

"Did your landlord know who you were at any point during your stay?"

She looked him straight in the eye, because this was the one lie she would tell. "I never identified myself to him. I used the name Emma Morris and did everything possible to make sure nobody in town learned who I really am. The people I met there were nice. They welcomed me. Nobody ever knew my real identity. As you can see, I've altered my appearance."

Her lawyer interrupted. "Perhaps you'd like to see what the private investigator Mrs. Richardson hired has found. If you hear this, you may be more understanding of her case." The attorney motioned with his hand to Dan. "Why don't you show them what you've got."

Her fate rested in the hands of the people around this table. Rose settled back into her seat, her fingers wrapped around the moon charm.

Chapter 26

Six months later...

Rose blinked into the noonday sun as she walked out of the lawyer's office onto Twelfth Street in downtown DC. The crisp air smelled of late autumn, and early Christmas decorations hung from storefronts even though Thanksgiving wasn't for two weeks.

She stepped down the sidewalk, her steps light for once. This morning's closing on the house she and John had in North Carolina had gone well. The sweet couple that now owned it reminded her of them on the day they'd purchased the place, a rosy future ahead of them. God, she'd been so blinded by what she wanted to believe.

She crossed F Street, debating if she should go spend a little time at the Smithsonian Museum of American Art, but instead continued toward the Hilton, her home for the next two nights while waiting for one last meeting with the Department of Justice to assist in their case against John.

Then she'd be free to take care of the one thing she'd been aching to do for six months. Though she and Leo had spoken regularly, she'd asked they not see each other. Besides her worry that he'd be dragged into this by the press, she wanted their reunion to be completely unencumbered by her problems. And she was two days away from being problem-free.

She hurried down the sidewalk but paused at a newsstand. The current issue of *Sophisticate* sat on a rack. As she grabbed it, she spotted this week's *Time* magazine with an article about last week's election results. John hadn't even been able to run for his Senate seat, the one he'd cared about more than the law. The party had ousted him as the facts about the straw donations came to light. Soon he'd face a grand jury.

Records revealed that the late night phone call had been to his campaign manager, who sang like the proverbial canary once cornered by the authorities. Seemed loyalty to a malicious politician had limits and he'd corroborated the story Rose overheard. She hoped they nailed John. What he'd put her through was horrible. He didn't deserve even a drop of her sympathy. The only good from this whole mess was meeting Leo and finding a temporary home with friends in the small Connecticut town.

She paid for the copy of *Sophisticate* and continued to the hotel, anxious to see her feature piece in the issue. A block later, she neared a Starbucks. She smiled. Caffeine of any kind always made her think of Leo. She went inside. Once she had a latté in hand she found a table near the window, shimmied out of her blazer, and cracked open the magazine.

Sophisticate and her editor had stuck by her these past six months. Even at the start, when her innocence remained in doubt by some. She was glad because it gave her a chance to really think about the feature story on falling in love. A chance to remember the night she'd fallen for Leo.

The friends she'd made in Northbridge remained in her heart as she rewrote the article, too. She didn't need to use what they'd told her. Still, writing it reminded her of how they'd welcomed her to the vineyard and let her into their inner circle.

Over the course of the past few months, she'd received letters from each of them. Supportive notes, since both her past and present were all over the news. Even though the press learned her real name and tragedy of her parents' death, the reaction from others wasn't as bad this time around. Maybe due to the passage of decades. Sophie's note shared how Leo even brought Bella to the farm one day so their dogs could play.

Before she started reading, she got out her phone and dialed her editor. On the third ring, Mia picked up.

"Hey. It's Rose."

"How'd it go today?"

"Fantastic. The house is sold. I have money in the bank. Life is good. Listen, I just passed a newsstand and picked up this month's issue."

"Your feature has a mention on the cover."

"I see. Thank you. I wanted to make sure you sent an advance copy to the address I gave you?"

"Yup. Both addresses. Guess you left behind some friends in Northbridge."

"You could say that."

Mia laughed. "Or maybe the subject of our article?"

"I'll never tell. Listen, I've gotta run. We'll talk soon."

She flipped open the magazine to her story.

A Potion for Modern Day Love
By Dr. Rose Richardson

Take one basset hound.
Add a power outage.
Answer 40 questions.
Mix well then sit back and wait.

"Write an article on this. See if it's possible."
My editor spoke those words as she handed me a study done about a successful experiment on making two people fall in love in one sitting. Was she crazy, I'd wondered? After reading the details, I was certain she was.

Two strangers falling in love based on a series of questions seemed preposterous. Besides, the notion I might find anything redeeming in the idea of such deep affection took an enormous leap of faith. My own marriage had just toppled around me.

Would I ever love again? Had I ever really understand unconditional love? With my own issues coming to a head, I searched for other angles to get my job done. All avoided my own feelings on the topic and instead I solicited others.

Then the strangest thing happened...my new landlord fell in love with my basset hound.

I had taken refuge from my failed marriage in a rented apartment. My landlord was a man who carried a two-ton chip on his shoulder. He didn't like me that much and the feeling was mutual.

As the days passed, though, I watched him take a liking to my cherished basset hound, Bella. Hers was an adoration I understood. She'd wooed me at the shelter with hopeful eyes and a spirit that wouldn't give up. Same way she'd probably lured him in, too.

Their romance was two-sided, obvious to me because my loyal companion made no bones about her love for him. "Aren't animals supposed to have a hidden sense about nasty people?" I'd often think, but Bella's overtures seemed to soften this man's soul, scratch away at the chip he carried. In fact, it left me curious about what might have caused the chip.

And as the pieces dropped, it revealed a man I could like, too.

Then—believe it or not—on a dark and stormy night, the home's power went out. Leaving the three of us alone with nothing to do. We played games. We roasted hot dogs over an open fireplace. And when we'd exhausted all possible forms of entertainment, I suggested we give those forty questions a try.

Rose shut the magazine and closed her eyes. Tears welled. All the tenderness she possessed for Leo was found in the remaining paragraphs. Love had been planted like a seed on that night and buried deep beneath complicated layers of history. Distance created a strange kind of ecosystem, where the seed fully bloomed into something she believed in…a relationship like none she'd ever had before.

She could only hope Leo read the article Mia had sent.

* * * *

Leo left Washington Square Park and strolled along Fifth Avenue with today's *New York Times* in one hand and Bella's leash in the other. She sniffed the scents of the city, her tail held high and gait purposeful.

He turned onto Ninth Street. The scenery changed to rows of red brick and stucco residential buildings. Towering trees spaced along the sidewalk clung to a few of their autumn leaves, but not as many as a few weeks ago.

Once at his building, he stopped in the lobby mailboxes to get yesterday's forgotten mail. They took the stairs to the second story apartment he called home. He'd purchased this place after his wife died. The quiet Greenwich Village neighborhood suited him. Calmer. More artsy.

Once inside the apartment, he tossed the newspaper and mail on the dining room table. He headed to the galley kitchen and popped a pod into the Nespresso machine. Damn Seth and his birthday gift. Leo loved the contraption, but refused to tell him how much.

He waited as a frothy cup of coffee appeared in seconds. Nostalgia for his old percolator in Connecticut hit hard and fast. Or maybe it was all the hope he held out for Rose, always making him think about Northbridge.

He didn't dwell on the idea. She'd return—when the time was right. In a few days he'd be done with this release tour of his novel. His publisher reported strong pre-orders, several stellar editorial reviews, and fantastic release day sales. All restored his lost confidence after the last book blunder.

Bella wandered into the room and watched him, an expectant glimmer in her bloodshot eyes. "I suppose you want a treat?"

She wagged her tail and stared him down, a shrewd negotiator for someone who couldn't speak. He dug out a treat and waited until she took it. "Let's see if there's any news about your mom in the paper."

Bella chomped away, clearly not interested.

Leo flipped the paper, until he spotted a short piece with the heading "Senator to Face Grand Jury." He carefully read each word, certain they'd indict John Richardson on charges of making illegal campaign contributions and fraud for using Rose's money without her knowledge.

Six months of patience. Not an easy task, but he respected the boundary she'd established.

Love for her possessed him. Their phone calls made him even more eager. Each night since she'd left, he went to sleep remembering the short life they'd shared up at the lake. He'd dedicated the book to Bella, for bringing them together and even sent Rose a copy before the release date. He smiled remembering the delight in her laughter when she'd called to thank him.

Sometimes they'd talk about her journey facing the murky matters of her life. Doing it alone mattered a great deal to her, a fact he understood more and more as the days passed and he read the papers about her journey.

Still, there were moments of doubt. At those times, he'd call Bella over. A sign Rose wasn't gone for good.

He folded the newspaper in half and got up to shower. He had a late morning interview with the *New Yorker*, lunch with Seth, and then his book signing at the Barnes & Noble in mid-town.

On his way past the counter with his coffee cup in hand, he stopped to flip through the pile of mail. At the bottom, he spotted a copy of *Sophisticate* magazine.

A slinky model on the cover wore a trench coat and carried a briefcase. Near her shoulder, an article teaser shouted, "New Rules To A Successful Career." He sipped his coffee and nearly spit it out after reading another feature: "31 Sex Tips: How to go from zero to ninety in the bedroom." He chuckled, not sure he could keep up with ninety, but somewhere around sixty or seventy sounded good.

He was about to walk away, but on the bottom a third article teaser caught his attention. "Dr. Rose shares how forty questions, a basset hound, and a blackout brought her love."

She'd mentioned a surprise during their last call but refused to say more. His heart lifted as he opened the magazine. He devoured each word, laughing at her descriptions of their evening, recalling some of the same emotions in himself that night.

When he finished, the urge to hold her seized him. He grabbed his cell phone from the counter, ready to dial her number and ask if she was ready. He stopped. Nope. She'd asked for him to wait for her return, so why ruin it now?

He continued to the shower, but hoped to God she didn't make him wait too much longer.

* * * *

"Thank you." Leo smiled at the young man with wire-framed glasses, an aspiring writer himself. "Good luck with your novel. Keep at it. No matter what."

Leo glanced out into the crowd for a split second at the long line, kept orderly by store staff. He'd signed books for the past two hours. His cheeks hurt from smiling and hand ached from writing. But in truth, he'd want it no other way.

He continued to greet his readers. As he finished with one customer, he turned away to take a sip of his water. A quick glance at the line showed it finally had an end. He reached for a book from the store staff who'd been assigned to help him, but instead the tall young lady, whose nametag read "Hadley," handed him a small piece of paper.

"It's important," she said.

He unfolded the note, expecting perhaps something from Seth. Although he could've texted or left a voice message.

Look up.

He slowly lifted his head, his heart pounding from months and months of saved up anticipation. Sure enough, Rose stood at the end of the line, a copy of his book clutched to her chest. A questioning smile rested on her lips, causing his heart to leap a mile into the sky. No longer dressed in the silly teen-wear, she wore a classy wraparound red dress clinging to her curves. The necklace he'd given her hung around her neck, the diamond charm sparkling and enhancing her beautiful blue eyes. Her hair had grown and was a light wheat color, still with layers but styled more professionally.

He dropped the note on the table and stood, half wondering if he'd totally lost it and she was a mirage.

She stepped from her place in line and her smile grew. "I promised I'd find you."

He moved toward her. "Is this your surprise?"

"It is. A surprise, just like the first time we met." She tipped her head to the line. "Not a good idea?"

"Are you kidding? It's great!" He took her hands in his. "God, I can't believe it's you."

"Did you get the magazine? I asked them to send it to both your New York and Connecticut addresses."

"Yes. At my place in the city. I just got it today."

He placed her arms around his waist and cupped her cheeks. Without answering, he kissed her. Softly at first, then more deeply, long and filled with all the passionate he possessed inside his heart for this woman.

He leaned back and stared into her eyes. "God, I've missed you."

"Me too."

"Come sit with me up front until I'm through."

He guided her around the table holding her hand. A store helper nearby offered to get a chair.

He kissed Rose again and quietly said, "I loved your article. Everything you wrote about those questions hit me the same way, too. Every single day I've thought about you. So did Bella."

"I did the same. How is my girl? I've missed her so much."

"She's good. Back at the apartment right now. We'll go there when I'm through."

"Sounds perfect." She touched his cheek with her hand, watching him through gleaming eyes. "One quick question. I'm here to collect on your note."

"My note?"

"The one that came with the beautiful necklace. You told me on the phone that you'd only tell me in person what it means...all the promise of a full moon."

Leo laughed. "Had you on the edge of your seat, did I? Good. That was my insurance to get you here." He took her hand and squeezed. "It's something my dad used to say all the time. He'd say, 'Life waxes and wanes, but the promise of a full moon sheds light on everything that is possible.'"

Her face softened. "It's perfect. And thank you. For the necklace, for letting me deal with unfinished business, and for taking care of Bella. Now I'm ready for any possibility."

Leo signed the remaining books while Rose waited. Every so often he'd glance her way and catch her watching him. He suddenly found himself thinking about a clichéd phrase, something about letting things go, because if they are meant to be yours they'll return.

The last customer left. Leo thanked the store and took off with Rose. They walked hand in hand down Fifth Avenue, Leo still stunned at how his day changed. About to flag a cab, he instead drew her away from the center of the sidewalk and against the side of a nearby brick building.

He cornered her there and kissed her the way he'd wanted to a thousand times in his mind. First a delicate tasting of her tender lips, then he fully covered her mouth, softly probing while breathing in her perfumed scent as his fingers threaded the silky strands of her hair. She slipped her hands inside his jacket, drawing him closer and sighing against his mouth. When he pulled away, he saw all the lust in her gaze he'd seen during the short time they spent as lovers.

He tucked a stray piece of hair behind her ear. "Another article in *Sophisticate* caught my interest."

"New rules to a successful career?"

"Nope. The one about going from zero to ninety in the bedroom. Care to check its accuracy?"

"Are you kidding?" A cool November breeze blew his blazer jacket flap open so she tucked herself against his chest and he held her tight. Looking up, she smiled. "What are we waiting for?"

Epilogue

"Are you ready?" Harry walked out of the back of the tasting room at Litchfield Hills Vineyard.

Rose went to him and straightened the knot of his tie. "I've never been more ready. Aren't you the handsome devil in that tux?"

Harry waved his hand and smiled. "You, my dear, are going to steal the show."

The gown she'd fallen in love had a simple elegance. The heart-shaped bodice fit firmly around her torso then flared at the waist, falling to her feet. Needlepoint French lace with a floral print covered her shoulders, arms, serving as an overlay to the dress. A satin bow belted her waist.

Harry cracked open the door and peeked outside. "Should I tell them to start the music?"

She nodded. Harry waved, presumably to Trent Jamieson, who'd be playing his guitar as she walked down the aisle.

Harry offered his the crook of his arm. "Your future husband has a little surprise for you."

"A surprise? Twice I've surprised him. I suppose I'm due."

As they carefully walked a candlelit path from the tasting room to the grassy lawn looking out to the lake, Rose took in the setting. Streaks of amber, gold, and gray pastel filled the dusk sky. Over the lake, a full moon rose on the horizon. A perfect late spring evening.

She scanned the seated guests, seventy-five of their close friends and family. New friends and old. Sophie and her husband, Duncan. Meg and Charlie sat with Bernadette, whose husband, Dave, stood at the end of an aisle formed by folding chairs to officiate. His smile warmed and welcomed, putting Rose at ease. Not far from Dave, Trent strummed his guitar. Veronica stood at his side, waiting to sing as part of their service.

Then there were the people who still stood by her side while her name got dragged through the papers, like Mia, Joanne, and two friends from North Carolina.

She glanced up front again, searching for Leo. Instead she saw Seth, the best man, and Leo's sister, Mallory, the only two people standing up for them. In Mallory, Rose found a sisterhood. Having her as matron of honor sealed their affection for each other.

She didn't see Leo right away, but when she glanced to the grass she found him kneeling, his back to her. He stood after a few seconds and turned. His gaze filled her with the same love it did each time he looked her way.

He smiled, a huge grin, and motioned with his head for her to look down.

On the ground, between Leo and Seth, sat Bella with a large satin bow tied around her neck. A black pillow rested on Bella's back, secured by a second white satin bow. Both wedding rings were tied neatly in the pillow center.

Rose's heart melted. The one time she had suggested Bella come to the service, Leo had replied, "A wedding is no place for a dog," so she'd let it go.

She hugged Harry, and met Leo in the center. Their hands joined. "I thought you said a wedding was no place for a dog."

Leo winked and gazed at Rose, a sparkle in his eyes. "Did you think I'd leave Bella out?"

"But I'd thought Seth was carrying the rings."

"So did I," Seth said from the sidelines, and everybody laughed.

Dave started the service, quickly overrun by Seth's panicked voice. "No, Bella. Stay. Stay!"

The dog walked the center of the aisle, not even a hint that she'd heard Seth's demands. She waddled over to Dave at her own slow pace and plunked at his feet, facing Leo and Rose. The moment drew more laughter.

Joy reached deep inside Rose, her heart filled with love for Leo and excitement for their future in Northbridge.

She touched Leo's cheek. "You know, I think you fell in love with Bella before me."

"It's debatable. I think she helped us along though."

Dave cleared his throat. "You two have a lifetime to discuss this. I plan to make this ceremony a little different than the last one the three of us participated in."

Snickers erupted from the select few who'd been privy to the house-cleansing ritual. Dave then performed a beautiful ceremony, including a reading of vows they'd each written themselves. Leo's talked about his own growth during the six months he waited for her and Rose cried. He'd learned love was limitless, even when we someday lose the people we care about. Rose's talked about the true meaning of home and how she'd found one with Leo.

When they finished, Dave announced, "You may now kiss."

Leo brushed her lips then slipped a hand around her back, tipped her and kissed her more deeply. Bella howled.

They laughed along with the guests. Rose couldn't remember a time in her life when she'd ever felt more at peace or more loved. She went to kiss Leo again, but this time Bella squeezed between them. Neither one complained. Instead of kissing, they squatted down to pet the dog who'd been smart enough to understand how they all belonged together.

~The End~

Please enjoy another glimpse into the world of Blue Moon Lake:

SHARE THE MOON

Sometimes trust is the toughest lesson to learn.

Sophie Shaw is days away from signing a contract that will fulfill her dream of owning a vineyard. For her, it's a chance to restart her life and put past tragedies to rest. But Duncan Jamieson's counter offer blows hers out to sea.

Duncan still finds Sophie as appealing as he had during boyhood vacations to the lake. Older and wiser now, he has his own reasons for wanting the land. His offer, however, hinges on a zoning change approval.

Bribery rumors threaten the deal and make Sophie wary of Duncan, yet she cannot deny his appeal. When her journalistic research uncovers a Jamieson family secret, trust becomes the hardest lesson for them both.

A Lyrical e-book on sale now.

Learn more about Sharon at
http://www.kensingtonbooks.com/author.aspx/31604

Chapter 1

*New Moon: When the moon, positioned between the earth and sun,
nearly disappears, leaving only darkness.*

November

The sabotaged kayaks beckoned. Sophie Shaw trod a thin layer of ice pellets on the lawn as she headed to the lake's edge, where eight boats waited to be returned to the storage rack. The fickle New England weather had offered sleet-dropping clouds an hour earlier. Now, a wink from the sun reflected against Blue Moon Lake.

She dragged the first boat up a small incline, annoyed some bored teenagers had considered destruction of property entertainment. Growing up she and her friends had respected the local businesses.

A UPS truck screeched to a stop in front of a row of shops on Main Street. The driver hopped out and ran into Annabelle's Antiques with a box tucked under his arm. Sophie glanced both ways along the road for signs of Matt, whose new driver's license and clunker car played to every mother's fears. Fifteen minutes earlier, she'd texted him for help with the boat mess. He'd replied "k."

Sophie's flats glided along the slick lawn. She gripped the cord of a bright orange sea kayak and, using two hands, struggled backward up the slope. Her foot skidded. The heel of her shoe wobbled for security but instead, her toes lifted off the ground and flashed toward the clear sky. The burning skid of the cord ripped across her palms just as her other foot lifted and launched her airborne. *Thud!*

Air whooshed from her lungs. Pain coursed through her shoulder blades, neck, and spine. The ground's chilly dampness seeped into her cotton khaki pants, raising goose bumps on her skin. Seconds passed without breath before she managed to swallow a gulp.

Lying flat on her back, she stared at the cornflower blue sky and spotted a chalky slice of the moon. The night Henry died, a similar crescent had hung from the heavens, barely visible nestled among the glittering stars. She prepared for the scrape that threatened to tear the gouge of her scarred heart. Seven years. Seven painful years. She closed her eyes and after a few seconds, the weight of sadness lifted off her chest.

Tears gathered along her lower lashes. She pushed a strand of unruly long hair from her face. Footsteps crunched on the ice pellets and headed her way.

"Matthew Shaw…" Fury pooled in her jaw as she resisted the urge to yell at her son. "You'd better have a good excuse for taking so long."

A man with cinnamon hair, short on the sides with gentle waves on top, knelt at her side. She studied the strong outline of his cheeks and the slight bump on the bridge of his angular nose that gave him a rugged touch, but he wasn't familiar.

"Are you okay?" He searched her face.

The stranger hovered above. Tall treetops, clinging to the last of their earth-toned foliage, served as a backdrop to her view. A vertical crease separated his sandy brows. She couldn't pry herself from his vivid blue eyes, in part stunned from the fall, but also by her first responder.

For several long seconds she stared, and then mumbled, "I think so. Just a little shocked."

A whiff of his musk cologne revived her with the subtle charm of a southern preacher casting his congregation under his spell.

He frowned. "Does it hurt to move anything?"

"Sometimes it did before I fell."

The stranger's face softened and his lips curved upward. "A sense of humor, huh? That's a good sign."

"I suppose." His deep voice relaxed her like a cup of chamomile tea, the balanced and certain tone of his words easing her wounded spirit. Maybe this guy was a sign her rotten luck might change. "So, where's your white horse?"

"In the stable. Today I came in the white Camry." He motioned with a wave of his hand to a corner of the parking lot.

She pushed up on her elbow to look and a sharp pain jabbed her neck. "Ow!"

"Careful." His smile disappeared. "I was on my way over to help when you fell. You hit pretty hard."

The heat of embarrassment skittered up her cheeks. Not only had he witnessed her spastic aerobics, but she never played the distressed-damsel-on-the-dirty-ground card. A woman proficient at fly-fishing, who learned how to drive in a pickup truck and who, in her job as a journalist, had uncovered a corrupt politician, should be up and running by now.

"Go slow." His request suggested doling out orders came easy. "May I help?"

She nodded. He slipped a gentle hand into hers. The chill coating her skin melted against his warm touch. His well-groomed nails and thick fingers suggested he didn't work outdoors, rather the clean hands of a man who spent his days in an office. No wedding band either. He helped her sit and studied her as if a question perched on the edge of his thoughts.

"Can I call someone?" He blinked. "Your husband?"

"Oh, I'm not married." She caught the slight twitch of his mouth. "My son's supposed to be on his way to restack the boats."

Since her divorce from Mike, she'd concluded the available men in Northbridge were as predictable as the assortment at the dollar rental video store, filled with decade-old hits she'd seen so many times they held little interest. This man was a refreshing change.

"Ready to try to stand?" He took her by the elbow and she nodded.

Once on her feet, their hands remained together.

He glanced at them and let his drop. "You'll probably think this is crazy but—"

"Sophie?" The owner of Griswold's Café stood across the street and wiped his hands on a stained white apron. He'd placed the call to her father to alert them about the vandalism at Dad's boat shed. "You okay?"

"I'm fine." She waved. "Thanks."

She returned to the newcomer's gaze, as blue as the deep Caribbean Sea and as shiny as a starburst.

He raised his dirt-stained hands. "You might want to check yours."

Sure enough, her palms carried the same smudges from the impact of her fall. "Hold on. I have something to clean us off."

She trotted to her car, hoping the backside of her blazer covered any mess on the back of her pants.

After finding a package of wipes in the center console, she cleaned herself spotless and peeked in the rearview mirror. Her dark chocolate curls scattered with the freewill of a reckless perm. She neatened them with her fingertips then grabbed her cell and tried to call Matt but landed in his voice mail. The second she hung up, the phone rang. Bernadette's name showed on the display.

"Hey."

"Is your speech ready for tonight? You're our star speaker."

Bernadette always latched onto a crusade. The first was in third grade, a petition over the slaughter of baby seals for their skins. For tonight's public hearing, Bernadette had promised everyone the fight of her life. Her special interest group's concern about the large-scale development on Blue Moon Lake proposed by Resort Group International was a sore topic for many local residents, especially Sophie.

"Better find a new star speaker. There's a change of plans." Sophie readied herself for a negative reaction. "I'm covering the story for the paper now."

"You? Has Cliff lost his mind?"

"No. The other reporter can't do the assignment. Her father had a stroke earlier today. Cliff wanted to take the story himself, but I insisted he stick to his job as editor and let me do mine. I even made a five dollar bet I'd get a headline-worthy, bias-free quote from the company president."

"Do you think you can? I mean, RGI stole that land right out from under your nose. What was it…three days before signing the contract?"

Those were almost Cliff's exact words, along with some mumbling about how the paper's cheap new owner had cut his staff and he saw no other choice. "Two days."

"Honey, why would you want this story?"

"I have my reasons. This won't be the first time one of us needed to report on something close to us."

"Yeah, but wouldn't some public chastising against the corporate giant be good for your soul?"

"In a way." Sophie hesitated then decided to tell her best friend the truth. "Look, this is a chance to redeem myself. Prove to Cliff I really *can* stick to my journalist's creed after…well, you know, what happened with Ryan Malarkey."

"Mmm, forgot about him. He makes all us lawyers look bad." A long pause filled the air. "Guess that's a valid reason."

Sophie still harbored guilt from the last time a story got personal and she'd been fooled into violating her hallowed reporter vows. "Hey, on a lighter note, it's raining men over here at the lake."

Bernadette laughed. "What?"

"Some kids vandalized Dad's kayak shed. He asked for my help and this handsome guy appeared out of nowhere to help me. Fill you in later. He's waiting."

On her way back to the stranger, she studied his profile. Men this desirable didn't drop out of the sky around here. Why was he in town? Visitors to Northbridge weren't unusual in the summer, but not late fall. He faced the water, looking in the direction of the rolling hillside of Tate Farm, the property under discussion at tonight's controversial public hearing.

She neared the visitor and he turned around.

"Are you the owner of this place?" He pointed to the wood-sided shed with a sign reading "Bullhead Boat Rentals."

"No. My father runs it with my brother. Dad's too old to be walking around in this icy mess and my brother is gone for the day." She handed him a wipe. "They also operate the local tackle shop and Two Rivers Guided Tours, guided fly-fishing trips."

"I remember the tackle shop." He cleaned his hands and tucked the dirty wipe in his jacket pocket. "My family came here for a couple of summers. Close to thirty years ago."

Sophie studied him again. Summer vacationers passed through here with the blur of a relay race.

He brushed a dead leaf off the knee of his faded, well-pressed jeans. "Such a great little town." He scanned the main street, unhurried and relaxed, then took a deep breath, as if to savor a nostalgic moment. "Quintessential New England."

Although she'd lived all her forty-four years in Northbridge, she looked around with him. A few cars parked on the road near a long row of pre-WWI buildings, now housing retailers who had serviced the town's residents for countless decades, such as Handyman Hardware and Walker's Drugs. The retail stretch was sandwiched between her favorite place to eat, Sunny Side Up, a metal-sided, trolley car-shaped diner and the weathered façade of Griswold's Café. The popular hangout for waterfront meals had a karaoke night the locals rarely missed.

She examined his profile again. Surely she hadn't forgotten someone with such a sexy full lower lip and strong chin?

"I can't imagine anybody being unhappy here," he said, his tone quiet.

She held in the urge to retort with a cynical remark. Every time she stuck a foot out of town, circumstances jerked her back. "Too bad you picked today to return. Most of our visitors enjoy the warmer weather."

"I'm house hunting."

"Oh. Well, we have a lot of summer residents."

"I want a year-round place."

The absent wedding ring held renewed interest. "Where are you from?"

"Manhattan."

She adjusted her crooked scarf. "Living here will be a big change."

"I know. I've always loved this place, though." He reached out and tenderly brushed a leaf off Sophie's shoulder. His gaze flowed down her body like a slow trickle of water.

An unexpected burn raced up her cheeks.

He lifted his brows. "Hey, I never knew the lake went by another name. The town website said the original name came from an old Native American word."

She nodded. "Puttacawmaumschuckmaug Lake." The long name rolled off her tongue with ease, the pronunciation a rite of passage for anyone born and raised around the body of water. "It either means 'at the large fishing place near the rock' or 'huge rock on the border.'"

"What?" He chuckled. "Puttamaum…"

She shook her head and repeated the difficult word.

"Puttacawsch—"

"Nope. It's a toughie. That's why a reporter who visited here at the turn of the century suggested in his column we change the name. He said the water's beauty was as rare as a blue moon, and the phrase stuck."

He grinned, easy and confident. "My kids will love this place."

Kids? Sophie buried her disappointment. "Are you and your wife looking at the other towns bordering the water?"

"No. I like Northbridge. Oh, and I'm not married," he said matter-of-factly. His gaze arm-twisted her for a response.

She wanted to fan her hot cheeks but instead regrouped while pointing across the lake. "If you have a spare few hundred thousand and want to help the town out, take a look at Tate Farm. A developer wants to buy it to put up a large resort. Maybe you can outbid the guy."

"Oh?"

"Uh-huh. There's a public hearing tonight."

The hearing would be her first chance to meet the corporate vipers from Resort Group International face-to-face and she couldn't wait to hammer firm president, Duncan Jamieson, with some tough questions. With any luck the zoning board would vote down their request so the offer she'd made, along with her dad and brother, would be back in play.

The stranger's brows furrowed and he stroked his chin.

"Don't worry. I'm confident our zoning board will vote no on their proposal and keep the nasty developer away. By the way, I'm Sophie."

He dropped his gaze to the ground for a millisecond then looked back up. "I'm Carter."

If Nana were still alive, she'd have said in her thick Scottish brogue, "Verra good sign, Sophie. Carter comes from the word cart: someone who moves things." Nana held great stock in the art of name meanings.

He'd certainly moved Sophie.

Matt's rusty sedan whipped into the lot, ending the lusty thoughts. Her son hurried over, unease covering every corner of his face. "Sorry I'm late."

"What took you so long?"

"Grandpa called to make sure I helped you." He dragged his hand through his messy dirty-blond hair. "We were talkin'."

She had her suspicions about the topic but rather than ask, she introduced him to Carter.

He turned to Matt. "What do you say we let your mom take it easy and we'll finish this job?"

Matt nodded and trotted to the boats.

At her car, Carter opened the driver's door. "Better hop in." His tone lowered. "Your hands were cold before."

Sophie's knees softened and she tried to speak, but no sound came out. Turmoil reigned inside her body as he jogged away from her and caught up with Matt.

She tried to shake off the lost control caused by this stranger. This little incident had stolen some of her strength and lately every morsel was necessary to stay afloat. On the roller coaster of life, she had been taking a wild ride. First due to a chance to own the vineyards, giving her a helping hand from her inner grief and fulfilling a life-long dream. Then two weeks ago, RGI had barged into town and yanked her offer from the table.

Carter pointed to a kayak and said something. Matt laughed. The scene made her miss having a man in their household. Her heart softened, awed by the way this knight who'd arrived in a shiny white Camry galloped in and took charge…and how she'd simply let him. Was something good finally stepping into her life?

Disappointment skimmed her chest. Who was she kidding? Nothing would come of this.

Her cynical nature hadn't developed overnight. Rather, she had soured over time. Lost opportunities, gone due to circumstances beyond her control: Mom's cancer, Sophie's unplanned pregnancy, her subsequent marriage to Mike, even her lost bid on the land RGI now wanted.

Time to forget this guy and concentrate on her job. She'd have to work harder than ever to stick to her journalistic creed, but any teeny, albeit truthful, crumb of negative news about RGI or its president, Duncan Jamieson, could sway the scale on the zoning board vote. Then the greedy developer would disappear from Northbridge forever.

Her family wanted that land. Land their ancestors were the first to settle back in 1789. Land where the winery plans of their dreams could come to life. The most important reason, though, was protecting the sacred place where her firstborn son, Henry, had died.

Meet the Author

Sharon Struth is an award-winning author who believes it's never too late for a second chance in love or life. When she's not writing, she and her husband happily sip their way through the scenic towns of the Connecticut Wine Trail. Sharon writes from the small town of Bethel, Connecticut, the friendliest place she's ever lived. For more information, including where to find her other novels and published essays, please visit her at sharonstruth. com, find her on Twitter @sharonstruth, Facebook, or stop by her blogs at Musings from the Middle Ages & More (sharonstruth.wordpress.com) and The Hungry, Healthy Writer (hungryhealthywriter.com).